MICHAEL A. HAWLEY

ONE DAY IN THE LINE OF DUTY.

DOUBLE

TWO COPS IN THE LINE OF FIRE.

BLUFF

ONYX

ONYX

$6.99 U.S.
$9.99 CAN.

ISBN 0-451-41047-5

9 780451 410474

50699

EAN

A wake-up call

The picture slipped from Harris's fingers. Meigs stooped to retrieve it, then handed it back. "Please don't get too pissed. MacRae freaked. He saw this picture in the gal's bedroom, on her dresser, and just grabbed it without thinking. Aw, hell, it's a picture of one of our own guys. MacRae's old partner, John Darby. He's Narcotics now, runs a proactive unit out of our precinct. Christ, Sarge, you know what this might mean? Jesus, it—"

Harris cut him off midsentence with the ferocity of a marine drill instructor. "I want a written statement from MacRae before he goes off duty. I want a written statement from you before you leave this porch. No exceptions, not one—you got that? No bullshit, no excuses, no nothing!" She paused and drew a deep breath. "Who else knows about this?"

"Just me and MacRae."

"Keep it that way for now. We don't need anyone from Internal Affairs in here any sooner than necessary."

Harris stopped. Her fingers twisted the photo. "Damn it," she mumbled in frustration. Ten minutes before, she'd had a simple case. Now she knew different. She tossed her booties and gloves into the trash container Roy had set up, downed her coffee in three gulps, and dashed for her car. Moments later she had the captain on her cell phone. She quickly explained the situation, then hung up.

Still holding the photo, she threw it violently against her windshield. "Bastard," she breathed through gritted teeth. "You lousy goddamned bastard!" Harris knew John Darby all right, knew him very well. Only an hour and a half prior, she had left him dozing in her bed.

The time was 0314. . . .

DOUBLE BLUFF

Michael A. Hawley

AN ONYX BOOK

ONYX
Published by New American Library, a division of
Penguin Putnam Inc., 375 Hudson Street,
New York, New York 10014, U.S.A.
Penguin Books Ltd, 80 Strand,
London WC2R 0RL, England
Penguin Books Australia Ltd, Ringwood,
Victoria, Australia
Penguin Books Canada Ltd, 10 Alcorn Avenue,
Toronto, Ontario, Canada M4V 3B2
Penguin Books (N.Z.) Ltd, 182–190 Wairau Road,
Auckland 10, New Zealand

Penguin Books Ltd, Registered Offices:
Harmondsworth, Middlesex, England

First published by Onyx, an imprint of New American Library,
a division of Penguin Putnam Inc.

First Printing, August 2002
10 9 8 7 6 5 4 3 2 1

 REGISTERED TRADEMARK—MARCA REGISTRADA

Printed in the United States of America

PUBLISHER'S NOTE
This is a work of fiction. Names, characters, places, and incidents either
are the product of the author's imagination or are used fictitiously,
and any resemblance to actual persons, living or dead, business
establishments, events, or locales is entirely coincidental.

To my loving wife, M'Liss, and children, Alex and Adrienne; their support and prodding made this work possible. And to Ken and Josephine Frandsen for their ability to be in-laws, friends, advisers, parents, and grandparents, and for having the uncanny ability to know what to be when.

One

The long, thin blade of the fillet knife angled before her eyes. No words came from the expressionless intruder, although a solitary bead of nervous sweat began to roll down one cheek.

They stood alone, face-to-face in the dimly lit bungalow. Sounds of a nearby freeway textured the late-evening air with a soft hum. She wanted to scream, to cry for help, but her body would not respond. Pure terror had frozen every synapse in her brain.

A telephone rang.

They flinched, but only one turned toward the sound. The other remained transfixed, the knife inches from her throat.

It rang again.

A slight, cruel smile crept across the intruder's countenance. "I guess you're not home tonight, eh, Christina?"

Another ring as the knife was drawn softly across the victim's throat. No wound appeared.

"Please . . . don't," she murmured numbly. "Anything, I'll do anything. . . . Just—"

Faint counterpoint to her breezy message on the telephone recorder: "Hi, I'm not home right now. . . ."

The intruder reached out to the girl's long black hair. Reflexively, she reared away, taking a backward step to regain her balance. Then another, and another, until her calves nudged up against the couch near the open kitchen doorway. The phone was somewhere in there.

"If you'd like to leave a message, just wait for the beep . . ."

The intruder closed the distance and again reached for her hair. While one hand fondled her tresses, the other held the knife taut against her throat.

". . . and I'll get right back to you, maybe. Ha, ha."

The girl shuddered. She was as far back as she could go. Suddenly her knees buckled and she dropped toward the tattered cushions. But before her body could come to rest, the intruder wrenched her back upward until she was standing on her tiptoes—stretched, as though at the end of a hangman's rope.

Beep.

The intruder pressed the knife harder. This time the pressure was enough for a layer of skin to give way. A slight trickle of blood quickly formed, and dripped slowly onto her exposed breasts.

"Hello, Tina? Where are you?" It was a cheerful masculine voice. "Hey, it's almost twelve forty-five."

"Did you feel that?" the intruder spat. "How'd you like it? I liked it. Shall we do it again?"

"I'll try to drop by in a little bit," the message continued. "You'd better be home, and you know why." The caller ended the message with a suggestive snigger.

In a last desperate bid for freedom, the young woman twisted and flailed with her arms. The efforts landing weakly.

"You little bitch!" The intruder gave a violent yank on Christina's hair as a sharp, searing pain tore through her. Her eyes darted downward and in horror she saw that the knife was now buried deep in her rib cage. Blood immediately stained her slight cotton nightshirt; large drops began to puddle on the floor. She staggered to her left and grabbed for the doorjamb. "Goddamn you," she moaned. "Goddamn you!"

The knife was thrust again. This time, though, she felt little pain. The blade entered at the top of her right shoulder and plunged deeply into her chest and lungs. By the time the next blows bore down, she was no longer aware. All thought and feeling had died quickly after the second thrust. The finely honed steel had partially severed her aorta, and like a dam bursting, blood poured into the thoracic cavity, sapping her consciousness. A moment later she collapsed where she stood, crumpling onto the linoleum. Like an engine with no oil, her heart seized and she was dead.

The killer stood over the body a moment, knife in hand, then calmly switched on the kitchen light for a better view. The knife was thoroughly washed, dried, and returned to the cutlery drawer. Satisfied with the handiwork, the intruder crept out the back door into the brisk night. A light mist had begun to fall.

Two

The blue Ford Taurus pulled in behind three patrol cars and an ambulance, all double-parked in a queue parallel to the dented Toyota Corollas and rusting Volkswagen Beetles. The emergency lights on the lead prowler were still rotating. Its blue beams throbbed rhythmically through the thick, damp air, casting flickering shadows on the rows of modest homes.

Seattle police detective sergeant Leah Harris exited the Ford and looked at her watch; it was 1:42 a.m. The page had come only twenty-three minutes before. *Good time*, she thought, just long enough for her to toss on a nylon jogging suit and a baseball cap to cover her short, reddish blond hair.

For a moment she stood beside her car, looking left, then right, absorbing the topography while steeling herself for what was ahead. She gulped a deep breath, and felt in her jacket pocket for her department badge. It hung on a necklace-length chain, like an oversize dog tag. She looped it over her head and reached to the small of her back for her duty weapon, a compact 9mm Beretta. Reopening the car door, Harris placed the gun under the driver's seat. She wouldn't be needing it now; it would only get in the way.

Moving briskly, her game face now on, the slender, thirty-seven-year-old detective bounced to the sidewalk, stepping past a huddle of onlookers to where three uniformed officers stood milling on the porch of the unassuming residence. Upon seeing her, their backs straightened. "Good morning, Sergeant," the oldest of the officers called out, his voice weary from yet another night spent working in the cold rain. "We've got us a beauty here."

Harris halted just below the trio and shot a look from them to the open door. She could hear voices inside that shouldn't be there. "Meigs, who the hell's in the house?"

"Grearson and Tully," he began defensively. "They're—"

"Get them out of there, now!" Harris cut him off. "And for God's sake make damn sure they haven't touched anything!"

She focused on the youngest officer. He was tall, a head and a half higher than her, with a muscular build. "Kelly, isn't it?" He nodded. "Get some barrier tape and—" Harris paused, looking toward the street. There were now over a dozen neighbors gathered, mumbling and pointing in their direction. "String it from there to there. And get those people away! No one crosses the line, no one. Got it?"

"Yes, sir."

"And don't step on the grass. Stay on the god-damn pavement."

"Right."

"And turn those frickin' blue lights off. Christ, we've got a big enough crowd as it is. We don't need any more attention."

"Yes, sir!" The young officer sprinted away as Meigs stepped down from the porch, fol-lowed by the two uniforms who had just exited the home. Harris rolled her eyes in frustration: both were veterans who knew better than to walk through a crime scene. She withheld the urge to reprimand. Her fourteen years with the department, working in an all-male enclave, had taught her just how fragile a man's ego could be. Whatever she might say now would only be taken as a snipe by some "kiss-ass bitch" who'd been promoted over them, and then only be-cause she was a woman. She had long ago given up fighting that battle.

Harris looked up at the men. "Where's your sergeant? I don't see his car."

Meigs laughed. "He's in the ER."

"Injured?"

"Yeah," Meigs said with a wide grin. "He got his fat ass bit by a dog about an hour ago."

"First time in two years," Grearson chimed in, "that he gets out of his car to back one of us up and—*wham!*—just like that, this mangy old mutt comes out from behind a bunch of garbage cans and takes a chunk out of his butt. Funniest thing I ever saw. I didn't stop laughing for ten minutes."

Harris frowned.

"Oh, he'll be okay," Meigs went on. "A couple of stitches, a few painkillers, and he'll be good as new. Hell, he might even be able to get his disability retirement. You know, not being able to sit down and all; he won't be able to perform the essential functions of a sergeant." Meigs snorted as he laughed at his own joke. "Always sitting down. Get it?"

Harris nodded slightly. It was funny, but she didn't dare let on that she agreed. "Listen, enough of this crap. You two need to seal off the alley behind the house, and don't"—she emphasized the *don't*—"go walking around inside the backyard. Grab the barrier tape. String it about thirty feet on either side of the property and stay back there. Don't move until I tell you, all right?"

"Right, boss."

Tully and Grearson ambled off while Meigs remained.

"Okay, we're going to be short on dicks for a while. Reedy is getting married again and they had a bachelor party somewhere down in the south end. It's probably still going on and they're probably all shit-faced. I've got pages in, but except for the lab techs, it might be a while until I can get a crew here." She paused and surveyed the street again. Kelly was starting to string the four-inch, yellow crime-scene tape printed with POLICE ONLY—DO NOT CROSS THIS LINE.

"Looks good," Harris called out approvingly, "but get those punks farther back." She pointed to a group of young men in hooded sweatshirts—skateboard types, leaning on her car.

Returning to Meigs she continued. "I want you to plant your ass right there at the door. No one goes in without my say-so. Keep a log. I want names, time in, time out, et cetera, of everyone. Start with you, the other two guys, and the medics."

Harris paused. She wished she could remember the name of the remaining officer now sidling up to Meigs. There was nothing more irritating for a line officer than to have a superior not know who he was. Trying not to look obvious, she stole a glance at his name badge. Mac something—but Mac what? Just then the Medic 1 ambulance unit started its engine. Harris ceased worrying about the name. "Stop 'em. They don't leave until I talk to 'em. Got that?"

The officer bobbed his head and darted off.

"Let's get out of the rain," Harris said, motioning for Meigs to step back up onto the front porch. They did, and she continued. "Start from the beginning. I know we've got a dead girl inside. When did you get the call? What was it for; what did you see when you first got here?"

Meigs drew a deep breath. "Well, Sarge, the call went out at oh-one-ten. Nothing special, just a report of a possible prowler. Christ, you know we get a shitload of those calls every Friday and Saturday night around here. You've worked this sector; you know drunk college kids stumbling home from a frat party. That's all it is usually. Anyway, I was just a block away, so I was on this place in ten seconds, but there wasn't a soul in sight, *nada,* nothing. I circled the block once, took a trip down the alley, lit it up with my lights, then came back here."

"How'd you find the body?"

"Community policing . . ."

Harris raised an eyebrow.

Meigs chuckled. "Ah, hell, Sarge, even I get out of the car once in a while. I needed a stretch anyway, so I came up here; the lights being on, I figured they were up and might have seen something. When I knocked on the door, it popped open just enough so I got a look-see. That's when I saw her lying there, blood everywhere and not a sound."

"What'd you do next?"

"Called for backup and medical, then tiptoed in, just in case she might still be alive."

"What else?"

"Hey, listen, Sarge, it was really pretty simple. One look at her, and you'll see what I mean. Blood all around and her chest and neck torn to shreds. It was obvious from the get-go there wasn't going to be too much anyone could do

for her. But for the record, I did check her out,
and no, I didn't touch anything or move her. I
then stepped back out of the house and waited.
Tully and Grearson, they got here at oh-one-
twenty, the ambulance five minutes later. We all
went back in then. The medics stayed for about
five, didn't do much, and our guys were finishing up a cursory walk-through when you got
here. Now, Sarge, you're up-to-date."

Harris glanced at her watch and mentally calculated the time differential. They had been in
the house for maybe fifteen minutes. Too long,
but she'd have to live with it. She relaxed a bit.
Five people had already traipsed through the
crime scene, but luckily no relatives or neighbors. There would be little contamination. A
chain of evidence could be maintained. She
glanced toward the crowd just beyond the barriers. Mostly college students, half-crocked from
a night of partying, emitting nervous giggles as
they eyed the scene before them. Harris looked
back to Meigs. "I'll wait for the lab techs before
I go in. There's no hurry now."

Meigs grinned. "Hey, don't worry. This one
ought to be a piece of cake. Hell, I've been one
of the first cops on scene to probably a hundred
murders. You've got a cute little Hispanic gal
whose boyfriend probably caught her sleeping
around. You know those hotheaded dudes with
their macho shit and all. Christ, I've seen this a
dozen times. Find him and you find the killer."

"I hope you're right. It'd sure make my life

easier." Harris sighed. "Say, what makes you think she's not married?"

"Easy. There's no beer in the fridge and no dirty undershirts in the laundry. She's got to be single unless she's a dyke."

The time was 0213.

Three

Harris hung up her car cell phone. She sat sideways in the front passenger seat, facing the houses, her jogging shoes on the wet pavement. Still waiting for the lab technicians, she had spoken briefly to several of the bystanders, all neighbors of the victim.

Her name was Christina and she spoke with an accent, one of them had said. A student, most thought—they had seen her on campus carrying books. She hadn't lived in the house long, six or eight weeks, probably with no roommates. Harris made a mental note of that. It was unusual for a student to live alone in a house—it cost too much.

At 0231, the white Chevy panel van assigned to the evidence recovery team pulled in behind Harris. She hopped out and walked back to them. As she did, the female in the front passenger seat rolled down her window.

Harris poked her head inside to speak to the

plump woman in a faded green lab coat. Harris knew Jane Fenton from dozens of cases they had worked on together. She was a skilled evidence technician, one of the best the department had: an encyclopedic brain for certain details, coupled with skillful collection technique. She provided the detectives with physical evidence that always withstood challenges in court. Several of Harris's cases had been won solely upon Fenton's skills.

The driver was a different story. Roy Stoddard had been a patrol officer for twenty-two years, until he had a head-on with a drunk driver while on duty. The accident had cost Stoddard his left leg, amputated three inches below the knee. Granted a disability retirement and fitted with a prosthesis, he had come back to work good as new as a noncommissioned employee six months later. When asked why, he'd always laugh and say that his pension check didn't cover the alimony he owed his three ex-wives. But from one look at his bloated red face and beer belly, it was obvious that he probably drank up that check by the fifteenth of every month, and needed another to get him to the first.

Harris quickly briefed them with what she knew, then laid out what she wanted done. "First, Roy, I want a video of the inside of the residence. A quick walk-through before we touch anything. Then go with photos, and then sketches."

Roy nodded sleepily and pulled out a half pack of Marlboros from his breast pocket. He withdrew one and rapped it against the side of his trademark Zippo lighter. "Soon as I have a smoke, Sarge, I'll get to it." He opened his door, stepped out onto the pavement, and lit up, exhaling cigarette smoke in her direction.

While his attitude aggravated Harris, she knew there wasn't much that could be done. Stoddard knew the rules. He could quote civil service and union regulations backward and forward. He knew exactly how far he could push, and practiced this skill as often as possible.

Ignoring him, Harris helped Jane pull two aluminum carry cases from the rear of the van and haul them up to the front porch. Opening the first, Jane removed several sets of latex surgical gloves and paper booties, handing a pair of each to Harris. Just as they began to put them on, Harris's pager went off. She recognized the number. "It's Gilroy. Hold up till I can brief him," she said, and hurried to her car to return the call.

By now, Stoddard had donned his protective gear and set up his video camera. Without warning, he tested the floodlight and caught Meigs looking right at it.

"Christ, Roy! Turn that damned thing off. You asshole, you blinded me."

Stoddard grinned wickedly, hefted the camera to his shoulder, and motioned to Harris, who had just returned. She looked down at her watch and back to him. "Let's call it 0234, Wednesday, November twenty-second."

"Hey, tomorrow's Thanksgiving," Meigs groused.

Stoddard ignored the comment, scowling as he entered the time and date into the machine. "Do ya want sound?"

"No," she replied curtly, remembering a previous crime scene Roy had filmed. "Keep it off. I don't need anyone farting on camera. Defense attorneys just eat that crap up."

Stoddard smirked, pushed the front door completely open, and began taping. Slowly he worked his way in, one step at a time. Harris followed, directing him where to point and where to step. From left to right, they did a pan of the front room, stopping only once as the body of the girl filled the lens. Harris swallowed hard at the sight. The floodlight clearly illuminated the savage wounds; the young victim's face was frozen in twisted agony.

Lividity had set in. Gravity had drawn the remaining fluids in her body down to the lowest points, creating bruiselike purple splotches where the internal pools had formed. It left the upper portions of the corpse an unnatural stark white. This told Harris one thing immediately: the victim hadn't been moved. Lividity, once set, never changed. She had died right where she lay.

Stoddard completed the pan and, with a nod from Harris, moved closer to the victim. "Start just before that first drop of blood and follow it to the couch. Then swing it back to where she's lying. Hold it on the body. Keep it still for a couple of seconds; then go ahead and film the other rooms."

Stoddard complied while Harris stood staring at the scene. Opposite the couch was a stereo CD player and a television set, flanked by two large speakers. There was a bookcase to the right, a fireplace on the left. A coffee table had been shoved to one side; a half-filled glass sat between a few magazines and some unopened mail.

"The ME's here," Jane called through the open door. "And a couple of your detectives—want them in?"

"Not yet," Harris replied. "Get your vacuum and do the front room and the kitchen while Roy's doing the pictures. When you get that done, let's get the usual blood samples and then see what we've got for latents. Tell our guys to go ahead and proceed with the FIs. Have Meigs let the ME know I'll be out in a couple of minutes, but it's going to be a while before we're ready for 'em."

Harris then bent to look at the items on the table. One piece of mail was addressed to Occupant; another was a telephone bill addressed to Ms. Christina Herrera. Harris leaned close to the glass; with her hand she wafted the odor of its liquid toward her nose. Vodka, she guessed. She rose as Roy reentered the room.

"Done. I'll do the stills now."

She followed Stoddard outside and headed toward an unmarked black minivan parked behind the other vehicles. The rain had stopped and the temperature had dropped several degrees, but Harris didn't notice. Her mind was singularly focused on the puzzle before her.

Two men sat in the van, engine idling. The passenger dozed while the driver nervously thumped the steering wheel, in rhythm to a tune Harris couldn't hear. Seeing her approach, he nudged his partner, then exited to meet her. Harris's attention, however, was drawn away from them to where Det. Philip Gilroy stood, waving her to join him. Gilroy was the youngest member of her team; baby-faced, he was only thirty-two. He was a natural though: a hard-charger with an instinctive nose for the job. Given direction, he'd track down every last shred of evidence on his route to an arrest. Presently he was standing beneath a street lamp seventy-five feet away, speaking to two young women.

The van driver stepped in front of Harris as she passed. "How long?" he asked in a grunt. Harris dodged by, ignoring his pained expression, her open palm signaling silence.

"Hey boss," Gilroy said as Harris joined him. "Thought you'd like to hear this right away."

He gestured toward one of the girls, who, like her companion, was dressed completely in black: jacket, sweatshirt, leggings, and boots. Her bobbed hair was also dyed ultrablack, while her nose, ears, and eyebrows had multiple piercings. Harris lost count of the number of holes at ten.

"This is Heather," Gilroy explained. Harris smiled kindly, taking in the girl's glazed, dilated eyes. An obvious smell of marijuana emanated from her clothes. "She lives with, ah—"

"Amy," the second girl interceded. "That's me."

Harris nodded acknowledgment.

"Right, with Amy in the house across the street."

"Right over there." Heather pointed to the dilapidated residence directly across from the victim's home. "I can't believe she is, like, dead. Weird. Really weird."

Gilroy glanced over at Harris. He raised an eyebrow slightly, then started again. "Heather says she saw our victim about six or seven hours ago, maybe around twenty-thirty."

"Yeah, Amy and me were on our way out to this party. It was eight o'clock, maybe eight-thirty. It was something like that; I saw her just standing in her living room looking out her front window. Like she was waiting for someone, I think."

"Yeah, I saw her too," Amy added. "She was just standing there, looking out."

"Was she alone?"

"I dunno. I didn't see anyone else. Could've been, but, like, we were on our way to this party and we really didn't pay much attention."

"Yeah, we really didn't know her, but she was in one of my art classes. I had a latte with her once. You know, being neighborly and all, but she was into a different scene. Like she had bucks, big bucks. You know the type. Daddy's got the money and he likes to spend it on his little girl."

"What about boyfriends?"

"I think she was hanging with an older guy, like over thirty. I saw him from a distance last week. He had this crew cut. Like in the military."

Harris leaned forward. "Can you describe him further?"

"Let's see . . . Maybe six feet tall, maybe more—good bod, though."

"What'd he drive?"

"A black Beamer. It was really cool."

"Was he Hispanic?"

"Naw, but the other dude who came by from time to time was."

"Who was that?"

"Another dude, maybe forty or more. He drove a dark green Lexus. Just like my step-dad's. Nice wheels. Anyway, he looked like a lawyer. You know, gray suit, shiny shoes. A downtown type. He'd drive up, honk his horn, and she'd come skipping out of her house, all decked out—Nordstrom's stuff, you know, shiny and slinky—and hop into his car. Four or five hours later, they're back and he'd just drop her off."

"Was that often?"

"Maybe twice a week."

Harris pulled Gilroy aside. "Go on over to their house and get a quick taped statement from them. I want as much detail as you can get on these two guys: cars, clothing, et cetera. We'll focus on them for now. I'll start looking through her personal stuff and see if I can come up with names and telephone numbers. By the way, who else came out with you?"

"Jennings," Gilroy replied. "He's around here somewhere. He went up the street when I came this way."

"Right, I'll find him. It's getting late; just get their statement, then back to the house, pronto. We'll need to nail down just who these two guys are and get on top of them right away, especially before they have time to work on their stories. That is, of course, if either of them needs to."

The time was 0301.

Four

Harris lifted the yellow barrier tape and proceeded to the front porch. Meigs was settled against the railing, sipping a cup of steaming coffee. "Smells good; where'd you get it?"

"MacRae ran down to the Seven-Eleven over on Forty-fifth. You want a cup?"

Harris nodded gratefully.

"I'll have him go get some more. Black?"

"Yeah, please. By the way, where's Tully?"

"They needed another unit at a bar fight over on Fifty-fifth. He drew the short straw."

Harris nodded indifferently and proceeded to put on another pair of booties and gloves before reentering. Both Jane and Roy were now dusting for latent fingerprints, oblivious to the girl's body that still lay crumpled on the floor like dirty laundry.

Jane looked up. "Hey, I think I've got the murder weapon. Let me show you."

Harris followed Fenton into the kitchen. A

drawer to the right of the sink was open; a solitary knife sat above it on the counter. "When we've got knife wounds as the cause of death, the most logical thing to do first is to find the knives that should be in the house, like here." She pointed, using a pencil from her lapel pocket.

Harris scrutinized the utensil. It was an expensive-looking fillet knife. It had a seven-inch tempered steel blade, with a high-impact, black plastic handle.

"Just a quick look at the wounds, and you can tell it had to be a slender bladed knife, but also something fairly long. This one fits the bill. Plus—and this is the clincher—notice where the tang meets the handle."

The two bent close to examine the object. At first Harris didn't see anything; then finally she detected a minute thread, lodged at the point Jane had described.

"From the victim?"

"I'm willing to bet on it," Jane said. "Same color as the nightshirt. I'll prove it for sure in the lab."

"Prints?"

"Naw, washed clean, but there's probably going to be some blood residue inside the handle area. A quick wash wouldn't have touched it."

"Sure looks like a domestic-violence setup. Young girl, two boyfriends. One finds out about the other and *voilà*, another statistic."

"I'd say that too, except for one thing."

Harris straightened. She had started to relax. The case had the look of an easy arrest, followed by a quick confession. In a crime of passion, evidence was always abundant and clear. But the tone of Jane's voice caused a warning pang in Harris's stomach. "Okay," she proceeded cautiously, "you've got something that's going to screw up our nice little theory, right?"

Jane gave a self-satisfied nod. "Kill the overhead light." Harris complied as Fenton bathed the countertop in the purplish beam of a small ultraviolet lamp. Splotches immediately appeared, brightly illuminated in the purplish light, interspersed with dustlike grains of particles, all barely visible.

"Those splotches are from drops of blood that have been wiped away. It was a messy kill. There had to have been blood spatter on the killer's hands, and in the process of washing the knife, some landed here. What you're seeing is the smudge pattern left after they were wiped away."

"And those little orange speckles?"

"Ah, that's the whole point. It's a kind of talcum powder."

Harris cast a quizzical look.

"I recognize the color; I see it all the time. It's the stuff inside the surgical gloves we're wearing—what makes 'em go on easier."

"Are you telling me what I think you're telling me?"

Fenton looked solemn. "Sorry."

"Shit, then this was a premeditated murder. Probably still a boyfriend, but there was some planning, some forethought."

"Yeah, not many people go around with surgical gloves in their back pocket just in case they need them."

Harris flipped the kitchen light back on as Meigs yelled through the open front door. "Coffee's on, Sarge. Come get it while it's hot."

Harris was glad for a break. She stepped gingerly over the body, and out to the front porch.

"Here." Meigs handed over the Styrofoam cup, and waited for Harris to take a sip. "I think we've got a problem," he then said with a sigh. "The lieutenant and Sergeant Riley ain't here, so I guess I'd better dump this in your lap. Sorry, Sarge, but one of the guys screwed with the scene. It was MacRae. He just fessed up and gave this to me." As he spoke, he pulled a Polaroid photograph from his coat pocket. In the dim light Harris could see it was a picture of a handsome, well-built man in his thirties. He was sitting on a bed, bare-chested, wearing only a pair of unbuttoned jeans. He was smiling, posed like a model for a seductive magazine layout.

The picture slipped from Harris's fingers. Meigs stooped to retrieve it, then handed it back. "Please don't get too pissed. MacRae freaked. He saw this picture in the gal's bedroom, on her dresser, and just grabbed it without thinking. Aw, hell, it's a picture of one of our own guys. MacRae's old partner, John Darby. He's Narcotics now, runs a proactive unit out of our precinct. Christ, Sarge, you know what this might mean? Jesus, it—"

Harris cut him off midsentence with the ferocity of a marine drill instructor. "I want a written statement from MacRae before he goes off duty. I want a written statement from you before you leave this porch. No exceptions, not one—you got that? No bullshit, no excuses, no nothing!" She paused and drew a deep breath. "Who else knows about this?"

"Just me and MacRae."

"Keep it that way for now. We don't need anyone from Internal Affairs in here any sooner than necessary."

Harris stopped. Her fingers twisted the photo. "Damn it," she mumbled in frustration. Ten minutes before, she'd had a simple case. Now she knew different. She tossed her booties and gloves into the trash container Roy had set up, downed her coffee in three gulps, and dashed for her car. Moments later she had the captain on her cell phone. She quickly explained the situation, then hung up.

Still holding the photo, she threw it violently against her windshield. "Bastard," she breathed through gritted teeth. "You lousy goddamned bastard!" Harris knew John Darby all right, knew him very well. Only an hour and a half prior, she had left him dozing in her bed.

The time was 0314.

Five

Sgt. Frank Milkovich drew the razor slowly across his right cheek as he gazed absently into the mirror. He was six-foot even, in good shape, though his light brown hair was beginning to gray at the temples and thin on top. He was still half-asleep, and barely noticed the overweight tomcat rubbing against his bare ankle. The orange-striped feline was purring loudly.

It was 0537, an hour earlier than he usually rose in order to be at the office by eight. Since being reassigned, he had grown used to the regularity of that schedule. Eight to five, with few callouts or late, lonely nights on stakeout. At forty-six, he was content to leave those to the young Turks. At this point in his life, he didn't even care that through bad luck and against his wishes, he had been forced into the position of acting Internal Affairs supervisor. In the past twenty-three years, he had been shot once, crashed three department cars, been spat upon, kicked, punched, and scratched too many times to remember. He felt tired, used up, like an old dog that preferred to lie on the porch rather than chase a passing car.

Unfortunately, he knew he had become what he had once most hated: a clock watcher—not of minutes or hours, but a watcher all the same; waiting for the next few years to tick away so he would reach the relief of retirement. Whereas other professionals, doctors and lawyers his age, were just entering their prime, cops were worn-out old men by fifty.

Milkovich finished shaving, dressed, then went downstairs to the kitchen. He grabbed a granola bar and washed it down with a glass of nonfat milk. That done, he fed the cat and exited through the back door of his modest town house to a carport in the alley. There, his unmarked police car sat. It was a four-year-old, dark gray, slightly battered midsize Dodge.

In twenty-five minutes he was in the center of the city, at his desk on the sixteenth floor of the Public Safety Building, two floors down from the chief. It was early still, and he was alone.

Savoring the quiet, Milkovich gazed out his window to the east. The building across was but one story taller than his floor, allowing an unimpeded vista of the suburbs that rose up the foothills like a creeping rash. But it was to the mountains beyond, still shrouded from the night of rain, that he fixed his attention. The first rays of sunrise pierced the thinning clouds, lighting the skyline's eastern fringes with a thin ribbon of scarlet. He loved that sight. It was the only thing he loved about the office.

Working Internal Affairs, IA, was—to his mind—the lowest form of investigative life: pond scum in the police food chain. It was here that he had landed four years prior, as a result of an unjustified disciplinary action. Unjustified—or was it? Was it even discipline? To Milkovich it was, although his reassignment from Narcotics to IA was officially publicized as a promotion, an irony Sergeant Milkovich had pondered at length. However, time had buffered his pain and blunted his speculations, although he firmly believed it was the current chief who had maneuvered him into this career abyss.

The chief was like that, well practiced in Machiavellian tactics. "Keep your friends close, but your enemies even closer," he was often known to say. And not unlike a capitalist in Stalinist Russia, if you bent Chief Miller the wrong way, it was off to the firing squad, or worse— banishment to some assignment that sucked the spirit from you. Curiously, Milkovich had been transferred here as merely an assistant to the lieutenant who ran the section, but that same lieutenant had fallen off a ladder at home four months prior and fractured his back. The chief had had no other choice than to appoint Milkovich acting lieutenant. And odds were, Milkovich worried, he'd keep the thankless job.

Milkovich swiveled around and pulled a fresh yellow legal pad from a desk drawer. He positioned it in front of himself, then took his coffee cup and walked down to the break room for hot water. Returning, he pulled an herbal tea bag from a small tin in his left file drawer, and set the cup to steep. Waiting patiently, he booted up his computer to check incoming e-mails.

Several moments later he heard the sound of approaching footsteps. Stifling a yawn, Milkovich leaned back in his chair, ready to greet Chief Miller with feigned heartiness.

Miller stepped into the office. He was fifty-five, balding, and twenty pounds too heavy. His complexion was ruddy and hard, giving him the look of a man about to have a stroke: a not-too-unlikely prospect. He guzzled coffee while on duty, guzzled scotch when off, and he chain-smoked all the time. A crushed pack of Camels poked out of his rumpled shirt pocket.

Milkovich coughed as the chief dropped heavily into the solitary chair opposite him; the odor of stale smoke seemed to seize the fresh air.

"G'morning, Frank," Miller said in his usual gravelly voice.

Milkovich eyed him; he looked tired. It was obvious he hadn't slept much the previous night.

Miller glanced hungrily at Milkovich's cup. "You got some coffee?"

"Herbal tea. Would you like some?" Milkovich knew the answer.

"You got to be kidding, that crap. It'll turn ya

queer!" The chief laughed and glanced outside.
"Lovely morning, glad the rain finally stopped."

Milkovich nodded in agreement, wondering
about the pleasantries. It was unusual coming
from Miller. There followed a moment of awkward silence; the chief fidgeted. This too was
something Milkovich had never seen in the man.
Miller's reputation throughout the department
was as an in-your-face type of manager: blunt
and loud, period.

Milkovich fiddled with his legal pad. "It's
early—you got me out of bed. So what's up?"
He tried to mask his irritation, but it still
showed.

"Well," Miller began slowly, rocking back in
his chair, "we have a potential problem with
one of our guys. If the press gets wind of this,
it could make life miserable for all of us." He
shifted forward to rest his beefy arms upon Milkovich's desk. Again there was a moment of
silence.

Miller frowned. "This got me out of bed, too.
I was trying to get a good night's sleep and I
get a call like this at three a.m. We had a homicide up in the university district last night.
Young Hispanic gal, around twenty or so. Got
knifed real bad. Someone just ripped the shit
out of her. Looks like a domestic. From what I
know so far, odds are she knew the killer—
probably a boyfriend. There weren't signs of
forced entry or anything else to indicate
otherwise."

"So where do I fit in?'"

"Christ, Frank, where do you think?"

Milkovich slowly set the legal pad back down. He began tapping it gently with his forefinger. He looked into Miller's eyes; though bloodshot, they were still a piercing blue. "So who?"

"John Darby." Miller grunted. "Do you know him?"

"I know the name, but no, I don't recall ever actually meeting him. How much of a suspect is he?"

"At this point, I'm not really sure myself, only that his picture was found at the scene: a Polaroid of him, half naked, sitting on the victim's bed. He may have nothing to do with this at all. Let's hope so for everyone's sake. But we've got to be real proactive with this one. That's why I want you on top of this right now. We've got a criminal investigation going, but you're going to have to do a concurrent internal. Even if he's not involved, I want to know why his picture was there. I don't like girlfriends of cops getting murdered, not in my town."

"Who's the lead on this?"

"Det. Sgt. Leah Harris."

"She's not going to like me butting my nose into her investigation. I can tell you that right now."

The chief's eyebrows narrowed. "I don't give a shit. Drop everything else you're doing and work this. By the way"—Miller's face became stern—"don't let this influence your investigation, but Darby's a good man. He's done good work. I have the greatest confidence in him, I'll guarantee you that." Milkovich caught the chief's not-too-subtle message. He feigned acknowledgment with a bob of his head while his superior continued, "But you know how the press is, for God's sake! Make sure you're doubly thorough on this. For the record, you can't give him any breaks. Not one. Got that?"

Milkovich nodded again.

"If he's innocent, clear him. If by some remote chance he's guilty—hell, I'll hang him myself." Miller paused for effect, then briefed Milkovich with the few other details that he knew.

He left as the sky to the east reddened in a corona of fiery orange, expanding outward like a slow-motion explosion.

Six

Milkovich sipped his tea and stared across at an art deco print, a birthday present from years past. One his wife—now ex-wife—had bought for him. It was all he had left of her. Too much drinking, too many odd hours, had ruined that marriage. The final push came after his reassignment to IA. For a year he had sunk into a mire of self-pity. By the time he had wandered his way out, she was gone. One weekend she had taken everything, stripped their apartment bare, leaving him only his clothes, a toothbrush, and the print. That pain, too, had subsided; only when he concentrated on the framed print did any remembrance of his marriage resurface.

Milkovich refocused his thoughts, jotting down the names he had so far: Darby, Harris, and Miller. Absently, he wrote them several times, ripped the page from the tablet, crumpled it, and started over. It was how he thought. With whom and where to begin? Suddenly he picked up his phone and dialed a three-digit number.

"Homicide," a strong voice barked. "Sergeant Lewis speaking."

"Hey, Dan, this is Frank," Milkovich said. "That knifing in the university district last night. Do you know if Harris's HIT squad is still out there?" "HIT squad" was jargon born of cop humor, a play on the acronym for Homicide Investigation Team.

"Naw, they knocked off a couple of hours ago to get some sleep. They're going to be back at it around ten, I think. Say, anything I can help you with?"

Milkovich knew what those last words meant. He heard it every time he started an investigation. "Anything I can help you with" was code for *What's going on, who's in trouble, and am I in any way a part of it; further, if I am, I know nothing, and get me my union rep.* Milkovich ignored the prying. "Find the address, and call me back. Also, for right now, forget I even called you. Got it?"

"Ah, Frank, come on. Who screwed up?"

Milkovich met the homicide detective's inquiry with silence. This was the part that he hated most about his job. Every phone call, every question, every action was viewed by the line troops with paranoia. His very presence at a precinct, over something as slight as a casual chat in the hallway with an employee, was whispered from officer to officer throughout the following shifts as they parked, car to car, during a slack moment. Each would mentally review all his actions over the past few weeks, trying to think of whom he might have pissed off, and what kind of excuse he could concoct to cover his ass.

"All right, I get the picture. I'll call you back with the address in a minute."

Milkovich hung up, swiveled to his right, and logged on to the department's computer network. He tapped in his password and a menu appeared, prompting him for another entry. *You have entered the Personnel Maintenance Program,* it read. Then in bold lettering: STOP! ONLY AUTHORIZED INDIVIDUALS WITH PROPER PASSWORDS MAY PROCEED. UNAUTHORIZED ENTRY MAY RESULT IN SEVERE DISCIPLINARY ACTIONS, BOTH CIVIL AND CRIMINAL.

Milkovich entered his code. Only he, the chief, and the personnel manager had unsupervised access to the data in this area. He entered Darby's name and in a moment the officer's vital statistics appeared:

Name: <u>Darby, John F.</u>   Current Rank: <u>Sergeant/</u>
<u>Investigations</u>
DOB: <u>03-01-63</u>
POB: <u>Panama City, Panama</u>
Hgt: <u>6'03"</u> Wgt: <u>200</u> Hr: <u>BLN</u> Eye: <u>BLU</u>
Hire Date: <u>11-15-94</u> Type: <u>Lateral Entry</u>
If Lateral, Previous Law Enforcement Employer:
<u>San Diego PD</u>

Milkovich tabbed to the next page, headed TRAINING:

College: <u>San Diego State University, San Diego, CA</u>
Degree: <u>BS Criminal Justice</u>
Date: <u>06-01-84</u> GPA: <u>2.75</u>
Police Academy: <u>State of California, Basic Law Enforcement</u>
Date: <u>04-18-86</u> Class Rank: <u>5/42</u>
Dept: Training: Community Policing (80 hrs), SWAT I & II (120 hrs), Supervisor I (40 hrs), Legal Issues I, II & III (60 hrs), DUI Detection (16 hrs), Pro-Act Team (40 hrs), Advanced Narcotics Investigation (80 hrs)

Milkovich paused to reread Darby's file, confirming there was nothing unusual about the record. Reaching for his tea, he finished off the cup and hit the tab button again. This brought up: EMPLOYMENT HISTORY

Previous Law Enforcement Employers: <u>San Diego PD 01-03-84 to 11-01-92</u>
Prior Military Service: <u>U.S. Navy 06-01-84 to Present*</u>
   *U.S. NAVY RESERVE—RANK: O-4, LT. CMDR.
   END OF FILE*****END OF FILE*****END OF FILE

Milkovich made a mental note of the navy experience. If and when he questioned Darby, it might be useful to keep it in mind. Persons with military experience responded well to authority figures, or at least pretended to.

Milkovich logged off the Personnel database and next checked his e-mail. There was only one new message. It read:

11.23 14:00:25 PST

From: Saunders/Computer Administrations
To: Investigative/Administrative Personnel

The FBI's confidential Internet Bulletin for the posting of criminal information, APBs, Missing Persons, etc., is now up and running. To access, simply log on to this Web site: http://www.fbi.in fo.bb./keylog/usr. Your initial password is SPD1234. Just follow the directions from there.

Milkovich finished the message and out of curiosity clicked on the hypertext. Several moments later the site appeared. As instructed, he entered the assigned password and submitted it. This brought him to a second screen, where he filled out a questionnaire on his identity and professional background. He was then asked to compose his own personal password. He paused and thought over several possibilities. Everything needed a password nowadays. How was he going to remember yet another one? While mulling that thought, he leaned back in his chair and his attention drifted to his desk calendar. He focused on it, and began reviewing his commitments for the week.

There were three investigations that he was currently working. The first was almost done: an excessive-use-of-force case, in which an elderly couple claimed they had been pushed and shoved by an officer at a domestic. The second was an internal-theft situation: someone, apparently an employee, was stealing dog food from the K-9 unit storage area. The last case involved a sexual-harassment allegation, reported directly to him by the victim just two days prior: a simple e-mail message requesting a meeting with him outside the department, at a crosstown café. He had tried to oblige, to connect with the young female officer while she was off duty, but had to cancel because of another complaint, which turned out to be unfounded. He had rescheduled the engagement for today.

Milkovich considered. Miller had told him to cancel everything, but his experience told him that he had better keep this one appointment. Odds were pretty long that Darby was somehow involved with a knifing murder, but Milkovich knew that a valid sexual-harassment case could be a time bomb ready to explode unless carefully defused. Milkovich made a mental note of the meeting time: 1530 hours.

He returned to his computer screen and the password inquiry. He pondered several possibilities, then typed in: *iaim46*. It stood for: *internal affairs, I am 46.* That entered, he was allowed into the national police bulletin board. He bookmarked the page for instant access, then got up and headed again for the break room with his cup and a fresh tea bag. As he approached, he could hear bits of conversation from the personnel staff who had begun to filter in for another day's work. He joined several middle-aged clerks who were seated at a round table next to a row of snack and soda pop machines. He listened to their chatter about kids, husbands, and coworkers. He said nothing, and wasn't expected to. As the top of the hour neared, they dispersed to their work areas. Milkovich followed one of them, an older woman named Betty, toward a locked office with a large room adjacent to it. Access to this area was restricted, guarded religiously by the woman he was accompanying.

"Just need a quick look at a file," Milkovich said as Betty fumbled with her set of keys. She grunted, found the right one, and unlocked the door. Flicking on the lights, she walked over to her desk, picked up a register, and handed it to Milkovich. "Sign in." He did; then they both entered the back room. It was filled with rows of heavy-duty, four-drawer file cabinets, all government gray, all locked shut.

"Open up the first D." Milkovich indicated.

"Anything else?"

Milkovich smiled and dismissed her with thanks. Betty nodded, mumbled something he didn't catch, and trudged out to her desk, leaving him alone in the room.

Reaching into the drawer, Milkovich pulled out Darby's personnel file and spread it open atop the cabinet. It contained a paper copy of what he had viewed on his computer screen as well as a bound stack of his semiannual performance reviews and commendation letters. Milkovich scanned these, but nothing caught his attention. Darby appeared to be a highly rated employee who had received the usual number of kudos from his supervisors. He had made sergeant quickly, though. He obviously knew how to kiss ass. Milkovich smirked and proceeded to the last page that rested atop a slim gray envelope. He straightened. Something was missing. Milkovich peeled back the flap in search of Darby's preemployment documents: a background investigation, psychological examination, and polygraph test. They were gone, the envelope empty.

"What the . . . ?" Milkovich shifted his gaze to the open file drawer and flipped through several of the adjacent folders. Darby's documents were nowhere to be found. *Could be a misfile*, Milkovich reasoned. With over two thousand employees, things like this were bound to happen.

Milkovich closed Darby's folder and placed it, as he had found it, back in its drawer. He then ambled out of the records room and was about to mention the discrepancy to Betty, when instead he simply bade her a thank-you and signed out. Maybe it was important, maybe not, but twenty-plus years of street experience had taught Sgt. Frank Milkovich one important lesson in police work—assuming something was a coincidence just might get you killed.

Seven

Sergeant Harris had tumbled into her bed at 0558. She had left the murder scene with dread, worried that John Darby might still be at her apartment.

Throughout the night she had continually fought the impulse to call him, to ask about the picture, why it was there and how it was that he had known the victim. Jealousy? She didn't think so—or was it? After all, she rationalized, they certainly weren't longtime lovers. She had started dating him only a month prior. And although she had known him for much longer, he had never seemed that interested in her before. Very professional, polite, but distant in a way that made Harris believe that he hadn't found her attractive.

One date had changed all that. A twist of fate, a chance meeting at a mutual friend's: a small gathering for a housewarming. Then a stalled car and a request for a ride home. It had been that simple. Much to her surprise, as she had pulled to the curb in front of his residence, he turned to thank her and half-jokingly suggested they have dinner—and soon.

She was floored, but readily agreed. Two nights later they met after work for drinks and a pizza. Cheap date, but she hadn't noticed. They sat across from each other for several hours, talking, laughing, as if they had been friends for years.

"Rule number one," Darby had said with mock sternness. "We don't talk about work or anybody we work with."

"Agreed," Harris remembered saying, but within two minutes their conversation had drifted in that direction. It didn't matter. For Leah Harris, what was said was just a blur. It was the closeness she remembered. The feeling that there was an immediate bond, despite their only having just begun to remove their emotional camouflage.

Three nights later they met again. The connection rekindled: dinner at a bistro, followed by a walk in the park at Pier 70. The smell of salt water on the air, waves gently lapping the bulkhead, then a kiss good-night.

Harris had tried to remain in control, to pace the relationship. No more than two meetings a week to start, she secretly pledged. She had tried to be unavailable on occasion, to be elusive, but in the end it was all a charade. She found herself waiting by her phone like a teen-

ager, anxious and worried that no call had come
from him that day.

And now what? The man with whom she was
so thoroughly infatuated might be a murder
suspect?

Her sleep had not been sound, but the
alarm rang for some time before Harris was
aware of it. She rolled over and punched the
off button, groaning in an effort to focus her
eyes on the time: 0940—four hours of sleep.
Her head throbbed as she tried to orient herself.

Propped on an elbow, she looked around the
bedroom. It was sparsely decorated, without
much personality. Her mother always complained of that, but Harris ignored her. Their
relationship was one of quiet conflict and constant misunderstanding, which both simply en-
dured in each other's presence.

Harris rose further, and with a yawn reassured herself that Darby was indeed gone. She
knew he would be. He was scheduled for navy
reserve duty and would be out of town for the
next three or four days. And yet . . .

Harris flopped back down and shut her eyes.
Conflicting thoughts raced though her mind. A
murder case to work, suspects to find and inter-
rogate. John was gone, not to be seen or heard
from for several days. But what about the picture; why was it there? She knew she'd have
to interview him, but questioned if she could
or should. Wasn't she too close?

The telephone rang. Harris jumped, then groped for the receiver.

"Leah? Oh, I'm sorry, you were still asleep." It was Darby.

Harris's heart surged at the sound of his familiar voice. Unprepared, she drew a deep breath, stuttering slightly, "John? Wh—where are you?"

"Jeez, Leah, I'm really sorry I woke you up. How late were you out?"

"Till five." She groaned. "And don't worry about waking me up. The alarm went off a couple of minutes ago. I've got to get going anyway."

"So what happened? Who's the victim?"

Harris's head was clear now. She had been caught off guard, surprised by his call. Darby had told her not to expect any contact while he was gone. Phones were usually unavailable; besides, he said the brass didn't like personal communications while on duty. Her shields went up.

"Hey, John, remember, no talking about work." She forced a laugh, hoping her subterfuge didn't sound too obvious.

"Never mind. I just thought I'd call and say good morning. I really enjoyed last night. At least, as long as it lasted."

Harris felt herself smile. "I did too," she whispered.

"Listen, Leah, I've got to run; I'm at the airport. The flight to San Diego leaves in a couple of minutes; they're boarding right now. I'll see you Sunday. Dinner at the same place?"

"I'd love it," Harris said.

"Good, gotta go. I'll see you then. Love ya."

The phone clicked dead before Harris had a chance to reply. For several more moments she lay there, her emotions swirling. With an effort, she switched into high gear, scrambling out of bed and quickly showering. With equal speed, she dressed and was soon out the door.

Harris headed her car toward North Precinct, rather than her downtown office. The HIT members had agreed to meet at the new precinct facility, only ten blocks from where the murder had occurred. They had set a 1000 start, to assess the case and plan their next steps before returning to the murder scene. Allowing for stragglers—Harris ruefully now included herself in that group—it would be closer to 1030.

Jane Fenton, Philip Gilroy, and Ed Jennings were already assembled in the conference room. They all had coffee, and someone had provided doughnuts. Their banter was at a minimum, everyone still groggy from their short night. Harris asked about Roy Stoddard's whereabouts.

Jane glanced at her watch with exasperation. "Who knows? The man does what he damned well pleases. You should count yourselves lucky that you don't have to work with him all the time. He hates work, he hates women, he hates life in general. He's a real pleasure to meet every morning. He usually hasn't showered and he reeks of cigarettes and bourbon."

"Don't feel bad, Jane," Detective Jennings commiserated, "Roy was my partner for five years. Shoot, that was a long time ago. I'm lucky I'm still alive, the way that guy drove. You know, in 'seventy-eight we had those big huge boats, I think they were Dodges, ah, Monacos, that's what they were. Big old boats, but with the police package. They put the four-forty engine in 'em, tuned 'em way up, and wow, in a straight line those cars were rockets. Of course their brakes were junk. You'd get to over a hundred and it'd take two city blocks to stop."

"So what's your point?"

"Well, one night when Roy was driving, we were on Second Ave., southbound, right at Pike. We spot this dude in a 'Vette, headin' toward Pine. His right tail light is burnt out. He's stopped at the light when we pull up right behind him. Roy looks at me, grins, and says, 'buckle up.' " Jennings paused, rolled his eyes, then continued. "As the light changes, Roy flicks on the overheads and floors it. That 'Vette burned a hundred yards of rubber taking off. Funny thing, we did too. We stayed right on the guy's tail past Cherry, past the King Dome, on into the industrial area, like we were in the Indy 500, drafting off of him. No kidding.

"Meanwhile, I'm on the radio trying to coordinate a stopping place with the other guys. Not to mention being scared witless! When we passed the Dome, Roy had the speedometer pegged at a hundred and twenty miles per hour. Thank God it was late at night and there wasn't any traffic."

"How'd you finally get him?" Jane was finally amused.

Jennings laughed. "Our gentleman just pulled over. He just gave up. Believe me, I'm not stretchin' this. But that's not the end of it. Roy always got ticked off with anyone who ran; it was this psycho thing in him. If you ran, at least in his mind, you deserved a pop in the jaw once he snagged ya. Well, this time was no different, except I think Roy was a little more worked up than usual. Must've had a fight with one of his ex-wives before he came on duty.

"Anyways, as the guy pulls over and sticks his hands out the window to show that he doesn't have a gun, Roy grabs for our shotgun. It was sitting upright in the rack between us. Bam! A round goes off right in our car, blowing a big ol' hole in the roof. Someone from the last shift had left it hot with the safety off, and Roy must've forgotten to check the chamber when we started our shift.

"Phew, was he spittin' mad. Not to mention that neither one of us could hear a darn thing now. Somehow I managed to keep him in the car. Two other units rolled up right then, and they arrested the guy for eluding. Meanwhile, we had to drive back to the precinct, show the sergeant what had happened, and write up a lengthy explanation, which in the end got us both three days off without pay. But I didn't complain; it took me that long just to get my hearing back."

They were all still laughing when Roy came stumbling in. He looked like he hadn't slept; his clothes were the same as the night before. He leveled a glare at the group. "What?" he grumbled, as though insulted. "Am I late?" He tossed a thick envelope onto the table, from which several dozen eight-by-ten color photos of the murder scene fanned out.

Harris looked at Roy questioningly.

He shrugged. "I thought you might want these right away, so I took them in and got 'em developed. And here's the video. I can pop it into that VCR." He pointed to the television in the corner.

Harris declined. "You didn't go home?"

"Naw, Sergeant. Hell, I usually don't go to bed until eight or nine in the morning anyway." He grinned, nodding to Jennings. "Hey, Ed. How's the wife and kids?"

"Just fine, Roy." Jennings was LDS, a Mormon. He didn't drink, smoke, or fool around. He had been married for thirty years, had six kids, and could have retired three years earlier, but loved his work. His position in law enforcement made him a highly esteemed member of his ward, a source of personal pride. He always took Roy's teasing with equanimity.

Roy walked over to the coffeepot, filled a dirty cup, and sat at the table with the rest of the group.

"So what have we got?" Harris was now all business. "A female, around twenty, Hispanic, with multiple knife wounds. She lived alone, but has been seen with two men, one at a time." Leah paused, feeling her heart jump as she reached into her purse and pulled out the snapshot of John Darby. She placed it on the stack of other pictures. "Here's a photo of one of them, I think."

Jane held it up. "Good-looking guy. Anyone we know?"

"Hey, that looks like, ah, what's his name?" Gilroy questioned. "I've seen him around here. Darby, isn't it? I think that's his name."

Harris nodded.

"Where'd that come from?" Jane asked suspiciously. "I didn't catalog a picture like that last night."

Harris leaned back in her chair. "Meigs gave it to me. One of the uniforms at the scene had snatched it, thinking to cover for the guy. They'd been partners once. Now Darby's a sergeant working here at North in Narcotics."

"Aw, shit." Roy grunted. "The Internal boys will be on us like flies on cow pies as soon as they get wind of this."

"They already know," Harris said, "or at least will know. When Meigs handed it over to me, I gave the captain a call right away."

Roy scowled. "That ol' captain is going to cover his butt A-SAP. As soon as you were off the phone with him, he was on the phone to the major, who hung up and dialed the assistant chief, who called the chief, who instructed the assistant chief to get an Internal rolling. Hell, all of that took less than twenty minutes. That'd be my guess."

"Well, regardless," Harris continued, "we still have a case to work. John Darby may be a suspect, and may not be. I'll take care of checking his alibi."

As soon as she said it, Harris knew she was close to crossing the line of ethical conduct. Her mind raced. She knew she couldn't keep their relationship a secret, yet she knew he couldn't have killed the girl. Her words came in a rush. "I know Darby fairly well." She felt her face reddening. "I've even dated him a little."

Jane shot a quick glance at her and slyly grinned. "Oh-ho, this is going to be interesting." She nudged her knee against Harris's. "Tell us more, please!"

"There's not really much to say." Harris tried to sound innocent. "I know him, and there's absolutely no way he could be involved in any of this. Why his picture was in the victim's house, I don't know, but I'm sure there's a good reason.

I'm betting you, though, that it's just a coincidence."

Harris confidently eyed each of the individuals before her. She could tell that they were all skeptical; but then, that was their nature. "On with business. Roy, thanks for the pictures. I appreciate the extra effort. Ah, Jane, did you find out about the autopsy?"

"Right. The medical examiner said they could do it this afternoon if there's a rush. They'd prefer Friday though."

"The sooner, the better. I want to know if she was on any drugs. I'll call them when we're done here and have them do it this afternoon. You need to be there. I'll try also."

Jane nodded.

"What about prints?"

"I checked on that on my way in this morning," Fenton replied. "When the body got to the morgue, they took a full set. They ran them through AFIS; no hits."

"I didn't expect there would be. Any latents?"

"We haven't had time to process them. The way this is going, it'll be another day at least before we can get to that."

"The other man"—Harris directed her question to Gilroy—"anything else on him?"

"Well, actually, yes, Sarge. Remember those two beauties with the nose rings I was talking to? When I was at their house getting written statements, a third gal came stumbling in. She was higher than a kite; this one had her belly button pierced, and her tongue." Gilroy gave an exaggerated shudder.

"What else did you see?" Roy asked sarcastically.

Flipping him off with his finger, Gilroy continued amid the laughter. "This little gal was all giggles. She could barely stand up, but after I convinced her that there really had been a murder across the street from her house, and that I really was a cop, she came down fast."

"Crack cocaine?" Jennings interjected.

Gilroy nodded. "She remembered seeing an older guy in a green Lexus-like car about seven p.m., parked at the Seven-Eleven across from McDonald's. He was using the phone booth and—" Gilroy stopped. He wanted to emphasize his next point. "Our victim was in his car."

"Are you sure?" Harris asked.

"She was certain. She had seen them there a couple of times before, doing the same thing."

"Hmmm. Drug dealer?"

"Maybe, but not in a new Lexus and in a business suit. Especially not in this neighborhood."

"Yeah, not in this day and age, but you'd think he'd have a cell phone in his car. Why the pay phone?" She paused. "Anything else?"

"No, but I think if you're all going back to the house, I'll start at the Seven-Eleven. Maybe someone there remembers him or her, and can get us going on an identification. Have we come up with any other information on the victim?"

Harris shook her head. "We found a purse, but no driver's license, Social Security card, or anything else. Just a couple of charge cards and about two hundred in cash."

"Pictures?"

"That's what I don't like," Harris said. "Everyone carries family photos. Christ, even the drunks on Skid Row have pictures; this girl didn't."

"Well, we might have missed them," Jane said. "Besides, we'll be able to spend all day in the house. Things will turn up; they always do."

Harris felt her enthusiasm returning. "Gilroy, you're right about the Seven-Eleven. Check it out, and see what you can find. If you come up empty, I guess you're going to have to start with all the Lexus dealers in the area. We've got a halfway decent description of the car and the guy. If he bought the car locally, we might get lucky. Jennings, you do the neighborhood sweep, door to door. I will be at the house for at least a couple of hours."

Suddenly there was a polite knock, and the meeting room door swung open. A secretary poked her head inside; she consulted her notepad, then announced to Harris, "A Sergeant Milkovich is here, from IA. He'd like to talk to you when you're finished." As she withdrew, Harris gave a roll of her eyes and groaned.

"Let the games begin," Roy pronounced, picking up the stack of photos.

Gilroy chuckled. "Sarge, that's what you get paid the big bucks for. We've got enough to get going—we'll let you deal with the ferret."

Eight

Milkovich stood lost in thought, his shoulder against the deep-set casement window, watching pigeons forage in the rear parking lot. He turned slowly as Harris entered. The door shut with a loud click.

"Have a seat," he proffered while reaching to shake her hand. He watched as she purposely took the one chair with its back to the wall. Milkovich sat opposite, a small oak table between them.

For a moment there was silence. He knew he was an intrusion, an upsetting incursion into the day's routine. To Milkovich, this was typical. No one in the department ever wanted to have to talk to him; they turned defensive, whether they knew anything or not.

"I know you're busy," he began in an effort to set a casual tone. "But I understand that there's a little wrinkle in the case you're working that might have an impact on the department." He smiled as he spoke.

Harris remained stone-faced. She knew what she would have to say, but she wasn't ready. She believed it was her job to find the killer and sort out why Darby's picture was there—not Internal Affairs'. They'd twist everything.

"Now I certainly don't want to interfere with your homicide investigation," Milkovich went on, "but I'm going to have to stay on top of anything that might implicate Sergeant Darby, or any illicit activity relating to our department."

"I understand," Harris said slowly. She felt herself being too rigid—her body language could expose her. She forced a weak joke. "God, I hate it when things like this screw up a perfectly good murder."

Milkovich noted the change. He had interviewed thousands of people. More was learned by how they spoke than what they said. "I understand you have the picture. May I see it?"

"Ah, I left it with the team."

"Okay, I'll check it out after we're done talking. Again, I don't want to interfere, but, well, what's your opinion at this point? Is Darby in any way involved?"

"No." Harris responded, knowing immediately she had replied much too strongly and quickly. "I mean, we have a prime suspect right now. He was seen with the victim just hours before the murder. Odds are, he did it. Of course, there's still the possibility that this is a random attack. It's way too early to tell."

"Have we had any serial killings lately?"

"No, we don't have anything going like that right now, yet we can't rule it out. This could be the start of one, or the return of a killer to a fresh, restocked pasture."

Milkovich inclined his head. "I see. Well, as I said, at this point I'm just going to be monitoring the situation. By the way, have you talked to Darby about this yet?"

"No."

"Any idea when you will?"

"Unless there's a drastic need, it won't be for at least three days."

"Three days?" Milkovich's eyebrows raised.

"He's on navy reserve duty, doing his weekend."

"Where?"

"San Diego."

"He's a friend of yours, isn't he."

Harris's jaw dropped. There was silence as they stared into each other's eyes. She was frustrated with herself, at how quickly she had been read. But she'd known he was good, very good. Despite the stories and gossip that had filtered through the department about the man—his drinking, his personal life, his detachment from every employee—within a couple of minutes he had figured her out. "Damn," she said under her breath, and sagged further with the stark realization that Milkovich could pull her from the case. One phone call, and she'd be off. She searched his face; there was an honesty about it that struck a chord. It was a face that had seen tragedy, and had been changed by it. The eyes were sad, but the rest of his features spoke of resolve. Strangely, Harris felt a sense of trust. Her confidence returned.

"Sergeant Milkovich—" she began.

"Please, no formalities. Just call me Frank."

"Okay, Frank, you're right about Darby. We are friends. I've dated him a few times. In fact, he was with me when the murder occurred. That's how I know he isn't involved."

"And the picture?"

"Good question, but that's one I don't have an answer for. I suppose he could have known her in the past. Christ, I don't know. But I sure as hell am going to find out."

Milkovich smiled shrewdly. "I bet you will. So what time did the murder take place?"

"We don't have a definite yet, but at this point we're assuming around midnight, though it's probably closer to one."

"And Darby was with you at that time?"

"Until I was paged out. He got to my apartment around ten, and was with me all the time."

"Okay, that's good enough for me, for now. Again, I don't want to interfere with your job— or your personal life."

"You're not. In fact, why don't you tag along with me to the victim's house? You'll get a better feel for what we're dealing with."

Milkovich had intended to do that anyway. He instantly liked Harris. She was smart, authoritative, a real professional. Yet he could also detect an appealing sensitivity that softened the hard edges. He looked at his watch as he stood up. "Let's go. I'll follow you." Ten minutes later, they were in front of Christina Herrera's bungalow.

Nine

The morning was warm for November. The streets had dried and there was a feeling that winter had not yet taken hold. There were still a few leaves on the trees and stunted blooms among the dying annuals. Milkovich exited his car and trailed behind Harris. They crossed over the barrier tape toward the bungalow. A lone police officer sat on the porch railing. He looked bored, and was.

The two stopped at the doorway to don gloves before entering. Jane was already inside. Roy was still in their van, talking on the cell phone and smoking a cigarette.

The body had been removed hours before. What remained was a chalked outline and a pool of dried, clotted blood. Milkovich glanced at the area, then moved on. He sensed something amiss, but was not sure what.

Harris went straight to the bedroom, and began searching the dresser. Though Roy had been through each of the four drawers before, she needed to check again. She was worried. Would there be any more pictures?

After doing a quick sweep of the house, Milkovich joined Harris. He watched as she finished the dresser and moved on to the closet. "Anything of interest?" He leaned lazily against the doorjamb.

She shook her head, and tried to ignore him. She didn't like being watched over, not by anyone. Finally she turned to him. "You ever work homicide?"

"Never. Did ten years in patrol, did burglary for a while, then narcotics."

"I guess you're not going to be too much help on this then," Harris jested.

"I'm really not planning on helping. I just need a simple yes or no answer. Was Darby involved? If it's no, I walk away. If it's yes . . . well, let's just hope the answer is no."

"Amen!" Harris agreed. "Come on, let's take a look at the kitchen."

As they approached, they heard the sound of a recorded voice, then the beep of an answering machine. Entering, they saw Jane at the far corner of the room. "Look what we missed last night." She pointed toward the telephone. The instrument sat inside a cubbyhole in the wall. An answering machine was behind, hidden in the recessed shadow.

Jane reached in, pressed the stop button, then rewind. "Do you want to listen to it? I've got a

cassette player in the van. It'd be easier to go
through the messages out there." She removed
the tape.

Harris glanced over at Milkovich. "I'll stay,"
he said, anticipating her question. "By the way,
is it okay to start disturbing things?"

"Go ahead, but don't mess things up too
much."

Milkovich watched the two women depart.
Standing motionless in the silence, he tried to
get a feel for what information the room might
hold. He had done this often on cases, just stopping and thinking, allowing his brain to catch
up and process all the sensory information that
was being constantly inputted. At least, that was
what he told his coworkers when they asked
what he was doing. He hated to acknowledge
that deep down inside was a small portion of
his persona that relied on gut instinct. Inexplica-
ble, but very accurate. Thus, from the very moment he had walked in, he knew something was
amiss. The totals didn't tally. He knew it, but
why?

Milkovich drew a deep breath, entirely
through his nostrils. It was then it hit him—a
faint smell, a vinegary acid odor, like that of
glue used to bond plastic PVC pipe. Quickly, he
eyed the likely places where he could find the
source: refrigerator, stove, one of the cupboards?
Then he saw it: the dishwasher, its door un-
latched. He moved close and could see that the
sheet metal screws securing the front panel were

nearly stripped. He bent down and sniffed. The smell was strongest at the joints. Grabbing a blunt butter knife from the flatware drawer, he removed the four screws, and slid the fascia panel off. And there it was, a small hiding space hollowed from the fiberglass insulation that lined the door. It contained a dozen marble-size balls of brownish black, claylike material. Milkovich held one up to his nose and sniffed. Now he was certain. The soft little marble he was holding was a quarter gram of Mexican black tar heroin.

Milkovich thought for several moments, then replaced the narcotic. He resecured the cover. The pieces were beginning to fit, but not all yet. With a sense of urgency, he began a systematic search of the premises, certain there would be more.

He checked the bathroom, the hallway, the dining area, then returned to the victim's bedroom. He opened the closet, the one Harris had just gone through, and suddenly knew what he was looking for. Below him on the wood floor was a throw rug. He kicked it aside and knelt in the dim space. With his fingertips, he swept the area, quickly detecting a slight near-invisible gap that ran two feet square. Milkovich reached into a pocket and pulled out his key ring. Bending low, he used his house key to pry at the wood. At first he was unsuccessful, but after repeated attempts, he managed to raise the small section of flooring high enough to get a fingerhold. "Got it," he mumbled, and lifted the cover off and set it aside.

Beneath was a metal plate, two quarter-size holes drilled on either end. Milkovich placed his thumbs into them and yanked. The plate popped away freely, exposing a hidden compartment. It was full, but not with what Milkovich had expected. Instead of more heroin or other drugs, neatly stacked bundles of one hundred–dollar bills filled the entire space.

Milkovich knelt to touch the pile. Judging by the size and depth of the storage area, he knew he was looking at close to a million dollars in cash. The euphoria of the find vaporized instantly as the implications of his discovery hit him. He had screwed up.

In a panic, he quickly replaced the metal lid and flooring, spread out the rug, and slipped outside to find Harris.

Ten

Sergeant Harris was beside the evidence van, her head poked halfway inside. Absorbed in listening to the answering machine tape, she didn't notice Milkovich approach. He had to tap her shoulder.

"What?" She turned, and her irritation subsided as she saw his urgency. With a slight jerk of his head, he led her a dozen steps away, then stopped. He didn't want anyone else to hear what he was about to say.

Harris reached his side. "Well?"

"We're screwed."

"What are you talking about?"

"Who owns this place? It's a rental, isn't it?"

"Yeah, some out-of-state holding company. They evidently own several houses in the area. I don't remember the name. I think Gilroy has it. So what's the problem?" Harris's patience was running thin.

Milkovich looked her directly in the eyes. His

face was grim. "I'm going to go out on a limb. God help me if I'm wrong, Sergeant Harris, but I'm going to have to trust you, even if I really don't want to." He paused, studying her eyes one more time. "I don't suppose you had a search warrant for today's entry?"

"We don't need one! We've had continuous occupation of the premises since the crime was discovered. What do you think all the crime scene tape and officers standing at the door are for?"

"That may work for a homicide like this, but this is different. Shit, I may have already messed things up."

Harris's annoyance changed to puzzlement. "What the hell are you talking about?"

"I found some heroin in there."

"Heroin!" Harris's interest skyrocketed. "Where? We've been through every inch of the place—twice!"

"It's Mexican black tar, not much, mind you, but damn it, I should have backed out right then. I know better. We could've had a telephonic search warrant in half an hour, and things would have been kosher. I could've gone through every nook and cranny then. Christ, I've been out of criminal work for way too long."

"How much heroin?" Harris pressed hard. "Where?"

"A couple grams, inside the dishwasher door."

"A few grams, big—" Harris stopped midsentence. She stiffened. She sensed that this was not about a couple grams of dope. A veteran cop couldn't have cared less about that. In fact, you'd expect to find some drugs or paraphernalia in a place like this.

She rephrased. "You found something else, after you found the heroin?"

Milkovich nodded. "Fruits of the poisoned tree, I'm afraid." He drew a deep breath. "You know that closet I watched you go through?"

Harris nodded cautiously.

Milkovich frowned. "A few minutes ago, you were standing on a million dollars, cash. It's gotta be drug money."

"Where?"

"There's a compartment concealed beneath the floor. Someone did nice work—Christ, come to think of it, it's cedar lined. Just like a hope chest."

Harris glared at Milkovich. Thoughts of Darby had been absent for a while. It had seemed obvious to her that he had not committed the murder. But now the equation was changing. She shivered, guessing what Milkovich was going to say—if not murder, then drugs. For a cop, getting caught in the latter could actually be worse.

"You were saying?" Harris anxiously prompted.

Milkovich didn't immediately reply. He had suddenly slumped into deep thought. He rubbed the back of his neck and mumbled to himself, "The god damn wrappers . . ."

"What the hell are you talking about?"

". . . like they all had the same third-grade nun teaching them penmanship."

"Milkovich!"

His lazy gaze vanished. "I gotta check a few things out."

"Check what out?"

"Look, Leah, I'll be blunt. Something tells me that Darby is up to his ass in this setup, whatever it is, and by the look on your face, the thought has occurred to you, too. He may not be linked to the murder—then again, he may—I don't know. What I do know is that we have some kind of drug house here: a victim linked to a narcotics officer, and one who travels back and forth to southern California on a regular basis. You tell me. What do you think?"

Harris wilted, her face noticeably pale. "I'm screwed."

"No, you're not. Not yet. Listen, we've got to keep this quiet. At least for a couple of days. You can't tell anyone. Jesus, you know how cops are. They gossip like a pack of politicians. If word gets out that I'm after a dirty cop involved in drug smuggling, everybody and his brother will know about it. I need time to confirm a few things."

"But I'm going to have to tell my captain."

"No, you don't," Milkovich corrected. His bearing was infused with an intensity Harris hadn't seen before. It instantly caught her attention. "Look at the manual. In an Internal Affairs investigation I have the authority of the chief to make any decision necessary that is in the interest of the department. And right now the best thing to do is to keep this under our hats. If there's one involved, there's going to be more."

"And if Darby calls me?"

"Act natural, but get a hold of me the minute you're done talking."

"But—"

"Just do it. Damn it, there's going to be enough talk with me being here. Make sure you keep a lid on the drugs; don't even tell your team members. Make something up, I don't care what. And keep a uniform on the house for another day. That'll buy us some time."

Harris slowly nodded her agreement—also to buy time. The pit of her stomach was near flood stage, churning with misgivings. She looked at her watch; it was 1159.

Eleven

With a certain self-satisfaction, Milkovich toyed with his private theory as he drove back to his office. For a number of reasons, he hadn't let on to Harris what he truly thought. He was still uncertain for one, but years prior, his very outspokenness about what he now suspected had infected Seattle had led to his transfer out of Narcotics. Those in charge, Chief Miller in particular, had been like ostriches with their heads in the sand. They chose to ignore his warnings. Maybe he had spoken too adamantly; maybe he had been too critical of the administration's response, or rather lack thereof. Maybe . . . Milkovich derailed that train of thought. The bitterness was not worth reliving.

His mind changed tracks. Today was what was important. Was he right? Was he accurately interpreting the data in the proper light? The bundles of cash, the markings on their wrappers, Darby, the victim, were all pieces of a puzzle that could fit together, but that likewise could be rearranged with little effort into a different order. What if? Milkovich kept asking himself. What if he was wrong about the money's source? What if this young girl had been murdered by a maniac and all his theories were bullshit? What if . . . what if the picture of Darby was a plant? God knows why it was there, but . . .

Milkovich pulled his car over. He had just run a red light and hadn't even been aware of it until he was across the intersection. He hadn't come close to hitting anyone, but a tremble wove through his body. He shook his head in disgust. He was being sucked in. He could feel it. The emotion was strong. His brain was focusing on this enigma, to the exclusion of all else. He was excited, nearly euphoric. He knew all too well this adrenaline rush. It had caused a divorce, a trip to alcohol rehab, and a stint with the department's shrink. And while he had conquered his demons, the price had been high. Professionally, his career had been lobotomized. Privately, his personal life had diminished to a sterile, orderly procession of uneventful days, none changing significantly from the rest.

But he was happier now, wasn't he? He tried to reassure himself. There had been so much pain back then, so very much pain. His mind drifted to the past.

It had started with the calls to his wife: "I'll be late, dear; it's important, I can't leave right now. . . ." He'd work an hour over, then three, then double shifts if he was hot on the tail of someone. "Honey, I can't come home right now. I've got this guy close to confessing. I just can't leave. . . ."

At first there was stoic resignation on her part. She had known he was a cop when she married him, but they were in love and that was all that mattered. She was the most important thing in his life. He'd told her that often. But the calls came with more frequency; the time away from home grew longer. Then it seemed that even when he didn't have a hot case, he would still stay after to talk with his partners, and they'd all go out for a couple of beers. Theirs was a closed society, and she had no way in.

Her resignation changed to tears. "Why are you crying?" he'd murmur soothingly into the phone. "I'll be home in a little bit." Yet even as he set the receiver down, Milkovich knew that his mind would not stay centered on her; rather, it was the case, always the case. And when he finished one, there was always another.

It had dragged on for another year. Tears became bitter resentment. The relationship was dead, all vital signs gone. It was but a matter of time, and when that time came, Milkovich was not surprised. He knew he was responsible, but he couldn't control the drive within him. On scent, he was alive and aware beyond normal stimuli. It was a narcotic that possessed his soul.

Then she was gone. A note on the kitchen table; the bank account split down the middle. He didn't bother to follow. At first it was easier without her. He wrote it off, a small chapter to edit from his life. But all too quickly, without the counterbalance of his marriage—tattered though it was—he began a free fall into his own personal abyss. The crash came one night: another door to break down, an arrest to make, but this time the spiral had him. Tunnel vision replaced readiness. He never saw the guy who shot him, who came from behind while he was questioning a suspect. All he remembered from that night was lying on the dirty floor, looking up into the eyes of a young female medic. Was she shouting at him? He couldn't hear; what was she saying? Why was she screaming at him? He tried to answer; did she hear what he said? Then there was nothing.

Milkovich wiped the nervous sweat from his brow. "Damn!" he cursed while angrily smacking the dashboard with his fist. In one stark moment he had uncovered feelings held at bay for years. Now what? he wondered. "I was good then," he said softly. "I was a natural. A goddamned natural. What happened to me? What have they done? God, what have I done?"

Then he felt it, a surge of adrenaline racing through his body. He straightened up and gazed into his rearview mirror. It was back. He could see it. The cocky confidence. It was all back, though tempered by a hard-earned maturity. He shoved the gearshift into drive and punched the gas pedal. He was going to crack this case open. He knew it; he could feel it. Frank Milkovich was alive again.

Twelve

It was 1238 when Milkovich entered the elevator. He thumbed his floor number and impatiently rocked on his heels as he rode upward. The door slid open and he quickly strode down the hallway. The same crowd of employees was in the break room, this time for lunch. He stopped, back-stepped, and turned in, heading for the coffeepot. He filled a spare cup, and bought a Snickers bar from one of the vending machines. The women watched in amazement.

"Going off your diet, Milky?" one of them joked. "And real coffee, not even decaf!" she jibed. "Deciding to join the human race?" He flashed a wicked grin and scooted out.

His desk was as he had left it, except for one thing. He saw it immediately—the legal pad that he had jotted notes on had been moved. It was now sitting faceup, centered on the desk. It was his habit to either secure notes in a locked file before leaving the office, or to at least flip them over. He was certain he had done the latter. He froze. Was this paranoia? He knew well that feeling, too; it was the constant side effect of the investigation high. He scanned the rest of his office. Nothing else seemed amiss.

"Frank." Milkovich whirled around, instinctively sliding his right hand toward the gun in his holster. "Whoa! A little jumpy today, eh, Frank?" Chief Miller stepped into the room. He gazed at the steaming cup of coffee still held in Milkovich's hand; he could smell the brew. "Coffee? Are we jumping off the wagon?"

Milkovich set the cup down, looking slightly abashed. "I needed a little change."

The chief chuckled, then turned brusque. "Brief me. What have we got so far?"

Milkovich relaxed, but just on the surface. He plopped down in his chair. "Well, Chief, I'm not really sure," he lied. He wanted time. "At this point we still don't have any tie-in except the photo. Darby is on reserve duty right now, and I think he's going to have a pretty solid alibi anyway."

"Good. He just doesn't seem like the kind of officer who would get himself into something like this."

"Listen, Chief, maybe by the end of the day I'll have something. I'll call you. Aw, shit, I almost forgot. I know you told me to drop everything, but I've got another case that's going to need an interview this afternoon. I'll be out doing that for about an hour; then I'll get back to this problem with Darby."

Miller patted Milkovich on the shoulder. "Hey, Frank, do what you think is right. You're the boss on these things, but let me know as soon as possible. Hell, even if it's three in the morning, I don't care. Call me. Got it?" He squeezed hard. It was a message being sent: *Don't move a muscle without my knowing about it.*

"Right, Chief," Milkovich acknowledged with mock obedience.

The chief departed, and for a moment Milkovich sat in silence. He stared at the misplaced notepad and pondered the exchange that had just occurred. Had Miller been going through his desk? But why? *There's a connection, there's got to be a connection; things don't just happen,* he reflected.

He sipped his coffee. It tasted bitter, yet possessed a fullness that he had missed. Looking at his watch, he reached for his phone, dialed a number, and waited for the ring.

"Narcotics, Cummins speaking."

"Jerry, it's Frank. I need to pick your brain."

"Oh, man . . . who screwed up now?"

"No, it's not that; I just need to talk to you about . . ." Milkovich hesitated. "Listen, Jer, you got a couple of minutes? I don't want to do this over the phone."

"Jeez, Frank, I'm really swamped. You can come down here if you like."

"That won't work—me walking into Narcotics. Hell, half the department will think you're all dirty."

"They already do," Cummins joked. "But I see your point. Hey, there's a new Starbucks down on Third. How 'bout there in fifteen."

"You got it." Milkovich hung up the phone.

Thirteen

"Oh, sure, I know him," the Vietnamese clerk said. The slight man was standing behind the counter, next to the cash register in his 7-Eleven store. "Very big man, very big."

Detective Gilroy chuckled to himself. Everyone was big to this guy; the clerk stood barely five feet tall. He turned serious, realizing he had hit pay dirt on his first call. He was on scent.

"And how do you know him? Does he come in here often?"

"Oh, yes, yes. Very often. Very nice man. Very important man."

Two teenagers entered the front door. The clerk turned and eyed them suspiciously, then turned back to Gilroy. "You police. Why you do nothing about these hoodlum kids? They all steal, steal everything. Must watch all time. Very bad, these kids."

Gilroy nodded halfheartedly. He pressed further. "This man, do you know his name?"

"Yes, he Mr. Herrera. He good man, helped me get my store."

"How's that?"

"He banker. Give me loan."

"Which bank?"

"That one," the man replied. He pointed out his front window toward the gleaming office building that towered above the others in the university business district, several blocks distant. Gilroy knew it. It was the regional headquarters for the Federated Bank of California.

"Mr. Herrera works there?"

"Yes, yes. He big man there, the boss."

"What kind of car does he drive?"

"First, you tell me what this about. Mr. Herrera my friend. I get him in no trouble."

Gilroy frowned, then tried a different tack. "He's not in trouble at all. A relative of his has been hurt. We want to let him know."

"Ah, I think best you just talk to him about this thing." He reached into a drawer below the counter and pulled out a business card. "Here," he said, handing it to Gilroy. "You call and talk to Mr. Herrera yourself."

Gilroy took the card and glanced at the inscription: *Federated Bank of California, Enrique "Rick" Herrera, Senior Vice President, Northern Operations.* He walked out to his car, grabbed his cell phone, and let Harris know. It was 1306.

Fourteen

Jane Fenton entered the elevator and rode down to the basement offices of the county medical examiner. She knew the way well. She had observed hundreds of autopsies in the twenty years she had worked for the police department. Most were routine. The cause of death and the circumstances surrounding it were usually known. Seldom were there any surprises, and Jane didn't expect this time to be any different.

She passed into the scrub room through a double door marked AUTHORIZED PERSONNEL ONLY. Fenton removed her coat, and began to put on a surgical gown, gloves, and mask.

A middle-aged woman entered, slender, in her late fifties; her graying hair was pulled back so tightly in a bun it looked as if she'd had a cheap face-lift. "This one yours?" she asked companionably. She too began to change into the protective garb.

Jane nodded. "We've got an early-twenties female. She was knifed last night in the U district."

"Anything odd?"

"No, I'm just curious about the angle of entry of the wounds, and the toxicology. Should be routine."

"All right then, let's get to it. Traffic is going to be hell if we don't get out of here by four. Damn holidays anyway."

Jane followed the pathologist toward the autopsy room. As they went through the last set of doors, the smell of strong chemicals hit her like a slap in the face. The gruesome nature of what she was about to witness didn't affect her, only the smells. The rotted flesh and sterilization fluids combined to make her feel as if she were standing in a vat of oily pesticides. She grimaced, felt her stomach turn, but pressed on. In a few moments her nausea passed. Her job depended on being able to acclimate to whatever environment she found herself in, and after two decades, that ability was now automatic.

Christina Herrera's body lay beneath a white plastic sheet on top of a stainless-steel examination table. Gutters lined each side, to capture the fluids that would soon spill out. There were four of these tables in the room, all in a line. They reminded Jane of chairs in a barbershop.

Surrounding each work area were sets of surgical tools, electronic devices, and other instruments. Video cameras, attached high on the far walls, were trained downward to focus on the operating area. The room was cold, but it wasn't just because of the temperature. The walls and the fixtures were hard—steel, ceramic tile, and linoleum. There was nothing compassionate about this room, nothing human.

They approached the body as the door behind them popped back open. "Dr. Reid." A young male assistant poked his head through the doorway. "She's all ready to go. I'm off to get some lunch; be back in half an hour. Anything I can get you?" The doctor turned her head and signaled no. He nodded and left.

Reid pulled back the sheet. The dead woman lay naked, her jagged wounds gaping wide. Internal organs and bone were visible; one breast was nearly severed.

Reid took a cursory look at the entire body, walking around it twice, eyeing the object like a sculptor with a new piece of marble. She posited, "There won't be anything under the fingernails; they're too short and I don't think she was raped. Look at the vaginal area, no violence. I'll do a thorough exam, but—"

She stopped midsentence and reached for a probe. It was a slender metal rod, over a foot long; it could have doubled as a knitting needle. She slid it into one of the wounds in the victim's right shoulder. It went in about six inches and stopped. She let go and studied the angle. She ventured, "Right-handed man, more than likely. This one came from behind. Her back was facing the killer."

Jane didn't comment.

Reid withdrew the probe and placed it back on the tray. Glancing up at the large clock on the wall, she pointed toward the camera, then at Jane. "Stay behind the line. If this ever goes to court, we don't need to confuse the issue."

Jane took up a position outside the camera's range. She chose to stay and observe the autopsy, despite having probably all the information she needed, other than the tox report, which would take a couple of days. What she anticipated, though, was the opportunity afterward to glean the pathologist's informal opinions. They were almost always right on the mark. Besides, she had a certain morbid fascination with the process she was about to view.

Reid pushed a series of buttons on the near wall. "Today is November twenty-second, the time is fourteen-oh-one, Dr. Phyllis A. Reid, MD, attending." She paused to assess the body. *"Before me is a white Hispanic female about twenty years of age. Hair is black, eyes brown, approximately five-foot-two and about one hundred pounds. Overall, there are numerous wounds about the left and right chest, shoulder and back area. Specifically . . ."*

Reid began with a detailed description and location of each cut, numbering them one through eighteen. She then closely examined further contusions and abrasions, and next, any noticeable scars from previous injuries. That done, she reached for a scalpel and began her first incision. Gently she placed the blade at the center of the sternum, and with one continuous motion slit open the body to the lower abdomen as though she were unzipping a winter coat. A gush of body fluids flowed onto the table and into the gutters. The smell hit Jane again. She winced as Reid retracted the opening and continued, "Wound five penetrated the left kidney at the adrenal junction. The puncture is about one centimeter wide. Wound eight . . ."

When she finished the overall description of the internal organs, she reached for an assortment of trays and set them beside her. With another quick flick of her wrist, she severed the liver, heart, and kidneys, removing each and setting them in the receptacles. Next she opened the stomach and examined the contents. ". . . and in the upper lateral area, there appear to be remnants of partially digested vegetable matter. Specifically, numerous pieces, one millimeter in diameter, of orange-colored vegetable matter . . ."

The autopsy continued as Jane's pager went off. She fumbled for it through the extra clothing, nearly dropping the device as she read the message. It was Roy. With sign language she indicated to Dr. Reid that she had to go. The doctor barely acknowledged, continuing to detail Christina Herrera's internal organs.

Jane exited and found a phone just outside the scrub room. She dialed their lab. It rang four times before Roy answered.

"What's up?"

"Thought you'd like to know, I've got a match on some prints. Darby's were all over the place. In the kitchen, bedroom, and toilet. Everywhere."

"Have you told Sergeant Harris?"

"Hell, no. You can. I just work here."

"Thanks, partner, thanks a lot." She hung up the telephone and slumped against the wall.

Fifteen

Sergeant Harris parked her Taurus in one of the few remaining spots in the parking garage beneath the sixty-story building. She followed the arrows to the elevator. Just as the doors began to glide shut, a male voice called out to hold the door. As if from nowhere, she was rapidly joined by a man in his early forties, well-groomed and wearing stylish business attire. He carried an expensive brown leather briefcase. Their eyes met for a moment. Harris automatically moved away, putting distance between them.

"Nice weather we're having," he ventured. Harris nodded, instinctively fingering the canister of pepper spray she kept in her overcoat pocket. He repushed the uppermost button.

"Business with the bank today?" His voice sounded friendly, but Harris sensed otherwise. She glanced at his manicured hands. The one holding the briefcase was clenched tight; the other lay restlessly on the polished rail.

With a jolt they began moving upward, passing other parking levels. Harris relaxed a bit. In a matter of seconds they stopped, the doors opened, and they were at the main-floor lobby. The man bade her a good day, and disappeared into the crowd of people.

Harris transferred to another elevator after checking the floor directory. This time she rode upward with a dozen others, all crammed shoulder to shoulder. As they rose and stopped along the way, the crowd thinned until she was alone. At floor fifty-nine, the doors opened opposite an elegant glassed-in foyer, discreetly lettered EXECUTIVE OFFICES FEDERATED BANK OF CALIFORNIA, NORTHERN REGION.

In the reception area, a young woman sat behind an impressive walnut wraparound desk. She wore an unobtrusive headset. "FBC, how may I direct your call? . . . One moment . . . FBC, how may I direct your call? . . . One moment . . ." She looked up. "Be with you momentarily." She then pushed an extension number on her control board. "Mr. Rath, your wife is on the line. Are you still in conference? . . . Right, I'll let her know . . . Mrs. Rath, he's still tied up with the loan meeting. I'm sure he'll call you when he's done . . . All right, I'll let him know." She pressed another button and moved the mouthpiece aside. "There," she said. "That should take care of the calls for a little while. Now, how may I help you?"

Harris opened her purse and withdrew her official identification. "Sergeant Leah Harris, Seattle PD. Is Mr. Herrera in?"

"Ah . . . no." The receptionist cast an appraising glance at the badge, then to Harris. "Do you have an appointment?"

"Not exactly."

"I believe he's expected back shortly." She turned to the clock on the wall. "This is his chamber of commerce meeting day. He is usually here by two, and—" She stopped and looked at a computer-generated schedule. "Oh, I'm afraid he'll be tied up for the rest of the day. Is there someone else who can help you?"

Harris's demeanor became severe. "No, only Mr. Herrera. And I think he will have time for me."

Sixteen

Milkovich waited patiently at the counter and was about to lean close and say something privately to Det. Jerry Cummins when the server approached. "What can I get for you two today?"

Cummins grinned widely. He was handsome, part Irish, part Native American, late thirties, with muscles that bulged from excessive weight lifting. It made his sports coat and pants look as if they had been shrink-wrapped on him. "How 'bout a double latte," he said, "with a little dollop of whipped cream and . . . do you have any fresh croissants?"

"Certainly."

"The kind with the little sprinkles of almonds on top?"

"Yes, I think we have a few left." She smiled brightly.

"Great, I'll take one of those." Cummins looked at Milkovich. "What are you going to have? It's my treat."

"Coffee, black."

"Just coffee?"

"Yeah, Jer, I don't like any of that fancy crap."

"You heard the man," Cummins said with a wink.

She winked back. "Take a table and I'll bring it right over," she said, then left to hustle the order.

The pair settled into a small corner table away from prying ears. Milkovich began first, his tone barely above a whisper. "Remember about ten years ago when those FBI agents came up here from San Diego and gave us guys in Narcotics the briefing on the Colombian drug cartels operating in southern California?"

Cummins whipped his head around. He had been eyeing the waitress. Suddenly he had an odd, questioning look on his face. "Yeah, I remember, but they were DEA. Say, what the hell is this all about?"

"What's the latest on the cartel operations? The Feds still trying to get into them down south?"

"Of course, but it's still nearly impossible to crack into one of the cells, as they call 'em. I bet they control ninety percent of the traffic in southern California—a big chunk of change, I might add. A huge market."

"Refresh my memory. . . . As I recall, the reason it was so tough to hook anybody was because of all the fire walls."

"Yeah, and all run very businesslike."

Milkovich nodded his head.

Cummins continued. "Real classy operation. Hell, if they went public and offered stock, I'd get some for my IRA." He chuckled.

Milkovich didn't. "What's the word around here?"

"Aw, Milky! You aren't going to start that again. Look where it got you last time!"

Milkovich frowned.

Cummins sighed. "Frank, like we tried to tell you five, six years ago, it hasn't changed. I still haven't seen any indication hereabouts, thank God. And it will stay that way, because the very system that makes it so hard to bust also limits its expansion."

"I know, I know. Then you guys haven't seen any evidence of it up here yet?"

"Naw, at least not the organization. We get their dope, but that's stuff that's been wholesaled out in LA. You got everybody and his brother bringing that crap up here. Bikers, gang-bangers, Chinese, Mexicans, you name it. Small, unstable operators, mainly. They trip down I-5 in their beater Buicks once a week and pick up a kilo or two. These guys are pretty much independent. Once in a while a bigger player does come into the area, but they don't last long. Especially if they're using the stuff besides selling. Then it's only a matter of time. Drugs, cash, and shit for brains make for a situation we can always exploit. But hell, you know all that!"

Cummins stopped. The waitress had their drinks ready and she delivered them with another wink and a smile. The narcotics detective beamed wolfishly, ogling her as she walked away. "Cute . . . nice buns."

Milkovich ignored the comment. As he reached for his cup, he sensed someone watching him. Slowly he turned his head ever so slightly to the right. In the opposite corner of the crowded café a man sat alone. For an instant, their eyes met.

Cummins read Milkovich's expression. "What's up, Frank?"

"Over there, the guy with the thousand-dollar suit. He's been giving us the eye."

"What's he doing now?"

"Nothing. He's picking up his newspaper and reading it. Hey, in a couple of minutes I'm going to go over and use the men's room. Watch what he does when I go by him, okay?"

"Sure, Frank. But what's going on? You're getting all hinky on me and I don't know whether you're flipping out, or you're on to something." Cummins hunched forward. "You know, Frank, I'll be honest. Ever since you stopped drinking and went into IA—what's that been now, four years?—I haven't recognized you. You've just been going through the motions; I—"

"He's getting up," Milkovich interrupted.

"Which way?"

"Toward the counter."

Cummins glanced over. "Nice suit. I don't know him, do you?"

Milkovich shook his head. "Maybe I am getting jumpy. . . . I'm working a case that reeks of . . ." He paused to look Cummins directly in the eye. Milkovich knew he needed help, an ally to check his thinking, cover him, to work in parallel without anyone knowing about it. But he hated to drag someone else in. The more that he shared, the more likely the wrong people would know. He began again, only to break off abruptly as the man turned and headed toward the side exit, just beyond their table. As he passed, his raincoat brushed Milkovich's shoulder. Milkovich froze and remained motionless for several seconds. Finally, through tight lips he asked, "Is he gone?"

"Your dude? Yeah, out the door and up Third."

Milkovich's eyes twitched with nervous energy; his tightly knit hands were clenched with bare-knuckle resolve.

"Hey, calm down," Cummins cautioned. "Your paranoia level is running a little high. What the hell is going on?"

Milkovich sensed the doubt in Cummins. Groaning inwardly, he started over. "I think we have an active cell in place. I found a cash house a couple of hours ago. Just like those Feds said it should look—a bedroom closet with a false floor. Cash, in hundreds and twenties, bundled neatly with audit markings in Spanish. There's got to be at least a million sitting in there right now."

Cummins's eyes widened. "Are you sure? There hasn't been any intelligence indicating this. Not a word."

"I'm sure of it. The wrappers on the hundred-dollar bills, they had the same distinctive tally marks on them, just like the ones those guys from San Diego showed us."

"Where's the house?" Cummins was now on his elbow leaning forward. "Is anyone sitting on it? Christ, I want in on this, Frank. This could lead us into a whole lot of great shit!"

"There's a problem."

Cummins winced and slowly sank back in his seat. He knew the problem right away. Dope and Internal Affairs. The two could mean only one thing—dirty cops. Cummins gritted his teeth. He looked at his friend and shook his head in disgust. "Do you really want to tell me? I could be a liability."

"I'm going to need help, Jer. I can't work this by myself. It's going to be too big."

"Whatever you need, Frank." The reply was without hesitation, although Milkovich wondered if behind the glib words his friend harbored doubts. "So what's the situation?"

"You heard about the homicide near the university last night?"

"Yeah?"

"A young Hispanic gal got knifed. I haven't

the slightest idea why, but we've got a link to one of our sergeants. That's how I got dragged in. An hour ago I was at the scene. I walked around and I could just sense it. Someone was living there, but not really. It lacked the personal effects that make a house a home. It didn't add up. When I stood in the kitchen, I got a nose hit off some black tar. It was stashed in the dishwasher. You know that feeling that there's going to be more? I was dead sure there would be. I could feel it calling out to me. That's how I found the cash. I walked right to it. Right where it was supposed to be. And guess what? The house, it's owned by an out-of-state holding company with no local connections."

Cummins's eyes widened as the tension in his bearing seemed to melt. "It's a fit, all right; you're on to something. But what's the link to the cop, and for Christ's sake, who is it?"

"I'm not sure of the link yet. Just some evidence that he's been in the house for other than official reasons."

"You're not going to tell me who?"

"Maybe, maybe not." Milkovich winked.

"You're toying with me," Cummins complained.

"A little . . ."

"Okay, then, but who else knows about the cash?"

"At this point, just me and the detective sergeant handling the homicide. And now you. By the way, we still have control of the house. At least for another twenty-four hours."

"Who's the dick?"

"Leah Harris. You know her?"

"A little. She's a hard charger."

"I think she's screwing the guy in question."

"Oh, shit! Figuratively or—"

Milkovich's expression remained passive.

"Damn! Don't tell me any more. I don't think I want to know any more about that part."

"To be honest, I don't either. Speaking of which, what do you know about John Darby? Ever work with him?"

"Darby? That's your man? Naw, Frank, forget it. He's a regular guy. I can vouch for him. He may be screwing a sergeant, but I can't believe he's into drugs."

Milkovich glanced at his watch. "Damn. Jer, I gotta go. I've got another interview in a bit. Nothing to do with this case, but I have to get it done today. Can you do me a couple of things?"

"As long as it looks kind of legal."

"Just do some checking with the guys down south. See if they know of anything about a cell up here. And ask around your unit. Don't get anyone suspicious, but there's got to be some information out there. Some of your informers have to know about it."

"What are you going to do with the house?"

"You mean the cash."

"Well, yes, the cash. Even if you don't connect it to anything, we can seize it. You said you found some heroin associated with it. That's enough. That million would make a nice contribution to the asset-seizure fund, and boy, would the administrative types be patting us on the back."

Milkovich frowned. "Sure, we could take it, but I want the people. The dollars aren't going to do me any good."

"Frank, Frank, Frank, this is a new era. Tight tax dollars. Zero funding. Asset seizures help put money into your paycheck. Doper money probably funds fifty percent of our entire narcotics operations."

Milkovich shook his head. "I don't need to get into that discussion right now. We could be here all day debating the ethics."

"But the house, what about the house? You're only going to be able to hold it for maybe another day before you have to release it or seize it. Especially if someone is going to push."

"That's not a problem. I doubt if anyone will even make a play for it. Hell, a million dollars, that's chump change for the cartel. If they have even the slightest idea that we know about the cash, they'll just leave it, and any trail leading to them will be untraceable."

"True, but I thought your only responsibility in all of this was the department's involvement. Sounds like you want back into Narcotics."

Milkovich shrugged his shoulders. "I don't know, Jer. Something stinks. I don't know what, but I'm going to find it. Just see what you can find out and I'll call you later." He looked at his watch again. "I gotta run."

The time was 1436.

Seventeen

Harris watched the elevator open. A lone man stepped out. She knew he would be Herrera. Although taller than she imagined, he was darkly handsome with broad, self-assured shoulders, and thoughtful brown eyes. He strode through the doorway, smiled at the two women, and started past.

"Excuse me, Mr. Herrera." The receptionist looked up from her control panel. "This lady is here to see you. She's a police sergeant."

He turned around and with a smile said, "Good afternoon; how can I help you?" It was a strong, sincere voice, no trace of an accent.

Harris stood up and extended her right hand. "I'm Detective Sergeant Harris with the Seattle Police Department." She flashed her identification. "I hate to impose, but I need a few minutes of your time."

"Sure, no problem." Herrera took Harris's hand and gave it a courteous shake. He glanced sideways at his receptionist, then back to Harris. "Follow me. We can talk in my office."

Herrera guided Harris toward a wide corridor, paneled in walnut and hung with original oils; she recognized several pieces by famous Northwest artists. They walked side by side toward a set of French doors and passed through to an anteroom. On one side were two workstations stacked with tiers of computers, fax machines, printers, and other electronic gear. The area had the look of a NASA launch room. A woman in her late fifties sat at one of the desks. She looked up in silent greeting.

"This is Doris," Herrera said to Harris. "Best executive assistant on the planet." He glanced over at the unoccupied station. "Where's Jean?"

"One of her kids had a toothache. She had to go get him from school. I doubt she'll be back today. . . . Don't worry; I can pick up the slack."

Herrera laughed. "Doris, you're not fooling me. You're just happy to have the office all to yourself for the afternoon."

Doris politely sneered and resumed her work.

The pair proceeded through another double doorway, into Herrera's spacious corner office. It was bright with daylight. Two sides of the room were all glass, permitting a panoramic vista of downtown Seattle, the Cascade mountain range, and the shipping on Puget Sound.

Herrera pulled the heavy doors shut.

Harris was momentarily speechless as she took in the stunning view. Her host said nothing, accustomed to first time-visitors goggling the sights. Harris played her part well. She needed time, anyway. To get a feel for the man, to make a determination as to whether he was going to be a suspect or a victim. The opening pleasantries would give her the opportunity for this assessment. Rushing would only be counterproductive.

While awaiting Herrera's arrival, she had mulled over several approaches. All were dependent upon her first impressions of the man. Now none of those preconceptions fit. Before her was an obviously influential, successful businessman, comfortable with himself and his stature, employed by one of the largest banks in the country. She calculated her odds, rolled the dice—she bet *victim*.

Herrera's work area was centered along one of the interior walls, where rows of awards and framed certificates were neatly arranged. He, too, had several computer terminals and other electronic equipment. Opposite, where the windows met, was a conversation area with a couch and chairs, all upholstered in rich burgundy leather. Herrera led Harris to this corner, crossing an oak floor inlaid with strips of dark mahogany.

They took seats across from one another, and after a slight pause, Herrera spoke first. "Now what can my bank do for the Seattle Police Department? A loan, perhaps?" He chuckled at his joke.

Harris forced a weak smile. "No, I think our department is fine. No, it's about another matter, I'm afraid."

"Yes?"

Harris drew a deep breath and sighed. "It's about Christina. I believe she's a relative of yours . . . ?"

Herrera's charming demeanor evaporated. He cocked his head cautiously and said, "She's my niece. Is she in some sort of trouble? I know she's had problems with her student visa. I thought that was all fixed."

"No," Harris replied. "It's not about that."

"Then what?"

Harris leaned close. Although she was well practiced at delivering death notices to family members, it was never easy. She could feel her stomach rumbling.

"Mr. Herrera, I am very sorry." Harris shifted in her seat.

Herrera froze.

"I am afraid that Christina is dead."

Shock and disbelief rippled across Herrera's face. "But—"

The room went still. Several moments passed before Herrera was able to continue. With a trembling voice he breathed, "My God—how?"

Harris gritted her teeth and replied, "She was murdered. It was sometime late last night, in her home."

"Murdered!"

Harris nodded solemnly. "I am very sorry. You have my deepest sympathies." Harris then reached out and took his hand; it was icy cold. She squeezed it gently. "It's a horrible world," she commiserated. "A very horrible world."

There was more silence. Harris let the news be absorbed while she studied the man before her. His eyes were clearly sad, near to tears. Too good for an act—*victim*, Harris mentally reconfirmed.

Herrera sank lower into his chair, only to suddenly rebound. Letting go Harris's hand, he leaped to his feet and drew a deep breath. His bearing straightened as his eyes narrowed. "Damn it, Sergeant, how could this happen? Who's the bastard responsible?"

"That's what I am trying to find out."

Herrera smacked the back of his chair, turned, and faced away from the Seattle detective, his gaze now fixed on a point well beyond the windowed wall. In a measured tone he asked, "What can I do to help?"

"I need to ask you a few questions. Are you up for that?"

He nodded silently and slowly turned back. "Sergeant, my time is yours." As he said this, he reached for the telephone resting on a nearby table and pressed it close to his ear. A moment later he said, "Doris, cancel whatever I've got for the rest of the day. . . . It's Christina . . . terrible news . . . she's—" Herrera's voice cracked. "She's dead." Harris could feel the shock from the other end of the line. She again shifted in her seat.

Herrera spoke a few more words, then hung up.

"Are you sure you are all right?"

Herrera nodded yes.

"Good. Your help is essential. First off, I think you may have been one of the last persons to see Christina alive. What time was it that you last saw or spoke with her?"

Herrera thought for a moment, then said softly, "It must have been seven o'clock last night, or maybe eight at the latest." His head lowered. "On Tuesdays I always pick her up to have dinner. That way I can keep an eye on her. You see, her father, my brother, is quite wealthy. She could have gone to any college in the world, and lived in the nicest accommodations, but she wanted to be independent, just like I was at her age." He sighed and continued. "I came to this country when I was only sixteen. I was penniless, but I knew the value of hard work and education." He turned and swept out his arm. "I guess she wanted to be like me. To do it on her own."

"How long had she been here?"

"About a year, although she didn't come to Seattle right away. I have an aunt who lives in

California. She stayed there for several months, before deciding on enrolling here. This was her first term."

"What about the house she was living in?"

"A dreadful dump. But I guess I would have thought it a castle when I was her age."

"Then she had moved in recently?"

"Oh, it's been maybe three months, maybe a little longer. When she showed it to me, I nearly had a coronary. I had to call my brother and lie about it. I told him it was a nice, safe place, close to me so that I could watch over her. Christ, what a joke that was."

"Then she found the place herself?"

"Why, yes." Herrera stroked his chin. "Why the questions about the house? What does it have to do with Christina's death?"

"I know this is going to be very hard for you, Mr. Herrera," Harris said in a persuasive tone. "But I'll be asking a lot of questions that don't seem to mean anything. Many won't, but I need to ask them to get a picture in my own mind of what your niece's situation was, just prior to her death. By doing this I can get a pretty good idea of who is, and who isn't, a suspect. Your answers will be very valuable in assisting me in this."

Herrera stepped around to the front of his chair and settled back in. "I see. Go ahead, fire away with whatever questions you like. I'll try my best to answer anything you need to know."

From behind her facade of compassion Harris had been carefully scrutinizing Herrera's every movement and word. Was it adding up? She wasn't absolutely sure. The questions about the house had seemed to cause some discomfort. But it was far too early to probe further in that area. Too early to show what few cards she held. She shifted to a different topic. "You said you were with her around eight o'clock last night."

"Yes, we had dinner, Chinese, at the Peking Garden. We talked for a while, and then I drove her home. I'm sure it wasn't later than eight o'clock when I dropped her off. She said she had studying to do. I came back to my office for a while to finish up some paperwork, then went home myself. That was the last time I saw or heard from her."

"Did she have friends?"

"She never really talked much about others. You know, she hadn't been here long, and she was something of a loner. Again, rather like me; although, a couple of weeks ago, when I came to pick her up, there was another girl at the house. She was just leaving; I didn't get her name. It must have been someone from one of her classes. She looked about Christina's age."

"Boyfriends?"

"I don't know. Maybe, but none she ever talked about. Certainly no one serious. She did mention going out occasionally. Pizza and movies, that kind of thing. I assumed it was with some boy she met at school. I didn't like to pry. That way I didn't have to lie to my brother when he called to check up on her. He has a heck of a temper."

"Did he call often?"

"Once a week like clockwork. Our family is like that. We're still close-knit even when separated by thousands of miles."

"You said you were penniless when you came to this country, but your brother is wealthy. Change of family fortunes?"

Herrera winced and stoically replied, "In Colombia, it is the custom for the eldest son to inherit the family business, while those of us born later get stuck with the crumbs. Though I love my brother Esteban, I could never work for him. It's a long story. . . ."

"He must be proud of your success."

Herrera cracked a slight, self-satisfied smile. "Perhaps a little jealous."

Harris smirked at the obvious sibling rivalry. She then cleared her throat and focused back on the investigation. "You know, we couldn't find Christina's wallet with her identification anywhere in the house. It must have been taken by the person who did it."

"Then she was killed by a burglar?"

"Possibly."

Herrera eyed Harris. "You don't think so, do you? You think it was someone else. I can tell."

He drew a deep breath and sighed. "Just how did she die?"

Harris hesitated. She didn't want to be too graphic, but at the same time she wanted to provide enough information to elicit a strong response. It was a critical part of her interrogation. She had become very good at judging the degree of complicity of the person she was questioning by when and how they asked for the details, and how they reacted to the answers she gave. She hunched forward and said. "She was stabbed to death."

Herrera closed his eyes and stiffened. His jaw quivered. Then slowly, like the sun rising, he opened them and looked at Harris. "Did she suffer long?"

"No. It was over in a matter of seconds."

"Thank God."

Harris nodded in agreement. "At this point, that's about all I can tell you. My people are processing the evidence left at the scene and interviewing witnesses. I feel confident we'll catch whomever is responsible."

"It must have been a madman. Who else would kill such an innocent young thing, and for no reason?"

Harris agreed, then asked, "Tell me more about your niece. What was her full name?"

"Christina Maria Anna Herrera."

"And her birthday?"

"Oh, ah—" Herrera rose and strode purposefully to his desk. "I think I wrote it on my calendar. I didn't want to miss it." He opened a portfolio and thumbed through several pages. "Here it is, March fourteenth. I knew I had written it down. And let's see, with her age right now, the year she was born would have to be 1980."

He rejoined Harris.

"What about her passport? You said she was on a student visa and you mentioned problems. What was that about?"

Herrera hesitated. "Ah, that was something my aunt arranged. I really couldn't tell you. Listen, after I break the news to her and she has had a chance to calm down, I'll have her call you immediately. I know she will be absolutely devastated, but if it is important, I know she will help."

"When will you be contacting her?"

Herrera's head hung low again. He sighed. "I was planning on flying down late this afternoon to spend the holidays with her and other family members. Now—my God, this is going to be a tough trip. Tell me, when can we have Christina? I mean, well, you know what I mean. I'll need to call my brother and see what arrangements he would like me to make."

"What is the best number for the medical examiner's office to contact you?"

He felt his breast pocket and withdrew a business card and a pen. He scribbled some numbers on the back and handed it to Harris. "My flight leaves a little after five. Here's my pager number and my aunt's home phone. Since I'll be gone for the next couple of days, they can use either of these to reach me. And please, Sergeant, don't hesitate to call either, especially if something turns up. I'd like to know as soon as possible."

Harris palmed the card, slipping it into her notebook and extracting one of her own. She passed it over. "Thank you for all your help. And please, you too feel free to call or page me anytime. . . ." Harris again took his hand in sympathy. "I really am very sorry about this. Such a terrible loss."

He forced a weak smile. "I only wish I could be more help. Christina didn't deserve this. She had her whole life ahead of her. . . . Damn all the bastards in this world!"

Harris nodded her agreement, rose, and strode solemnly for the door. Herrera remained, his head bowed, in deep thought. As she crossed the room, the sun broke through the partly cloudy skies and lit up the opposing wall, reflecting brilliantly off the plaques and burnished trophies. The glare caused Harris to squint, but as she passed by she was able to read some of the memorabilia. The largest certificate was from Yale Law School. Just below that was a degree from Harvard—a Master of Business Administration. But it was the framed photo just below that caught Harris's eye. It was of two men in golfing togs: one was the vice president of the United States. He was mugging for the camera with what appeared to be his best friend. Harris got closer and confirmed that the vice president was arm in arm with none other than the person she had just spoken with. The other golfer was the banker, Enrique Herrera.

Eighteen

It was a sickening ride down from the fifty-ninth floor of the Federated Bank building. Harris slumped against the elevator wall and mulled over her encounter with Herrera. She was now certain the emotions she had witnessed were real; the pain, the grief had not been faked. This, at least temporarily, removed Herrera from the suspect list. That left only one name: John Darby.

When the doors opened, Harris slowly stepped out into the lobby crowd and crossed to the parking garage elevator. It was full, but she squeezed in just as the doors closed, taking little notice of the other occupants.

There was a slight bump before the door opened at the first level. She rocked backward, and her shoulder blade brushed the chest of the man behind her. She felt it instantly—the slight, hard bulge of a gun butt in a shoulder holster.

Harris's mind instantly refocused.

Two passengers exited, creating room for Harris to move to the side. She stole a quick glance, and her nerves jumped. The man with the gun was the same person who had ridden up with her from the garage. Their eyes met; he smiled. Adrenaline surged through her body as she surreptitiously studied the faces of the other passengers; none looked threatening.

At the next level, four disembarked, leaving herself and the suspicious stranger. Stealthily Harris slipped the handles of her purse over her wrist and grasped the slack tightly. This while judging the distance from her leather bludgeon to his jaw. The elevator stopped, and the door glided open. Harris was ready.

For a second they both stood there, unmoving. With a courtly sweep, the man broke the silence. "I believe this is the bottom level. Please, after you."

Harris stepped out, spun to her right, and pretended to be looking for her car while closely studying his movements. He exited and passed her by, but several paces beyond, he stopped and turned back. "I think we came in together. You parked over there." He pointed to the area where her Ford sat.

"Oh . . . yeah, thanks." She watched as he walked over to a green BMW.

Harris jogged to her car. She could see the German car backing out. "K-L-M six-seven-eight," she repeated aloud as she unlocked her door and got in. She grabbed a scrap of paper and scribbled the plate number as she pressed MEMORY on her cell phone's speed-dial. Nothing happened. She swore softly—NO SERVICE showed on the phone's display. She was too deep in the parking garage.

Harris put the Taurus in gear and jammed the gas. Her tires squealed as she spiraled upward toward the exit and daylight. Once there, she hit redial. Gilroy answered on the first ring.

"Where are you, Phil?"

"Almost to HQ," he replied, instantly recognizing his boss's voice. "What's up?"

"Got your pencil?"

"Go."

"Get down to Immigration. Christina Maria Anna Herrera, three-fourteen, nineteen eighty. Run her the way you usually do, and see what they have. She should have been here about a year."

"Right." Gilroy hesitated, then broached, "So how was your meeting with Enrique? Do we have a suspect?"

Harris groaned. "I don't think so. He was nervous about something. But then we all are, aren't we?"

"What's the Immigration angle?"

"Herrera let slip that our victim had problems with her visa. I'm wondering if she might be an illegal or—"

"Huh?"

"Just a thought. That might be the reason for the nervousness."

"Hmmm. If she was, that might open up a whole new box of motives and suspects."

"Yeah, it just might."

"So you don't think Herrera had anything to do with this."

"Naw, his story was good, but damn . . ."

"What's that, boss?"

Harris sighed. "The man's got the coldest hands I've ever felt. Jesus, they were cold."

It was 1500 hours.

Nineteen

Milkovich sat alone on the park bench. A hundred feet distant, two young mothers pushed their small children on a swing set in a playground across from him. Their gleeful cries drifted his way, and he envied their pure joy as they rose and fell in the cooling November air.

He glanced at his watch, then down the wide, paved jogging trail, anxious for his appointment to appear. He wished that he had canceled the meeting after all. It should've been put off in favor of this new case—especially based on the circumstances he could now articulate. He'd have to make it quick, but sincere. It would be just enough to satisfy the officer that the department was taking her allegations seriously. And then, back to Harris. Time was getting critical.

Deborah Griggs approached on the path from the north. She had an eager German shepherd puppy on a leash. It strained at its collar, pulling along the short, stocky twenty-something woman.

Milkovich knew immediately that she was the person he was here to meet. She had the look—jeans, a black leather jacket, short-cropped reddish hair, freckles, and an open smile. Her outward innocence made a sharp contrast to the reality of the situation. It struck Milkovich that despite the problems that appeared to be impacting her life, she seemed buoyant, almost childishly carefree.

Griggs slowed as she neared, causing the puppy to pull even harder, making its eyes bulge and its tongue lap furiously at the wind. She yanked back hard. "No! Bad dog!" The puppy lunged forward until its large front paws were clawing at Milkovich's shoes. "No, Bullet," she yelled again, but the dog continued to ignore her.

Milkovich smiled. He grabbed a large fold of fur on the dog's neck and gave him a friendly rub. The dog inched forward, then proceeded to lick him furiously, its tail flapping wildly like a metronome on full speed. "Nice pup," Milkovich said, still stroking the fur. "Have you had him long?"

Griggs yanked again on the leash. "I'm sorry, Sergeant. I hope he's not bothering you. I only got him a week ago. All he wants to do is play." The dog lunged between Milkovich's legs. This time Griggs pulled him back with both hands. "Damn it! Sit, you dumb dog!" The puppy reeled back onto its haunches and stayed. "That's better. Good dog . . . good Bullet." She patted him in praise.

Milkovich shifted to the right side of the bench. "Have a seat."

Griggs complied, but first tied off her pup at the other end. The shepherd lay on the grass, eagerly eyeing the children across the way with a look that said he wanted to go play with them.

"He's going to be a big dog, judging by the size of those feet."

She nodded with pride, then turned serious. "Thanks for meeting with me. I know you're busy, but I've got to tell someone. This situation just can't go on. It's not right, it's not fair, and it's making my life absolutely miserable. I want to be a cop. I love the work, I really do, but—" Griggs paused to reach inside her leather coat. She pulled out a bound notebook and held it out to Milkovich. "I don't want to tell you any more until you read this. I'll start crying if I do. I've been an emotional wreck. Read it; it won't take long."

Milkovich grasped the thin volume and looked into her eyes. They were beginning to water. "All right." He opened the journal and randomly selected an entry near the beginning. It was in pencil, but the penmanship was neat and easily readable.

Oct. 22nd: It happened again last night. Why won't she leave me alone? It started at 2330. She pulled up beside my car and told me we should take a break together. I told her I had paperwork, but Paula insisted. Well, she's the boss. We got a cup at the 7-Eleven and then parked car to car. At first we just talked. Paula can be real sweet and understanding. She knows how tough it is for us. So even though I was real tired, I agreed to go with her to an after-hours club we'd been to before, when we got off shift at 0100.

We met there later. The place was empty. Usually is, on a weeknight that late. Again we just sat and talked. Then just out of nowhere she leaned over and gave me a long, deep kiss.

It was great; still, something made me uneasy. Jennifer had told me a lot about Paula, that she liked to prey on rookies. Groom 'em, treat 'em nice, then toss them aside when she's through with them. Just like men. But I couldn't resist; she just understands me so well. I can tell her anything. . . . I went home with her again."

Milkovich finished the page. He affixed a detached, professional expression on his face and looked up. Griggs was thin-lipped, nervously watching for his reaction. He gave a concerned sigh. He knew where this was going to go and he didn't like it. "You're—" he started, but she cut him off.

"Yes, I am, but it's no secret. There are a lot of gays and lesbians on the force and we do a good job. But this isn't about that. It's about human rights, and mine are being violated by that bitch Sergeant Anderson. Read further; you'll see what I mean."

Milkovich flipped the page, thinking, *Christ, why me? Why is it always me?*

Oct. 23rd: Work has been hell. I know it was a mistake to sleep with her again. What an idiot I am. She wants me again tonight. She won't leave me alone.

Oct. 24th: I gave in. Why, I'll never know. . . . Oh, be honest; she's beautiful and thinks I am too.

Oct. 28th: I don't believe Paula. There I was last night, on duty, just finishing up a DV report, and she pulls up. "I need to talk to you," she says. She had such an emphasis in her voice that I think it's something really important. She motioned for me to follow her, so I shifted into gear and she led me to a spot right behind the University Village Safeway. It's dark back there and I'm wondering what the hell is up. Then Paula gets out of her car and jumps into mine. Now we're sitting side by side and before I can say anything she leans over, grabs me, and gives me a long, wet kiss. And while she's doing that, she's rubbing my crotch. I tried to pull away, but she held me tight. Finally she lets go. I was horrified, but all she could do was laugh. "Jesus, Paula!" I screamed. "We're on duty!" She just shrugged her shoulders, then hopped out of the car.

Oct. 29th: It's getting out of hand. First she tries to get a piece of me while we're on duty, then what happens? She shows up at my apartment at 0400. She's drunk and pounding on my door.

Christ, I had to let her in or she would have woke up everyone in the building. . . . Big mistake. She talked me right back into the sack. . . . Damn! What am I going to do?

Milkovich flipped another page without looking up.

<u>Oct. 31st:</u> At the Safeway again. She grabs me, unbuckles my gun belt, then hers. She yanks at my pants. She shoves her hand down my crotch. Oh, Jesus, I'm thinking, what if we get a call—it's busy, it's Halloween.

<u>Nov. 4th:</u> Three days off and no Paula. I haven't answered my phone or my door. Maybe she's done with me. What a crazy bitch.

<u>Nov. 5th:</u> First night back to work. It's slow. Paula's been watching me. Every half hour we cross paths. It's almost the end of the shift and she's on the radio looking for me like it's something official. I've got no choice. I tell her to meet me in the parking lot of the 7-Eleven. It's well lit. She can't pull any crap there.

We park car to car. Her window comes down and she's got this wide-ass grin as she stares me right in the eye. "Have you been avoiding me?" she asks innocently. She's just like a cat playing with a mouse. What a bitch! I say, "No."

"Good," she says. " 'Cause I just love your pretty little ass."

I can't take it anymore. I break. She's not going to ruin my life. I stare right back at her. "Sergeant," I say, "leave me the fuck alone. You're my boss and that's it. I don't want to be with you, sleep with you, or anything else. Christ, Paula, all you're doing is using me."

Her smile vanishes. Her face is red. Now she's the Wicked Witch of the West. "Listen," she says in a voice so low I can barely hear it. "You're right, I am the boss out here. And you know what? You're still probationary. I can make or break you, and there isn't one damn thing you can do about it. Do you understand that? It's simple, very simple. You do what I tell you, when I tell you, and you've got a career here. You don't and . . . well, your next fitness report is due in at the end of the month. Let's just say that my opinion of your abilities may change."

That was it. I wasn't going to take any more. I looked right at her. "You lousy bitch," I said. "Don't you try that shit on me. I've had nothing but excellent ratings. I'm doing a good job and I'm going to keep on doing it no matter what kind of crap you try to pull . . . 'cause you know what, Paula? I'll talk. I don't give a shit. I don't have anything to hide."

Suddenly there's a plastic smile back on her face. "Fine," she says. "But you've totally misunderstood me. I like you a lot. Really I do. I just want to be with you, that's all. Maybe I just came on too strong. Maybe that's the problem. I can cool it if you like. I just thought you were enjoying it as much as me. We can go slower. That's not a problem."

"Paula, you just don't get it," I say. "It's not right. It'll only be trouble and—"

"There's somebody else," she says, cutting me

off. "You have another lover, don't you? That's it. That's the problem. I can tell. You're a lousy two-timing slut bitch. It's written all over your face. Fuck you!"

She started her patrol car and blasted out of there, almost hitting another car that was coming in.

<u>Nov. 6th:</u> No Paula. She's called in sick. What a relief.

<u>Nov. 7th:</u> No Paula again.

<u>Nov. 8th:</u> Paula's on duty, but I don't see her.

<u>Nov. 10th:</u> No phone calls. No one banging at my door. Maybe she got the message. Jesus, I hope so.

Beep . . . Beep . . . Beep. Milkovich glanced down at his pager, then back at Griggs. He sighed and shook his head.

"Do you need to make a phone call?"

Milkovich looked again at the number displayed. He didn't recognize it. "I'll finish this first. You have a hell of a problem. Christ, the department has a hell of a problem!"

<u>Nov. 13th:</u> I saw Paula for the first time since the 5th. She walked right past me in the precinct hallway. Didn't even look at me. It was as if I wasn't there, which is just fine with me. I think it's over. Thank god!

<u>Nov. 14th:</u> I'm just coming out of Bailey Hall from the sociology class I'm taking and I see her. I'm sure of it. She's across the quad. A hundred yards away, but I'm sure it's her. I know it. I start

in her direction, but she disappears into a thick crowd of students.

Nov. 15th: I didn't sleep last night. I never told Paula I was taking that class at the university. Was it just a coincidence? Was it her? I need to calm down. She hasn't bothered me at work. I don't exist, which is just fine for me except that my performance evaluation is due soon. She'd better not screw with me.

Nov. 17th: She was there again, watching me. I know it was her. I am sure now. Our eyes met for just a moment. I was getting a latte at the Bailey Hall espresso cart. I turned and there she was, not fifty feet from me. I started her way again, but she ducked out on me just like last time.

Nov. 18th: She's following me everywhere. I don't see her, but she's playing a new game with me. She's parking her Mustang outside everyplace I go. I know it's hers; I ran the registration. This is getting absolutely ridiculous. Christ, only another month and I'll be off probation and I can transfer to another precinct."

Beep . . . Beep . . . Beep. Milkovich set the notebook down one more time and looked at his pager. It was the same number as before. "I'd better answer this one. Let's walk to my car."

Griggs nodded, untied her dog, and the two proceeded silently, Milkovich clutching Griggs's journal tightly in his hand.

Twenty

"We need to talk," Harris said from the other end of the crackling cellular phone line. "Where are you?"

"In a parking lot at the arboretum. The one where East Twenty-sixth runs into Lake Washington Boulevard. Did you meet with Herrera?"

"I did."

"So?"

"Cold hands."

"What do you mean by that? Is he a suspect?"

"No, I don't think so. The guy is as American as Mom and apple pie. Yale Law School, Harvard MBA. He's even got a picture on the wall of himself arm in arm with the vice president."

"Of the United States?"

"Yeah. They looked like two old fraternity brothers having a good yuck on a golf course."

"Did you say Harvard?"

"Yeah, MBA."

"I'll be a son of a bitch."

"Now what?"

"You're right, we do need to talk, but not on a cell phone. How soon can you be here?"

"Twenty minutes maybe. The traffic is murder. I think everyone is leaving work early because of the holiday."

"I'll wait. Just get yourself over here as fast as possible. There are some things I need to go over with you."

Milkovich hung up and climbed back out of his car. Deborah Griggs stood patiently against the trunk of the vehicle, petting her dog. She could tell by the worried expression on Milkovich's face that something was up. She straightened. "An emergency?"

Milkovich nodded. He was still holding her book. "Something has come up. Where can I meet you later on?"

"I'm working a cover shift," Griggs replied. "Starts at eighteen-hundred."

"Do you have a pager?"

She nodded.

"Good, I want to get together with you on this as soon as possible. From what I've read so far, we need to deal with this right away."

"We can meet tomorrow. You can finish reading my notes, then if you have any questions—"

"I hate to wait even that long, but we may have to. By the way, does anyone else know about this situation?"

"You mean in the department?"

"Anyone."

"Well, not in the department, I haven't told anyone there, but, uh, I have discussed it with a few friends of mine. Just general stuff. No one knows the details."

"Okay. This is going to have to be handled very carefully. Listen, I'll try to get hold of you tonight sometime; if not, then tomorrow, I promise. By the way—" Milkovich stopped. He stepped close to her and placed a reassuring hand on her shoulder. "It took guts for you to come forward. I want you to know that. And as soon as I take care of this other issue I have going right now, you're going to be top priority. If I can prove your allegations, Sergeant Anderson is not going to get away with anything— got that?" He squeezed her shoulder gently, then pulled back.

"I feel better already," she breathed. "Come, Bullet." She yanked on the leash.

Thanking Milkovich one more time, she headed back onto the jogging path and disappeared down the darkening lane.

The time was 1608.

Twenty-one

Impatient with the slow elevator, Detective Gilroy saw the door marked STAIRWAY and burst through it. He ran three flights up, then down the hallway of government offices to the end, finally slowing at the door marked DISTRICT 9 HEADQUARTERS—IMMIGRATION AND NATURALIZATION SERVICE. He went right past the reception area—they knew him by sight—and proceeded through the maze of office cubicles to a corner where his older sister Donna sat, studying a pile of documents. Pictures of her three teenage children lined the half-walls that separated her from the dozens of other workers doing similar tasks. She looked up wearily.

"You're not coming for Thanksgiving dinner, right? I can tell just by the look on your face."

Gilroy stopped as he reached her side. "I'll try, sis. It's hard to say right now. We're working a hot one, but—"

"Phil, they're always hot. Don't fool me. Mom

would be steamed if she were alive and knew you'd missed five Thanksgivings in a row."

Gilroy groaned. "I'll try." He knew he hadn't sounded convincing, but the urgency of the situation displaced any guilt. He reached into his pocket for the scrap of paper with Christina Herrera's full name and birth date. He passed it to Donna.

"Everything we got?" she asked, already knowing what he wanted. She had done it many times before for her brother. Though it technically violated policy, her supervisors ignored this minor rule breaking. The exchange of information benefited both the immigration office and the police department. Further, Gilroy always made certain that any illegal aliens associated with any of the cases he was working were promptly detained. That was the *quid pro quo*— access to their private information without having to generate the necessary, time-consuming paperwork.

"Anything and everything," Gilroy confirmed.

She glanced at the clock on the nearby wall. It was nearing 4:30 p.m. "A few more minutes and you'd have to wait till Monday. They're doing maintenance on our system over the holiday. I got an e-mail that they were going to start right at five o'clock."

"Then let's get it in, sis. It's really important."

She nodded, tapping the information into her terminal keyboard. "It'll be a bit. The system's been moving slow all day." Looking back up, Donna asked, "So is she a victim, witness, or suspect: animal, mineral, or vegetable?"

"Victim."

"Too bad, she has a very pretty name."

"Had a pretty name."

"Oh."

"She was knifed last night in a house in the university district. The boss thinks it was a lover or something. Me, I'd say psycho. The dude just ripped the guts right out of her. Only a psycho does that. Poor kid."

His sister glanced at her computer screen, then back to him. "Slow, just like I told you . . . So how is your boss, anyway? You still haven't told me how you like working for a woman."

"Let's not discuss it."

"Aw, come on," she teased. "It can't be that bad. I've always had to work for men."

"Hell, I guess it really hasn't been that bad. You know, I was worried at first, but . . . it's okay. She's lightened up quite a bit and—"

The terminal beeped.

Both turned their eyes to it. It displayed: *No computer record found.* Gilroy grinned. "The boss was right; something isn't adding up."

"Probably an illegal," Donna said. "But are you sure you got the right name and date of birth? How about a Social Security number?"

"Naw, that's all I had. She's just not in the system."

Donna leaned back in her chair, then suddenly

shifted forward. "Say, what was the birth date you gave me?"

"March fourteenth."

"Uh-oh, sorry, I fat-fingered the date, see." She pointed to the top of the screen where her initial entry was still showing. "See, I put in the twenty-fourth, not the fourteenth. Let's try it again."

Gilroy bit his tongue. His sister had always been a bit of a scatterbrain.

"There, it's in right. Now we wait again." She rolled her chair away from the desk. "You want a diet Pepsi or something? I'm going to go grab one from the Coke machine."

Gilroy declined. He stood alone at her desk, staring blankly at the screen. This time the wait was short. At the beep, he leaned close and pressed the space bar. Instantly Christina Herrera's record appeared: date of entry, port of entry, student visa, current address, et cetera. "I'll be damned." Gilroy sighed. "She is real— and legal."

Gilroy swung around and took his sister's seat. He scrolled through the information, scanning it for any odd tidbit that might shed light on their investigation. Halfway down, he came to an abrupt halt. "Bingo." A self-satisfied smile flashed across his face. "Now that's interesting." He pressed the print key, waited for the hard copy, then quietly left without even saying good-bye to his sister.

Twenty-two

"Harris," she said answering the ring of her cell phone.

"It's Gilroy. Can you hear me? We've got a crappy connection." The line crackled loudly.

"I'm in a hole; hang on a sec." Sergeant Harris gritted her teeth in frustration. Traffic was still moving slowly. "There, I'm going back up the hill off Twenty-fifth. Can you hear me now?"

"Yeah, great."

"So?"

"Christina Herrera is for real, or I should say, was real. Everything matches, addresses, dates, and vitals."

"Well, it was just a thought. At least now we can get copies of her fingerprint cards from the FBI for an absolute ID."

"Already done. I was on the phone the minute I got back to the office. They're faxing her cards as we speak, but it's going to be academic. Roy was up here and I showed him her classification from the printout I got. He checked it against the prints they made from the body, before the autopsy. Every finger matched."

"Hmmm."

"Something else, boss."

"Now what?"

"There was a problem with her visa. Seems her father, Esteban Herrera, is *persona non grata* in this county. Given she's from Colombia, I'd lay dollars to doughnuts it's about drugs. What do ya think? Want me to poke further into this? It might be just the ticket to explain things!"

Harris froze.

"Well?"

"I'm thinking."

Although Harris's natural inclination was to fill her subordinate in about the money and drugs discovered at the victim's house, she held back. But not because of Milkovich's directive. It was Darby. Each new development seemed like quicksand. And the man she thought she knew was sinking deeper and deeper into this mire. Her next thought was even more troubling: Was her thinking biasing the entire investigation? Was she not pursing him as she knew she should?

"Damn."

"What's that, boss?"

"Nothing." Harris cleared her mind. "Listen, two things before we work this Colombian connection. First, check the list of registered sex offenders who are living within ten miles of our scene, and also check any new releases—anyone who got out of the joint in the last thirty days and hasn't got a permanent address yet."

"So you're thinking psycho? Even with this new angle?"

"My gut says no, but we've got to clear the possibility. Besides, Herrera is going to be in California for the next couple of days. He's got a flight that leaves in about an hour. It's too late to try to talk to him face-to-face about it. Besides, I'll want more details before we confront him. That is, if we need to."

"Okay, so what was the other thing?"

"Do you know a Sam Godwinn? He's with the Naval Criminal Investigative Service?"

"No."

"Okay—listen, go to my desk. He's under N. Find the number and call me back."

"Got it. Oh—Jennings checked in a few minutes ago, too. He finished doing the sweep of the neighborhood and got the search warrant done for the victim's house. He was wondering where you were. I think he wanted to call it a day and get home to his family."

"Have you got his cell number handy?"

"Sure."

"Do me a favor. Call him. See if he can get the warrant signed; then he can go. You can stay on though, can't you?"

"No problem. Hang on, boss, I'm putting you on hold. I'll find that number and be right back to ya."

"Thanks." And Harris continued on her way.

Twenty-three

The body cavity was hollowed out, the organs removed to be weighed and sampled. The smell of burned bone still hung in the air from the electric saw Dr. Reid had used to cut open the top of Christina Herrera's skull and extract her brain. The autopsy was now complete. The items removed would soon be placed back into the abdominal cavity. Christina Herrera would then be sewn together with a rough stitch and refrigerated to await burial, or the columbarium.

Jane Fenton had watched patiently through two and a half hours of Dr. Reid's solitary dialogue with the microphone and video camera. Reid had worked with a cold precision, detached, machinelike, without the slightest hint of emotion or recognition that before her was a once vibrant human being. She looked at the clock. It was 1648. She sighed, shifting her weight to another foot, then yawned.

For the first time since she'd started, Dr. Reid

glanced at Fenton and formed a slight smile. She reached over and shut off the recording equipment. "There, another one for the books, except for the lab samples." She walked over to a large bin labeled BLOOD CONTAMINANTS, yanked off her red-stained gloves, and tossed them in, followed by her lab apron. "Coffee?"

"Sure," Fenton readily agreed. She knew it was the price she would have to pay in order to get the doctor's preliminary findings now, instead of waiting a week for a written autopsy report.

They both exited into the scrub area. From the main hallway, it was a short distance to Reid's office, where a new smell offended Fenton's nose—old, thick coffee. The kind that had been brewed first thing in the morning, then sat cooking all day on a hot plate. Her stomach turned. It was the part of the ritual she hated most.

They entered the small, cluttered room filled with teetering stacks of old medical journals, newspapers, and textbooks. Reid removed a pile from the lone visitor's chair and placed it on the floor. Jane gratefully sat down, adjusting herself catercorner to the desk. Reid reached behind another set of documents, perched precariously on the edge of a shelf, and pulled out two stained coffee mugs. Filling them, she handed one to Jane, then settled tiredly into her swivel chair. Holding the cup with both hands, she raised it to her nose, savoring the same aroma that was making Jane queasy.

"Doing anything for Thanksgiving? Any plans?"

Fenton shook her head. "No, just me and my cat—and my cat is such a loner, he prefers me at work."

"No family?"

"An ex-husband in Portland, but if I saw him, I'd probably pop him one on the chin. We broke up five years ago, and he still owes me money."

"That's too bad. It's not good to be alone, especially on holidays."

Fenton forced a sip and swallowed quickly. "It's all right," she replied philosophically. "I still like my job, I make enough to get by on, and I can do pretty much what I want to. Really, I like it this way. How about you? A lot of family in the area?"

Dr. Reid grinned. "Four younger sisters, all of them married, some still with young kids, and all with baby grandkids. When everyone gets together, we need a dining hall. It's wonderful pandemonium. I always look forward to the holidays."

Fenton smiled halfheartedly. The vision of all those children screaming and running rampant while she was trying to eat disgusted her. "So, Dr. Reid . . ." Jane was hoping to focus the conversation. "What do you think about the girl you just did the autopsy on? Anything out of the ordinary?"

Reid gazed up at the ceiling for a moment, then back. Her chair creaked. Finally she spoke in a measured cadence. "This is unofficial and very preliminary. Things could change with the lab results. You understand, right?"

"Of course."

"Well, then." Dr. Reid sounded as if she were beginning an academic lecture. "Your victim was killed by multiple stab wounds, by a knife with a seven-inch blade. That blade was slender, no more than two centimeters, three-quarters of an inch, in width. My bet would be a standard kitchen fillet knife, but one of high quality, since the wounds showed no warping in the penetration. A cheap knife will do that—the steel bends on impact and causes the wound channel to be banana shaped."

Fenton nodded knowingly.

"Any one of a number of the wounds would have been fatal—several major arteries and organs were punctured. Bleeding was profuse, especially internally. I would say that within ten to twenty seconds of the initial attack, she lost consciousness, with death following soon thereafter. A minute or two at the most. As you probably saw when you first encountered the body, the right hand has a lone resistance cut along the palm. She must have reached for the knife, grabbing at the blade in self-defense. Remarkably, there is only the one. No other signs of a struggle, no contusions, lacerations, or other marks. That's unusual, I think you'll agree. It certainly points to a killer who knew the victim. At least that's been my experience, and probably yours. In a stranger kill, with a knife, there is always more preliminary violence to the body. The victim needs to be restrained more by the killer, just due to the simple fact that the victim knows right away there is a problem, and becomes defensive. That is in direct contrast with a killer who is known to the victim—the victim will allow the killer much closer before becoming resistant. I'd say that's the case here."

Fenton continued to nod. Based on what she had seen, she had already drawn the same conclusion, but she listened respectfully.

"However, I did note something of interest that may be pertinent to your investigation. Around both wrists there was some very faint bruising, consistent with her hands being tied or cuffed."

"Cuffed?" Jane's voice betrayed her surprise. This was something she hadn't seen. How had she missed it?

"What is interesting here is that, in my opinion, the bruising in this area is probably not associated with the attack. First, the coloration was such that the marks were at least twenty-four hours old when death occurred. Second, the severity of the bruising is not consistent with a homicidal incident. If the victim had been handcuffed, then knifed, the bruising in this area would have been extreme. I've seen it many times. People being murdered do try to resist, even when bound. Finally, if the victim had been cuffed at the time of the murder, she could not have incurred the resistance wound to her hand. That wound could only have happened with someone whose hands were free."

"Could she have been cuffed, then let go just before she was killed?"

"I would say no. Again, the bruising to the wrist was at least a day old. Now, of course, that is not to say the killer wasn't responsible for those, too. If the killer was her lover, then perhaps they had engaged in a sexual act the previous day in which handcuffs had been used. That's possible; lots of things are possible. My only point here is that those markings were not part of the actual homicide, and, between you and me, they are much more consistent with an act of consensual bondage than with forced restraint. But don't quote me on it. By the way, did you happen to find a pair of handcuffs at her residence, or perhaps a leather strap of some kind—you know the implements. Anything like that?"

"No, nothing kinky at all, and Roy and I tossed the house completely. Nothing to indicate this."

"Hmmm. Well, then . . ."

"Ah, jeez," Fenton uttered softly with the realization that Darby would have cuffs. She pressed Dr. Reid. "Was she sexually assaulted? Can you tell?"

"In my opinion, no." Reid thoughtfully sipped her coffee. "There was no vaginal violence consistent with an assault, although there was some semen present. The killer may have had intercourse with her before he killed her, as could have someone else, for that matter. It will be impossible to tell exactly when. However, based on the quantity present, I'd speculate that she did have intercourse within four to six hours of her death. But again, I have to believe it was consensual. Even in a rape where the victim submits without the slightest struggle, inevitably there will be vaginal bruising that just doesn't occur in normal sexual contact. Further, there are usually other types of violence about the body, like bite marks or bruising from slaps or blows. Then, too, the attacker will usually hold the victim down, and there tend to be marks on the victim's arms when this has happened. In this case, there's nothing."

"Then we'll get a typing on the semen? What about DNA?"

"The typing will be ready in a few days, no problem; but like blood, if it's from a common group, it won't be of much evidentiary value. Now DNA will take a while, and—"

The telephone rang, startling the pair. Dr. Reid picked it up. "Yes?" She listened intently for a few moments, then hung up, frowning. "DNA is going to take a while longer."

Fenton raised a questioning eyebrow.

"That was one of my techs. I had him take a sample of the semen and examine the sperm under magnification. There is none, which means one of two things: either the man is sterile, which is unlikely—even someone sterile will have a minimal count—or he has had a vasectomy. That'd be my bet. Unfortunately, with a vasectomy, doing a DNA test becomes a little more complicated. I'll get the sample shipped off to the lab on Monday, but under the best of circumstances, it'll be three weeks before we have any results. And that's if you have some political pull at the state lab. So my official advice, off the record, is that if you're in a hurry, just look for a guy who's been snipped." Dr. Reid chuckled briefly, caught herself, and resumed her formal manner.

"Until we get the tissue and blood tests back, that's about all I can give you. With the holiday and all, it'll be next Monday or Tuesday before I have anything on that. That's about it for now. I hope it's been some help."

"It certainly has," Jane enthused. "And what about the time of death? A possible suspect's alibi may hinge on that."

"Oh, dear, That's going to be a problem. I'm afraid my official pronouncement on that issue will not be very precise. The core temperatures taken at the scene were accurate and properly done, but in the technician's report of the body removal, there's a note that the victim was lying right next to a heater vent in the wall. The ambient temperature in the room was seventy-four degrees. That means the heater was on, and blowing hot air on her. There's no way I can give you an accurate time of death with this."

Fenton's concern wreathed her face.

"If I had to testify in court, all I could reasonably say was that Christina Herrera died sometime after six o'clock yesterday evening. I can't do any better. There's just no way. Hopefully you'll be able to pin the time down better from witnesses. If not, we're out of luck!" The ME sat forward, elbows on the chair arms, her hands clasped together. "So now, how consistent is the evidence you have with what I just postulated?"

"Bull's-eye."

As she had listened, Fenton had been mentally collating what was being said with what she already knew. Darby kept coming to mind, except there was no apparent motive. Something wasn't adding up. She knew she wasn't as sharp as she should be—the couple hours of sleep hadn't been enough to belay the fatigue that was beginning to set in. She drank some more of the dreadful coffee, ruminating. Then it clicked—the talcum powder. That was it, the curveball in this whole game. She threw it back at Dr. Reid.

"We recovered a knife exactly as you described from a drawer in the kitchen. It had been wiped clean, but there were traces of blood that will likely match the victim's."

"Ah, then we have an angry lover. A spur-of-the-moment jealous rage. That will work. The number of wounds and their type are all consistent with this type of attack—"

"But," Jane interrupted, "there were also traces

of talcum powder—of a type consistent with Dyna Med brand surgical gloves. They're commonly found at any drugstore. The kitchen counter had been recently wiped clean of blood, but the talcum residue remained."

Reid set her coffee down. "Premeditated . . . That changes everything. You still might have an enraged lover, but he's going to be one cold SOB."

"Then a psycho?"

"Could be . . . it just could be."

Twenty-four

It was dark now. The sun had set quickly behind a thickening band of clouds. The park was empty, except for a few solitary joggers finishing their runs. Milkovich stood braced against the hood of his car, the radiating heat warming his backside and tempering the cool, misting air.

Harris pulled in and stopped opposite him. She lowered the passenger window. "Hey," she called out, "you're getting wet."

Milkovich shrugged. He liked standing in the rain, especially a light drizzle like this one. It awakened many sweet smells, cleansing his lungs and his mind of the day's worries.

"Come on, get in. I'm not getting out."

Milkovich savored a last languorous breath.

Slipping into the passenger seat, he brushed away the rainwater, chancing to look at Harris just as the headlights of a passing car briefly illuminated her face. Her green eyes were sparkling. Milkovich was surprised that he'd missed noticing how striking they were. He continued to stare after the lights had faded.

"Well," Harris said uneasily. She could feel his gaze, despite the dark. Unthinkingly, she brushed her tousled hair back with her hand.

The rainfall became heavier, its increased patter rousing Milkovich. He blinked and looked away, embarrassed by his momentary fixation. When he turned back to speak with her, he kept his eyes averted.

"So?"

"I know you're thinking Herrera is clean in all of this, but—"

"Actually I'm not so sure now."

"How's that?"

"While Phil was checking with Immigration, he came across the fact that her old man, Enrique's brother Esteban, is not particularly welcome in this country."

"Figures." Milkovich sighed.

"Figures what, damn it? You know something, don't you? What the hell is this all about? When you first saw the money, you mentioned something about the tally marks being all the same. Then you wondered about who actually owned the house. Then there was Darby making regular trips to San Diego. And now, just a couple of minutes ago, you fixated on the fact that Herrera is a Harvard MBA. What the hell gives here?"

Milkovich's eyes narrowed and he grimly said, "We've stumbled onto a Colombian drug cell, that's what gives. Something that's never supposed to have been possible here in Seattle."

Harris stiffened.

"Like I told you before, I worked Narcotics. . . . Ten years ago, the department brought in some high-zoot FBI guys, or maybe they were DEA. Hell, I don't remember—they all look alike. Anyway, they were out of San Diego and here to give us drug cops an intel briefing. See, back in the eighties southern California was awash in cocaine. The Colombians were dumping the stuff onto the market like crazy. The unit these guys had been working in had been making busts of a hundred kilos at a time. And it was uncut, a hundred percent pure. Street value on lots that size were in the tens of millions—and it was everywhere down there."

"And what the hell does this have to do with us now?"

"Let me finish."

Harris sighed, then gave a slight wave of her hand to proceed.

Milkovich nodded a thank-you and went on. "Suddenly the pops got smaller and less frequent. Information dried up. No one would talk. The drugs were still there, all right, but these guys could only catch the small fry. Evidently, around 1986, the drug bosses back in Colombia got smart and organized—kind of like the Arabs did with OPEC. They got some guru with a Harvard MBA to customize a business plan just for them. Essentially, they embarked on a vertical and horizontal integration of their operation."

Harris raised a skeptical eyebrow.

"No, really. See, instead of simply manufacturing and wholesaling it out in large lots, they figured a way to establish cop-proof franchises near the actual consumption points."

"And how were they cop-proof?"

"That's the missing piece of the puzzle. No one has figured it out. But from time to time, just like today, us cops stumble across a house, like our victim's, with large chunks of change stashed away with no outward connection to anyone. The residents aren't aware the cash is there."

"Yeah, right."

"It's true, the renters are actual residents. In exchange for the free roof, they get lost for a couple of hours whenever it's time to make a deposit or withdrawal. Someone else in the organization does all the transfers, and the two parties never meet or know anything about each other. Don't ask, don't tell."

"So where are the drugs kept?"

"As far away as possible and under the control of separate players."

"But how do you keep all these people quiet? Someone is bound to talk."

"Ah, this was also part of the plan. Only blood-linked family members are ever used. Cousins, aunts, uncles, brothers, and sisters.

Squealing in this context will not only get you killed, but your own mother will spit on your grave."

Harris looked at him with sudden comprehension. "You think Herrera is your MBA?"

"Could be. Look, we've got a Colombian expatriate with an MBA. Not only that, but it's from Harvard. His age is right, he's obviously wealthy, and we have him associated with drugs, or at least money laundering. In my book, if it waddles and quacks, it's a duck, no matter how many people say it ain't so. And this guy Herrera, I think he's foul—pardon the pun."

Harris glanced at her watch. "He'll be out of reach for a little while."

"How come?"

"He told me he was flying to his aunt's place for Thanksgiving. By my clock he should be lifting off from SeaTac just about now."

"That's okay; we're going to need time to figure the best way to work this."

Harris hesitated.

"You don't think I'm on target?"

"Oh, it's not that. It's . . . Well, just before I pulled in here, I got a quick briefing on the autopsy from my evidence technician. There was no sexual assault."

"Good, a rape wouldn't fit into my theory of a drug deal gone bad, especially with family members. Anything else?"

"Yeah." Harris frowned, and with a sudden

rush of anger slammed her right palm on the
dash. "That goddamned, two-timing fucker!"

Milkovich flinched. "Darby?"

"You're damned right Darby! The autopsy
confirmed one thing: within a few hours of her
death, Christina Herrera had had intercourse
with a partner who's been clipped." Harris
banged her hand again. She could feel herself
blush, and was grateful for the darkness.

Milkovich remained silent, not wanting to
push.

"That fucking bastard." She shook her head
in disgust. "John Darby had a vasectomy. . . .
Shit, the bastard told me so, the second time we
slept together."

"He might have lied."

There was an awkward silence. "Christ, I saw
the scars!"

"Oh." Milkovich looked away. Her bluntness
caught him off guard as he briefly visualized the
implication of her last statement. "You know, it
could just be a—"

"Coincidence! Jesus Christ, Milkovich, you
just got done telling me if it waddles and
quacks, it's a duck. Well, John Darby is my fucking duck."

"But didn't you tell me earlier today that he
was with you at the time? How could he have
screwed the victim, if that was the case?"
Screwed. Milkovich regretted it the moment he
said it. Poor choice of words.

"Because, damn it all, we're not going to have

a solid time of death. Right now, we know for certain she was alive at around twenty-hundred. The grunge queens from across the street saw her about then. Beyond that, we don't know shit; she could have been killed anytime after that, or all the way up to an hour before her body was found. With the heat being on her— oh, I forgot to tell you that, too—jeez, I'm losing it. The body was right next to a heater vent, pumping hot air on her. It kept her body warm, so now normal core temperature degradation is useless. On top of that, the hot air dried all the blood on the floor at an accelerated rate. We can't even make a ballpark guess from that."

Milkovich pondered. "We're back to Darby again. But I thought you said he was with you last night."

"After twenty-two-thirty," Harris snapped. "He would work out at his gym, then drop by to—"

"I get the picture," Milkovich cut in. "But that should be easy enough to check out."

Harris glanced at her watch again—1658. "Ah, Christ," she moaned. She grabbed for her cell phone, studied a note clipped to the visor. She then punched in the number she'd recorded. The phone began to ring. She continued from the side of her mouth, "I was beginning to have my doubts about John a little while ago. I've got a friend in the Naval Criminal Investigative Service who, if they haven't all left for the day, can—" She stopped, her eyes drifting past Milkovich as she concentrated on her call.

"This is Sergeant Harris, with the Seattle Police Department. Is Special Agent Godwinn in? No? Darn. Say, who's in charge of the office now? Greg Ericksen—is he in? Gone too . . . ummm . . . What did you say your name was? Fisher? . . . Mel Fisher? Okay, Mel, I need some help. My name? Leah Harris; I'm a sergeant with Homicide, SPD. I need a name run on the worldwide personnel locator. No, I don't have time to put the request in writing—I really need the information now. Yes . . . yeah, I know you're not allowed to give that type of information over the phone; but look, Mel, I really do need your help. Call my office, talk to my boss—they'll confirm who I am. . . . Wait, hold on. How about this . . . Do you know Sam Godwinn at all? Do you know what his call sign was when he was flying? I do—it was Windbag." Harris chuckled. "Now if you know Sam, then you know how apropos the tag was and is. . . . See, you agree. . . . Okay, Mel, it's almost Thanksgiving; I bet you want to go home, and if I have to go through channels to get the info, you'll be there all night. Am I right? I promise your name won't come up—promise."

There was a pause. Harris grinned excitedly while absently placing her right hand on Milkovich's shoulder and giving it a gentle squeeze. Her eyes remained fixed on a distant point outside.

Milkovich froze, unsettled by the soft touch. Instinctively, he wanted to pull away—yet he remained, mesmerized by the brief physical contact.

"Darby . . . D-A-R-B-Y, first of John, common spelling. The middle is, ah, is F. I think that's for Francis. He's a reserve officer, a lieutenant commander. His DOB? I've got it written down here, just a second."

"It's March first," Milkovich interrupted, "1963." He remembered the date from the personnel file he had seen earlier.

"Thanks," Harris mouthed as she gave the date to the NCIS agent. She absently squeezed Milkovich's shoulder one more time. "OK, I'll wait. Yeah, no problem. Take your time."

Just then, Milkovich's pager went off. Harris jerked her hand away, realizing at that moment that she had been touching him. From the corner of her eye, she desperately tried to see if he was annoyed. She couldn't tell. He was already looking down at the faint light of the message screen, trying to discern the alpha message.

"Christ," Milkovich grumbled, "this is getting to be one of those days."

"You need to make a call?" Harris asked, her hand over the receiver.

"Yeah, it's the chief. I'll go use my car phone. Let me know what you find out." Harris nodded as Milkovich slipped out and made a dash for his vehicle.

Twenty-five

Officer Meigs leaned wearily against the front door. He angrily puffed on a cigarette, cussing the dampness and the decision by the watch sergeant to have him pull the next shift standing guard. "The asshole," he muttered. "This shit is for rookies." For the next eight hours he couldn't leave the premises. He swore again, then poured his first cup of coffee from a borrowed thermos. The aroma soon reached his nostrils and calmed him down a bit. Maybe this wasn't so bad. Eight hours here, and then four days off. No paperwork, no bitching from citizens, and he could stay dry. Of course, on nights like this, he rarely got out of his car anyway. Why get wet, he'd always rationalized, just to write a two-bit ticket for speeding? Leave that to the rookies and the brown-nosers trying to make sergeant.

He took a sip, savoring the hot liquid as he gazed across the street to the house occupied by

the three young women. He could see one of
them standing in front of the window, silhouet-
ted by the living room lights. He could hear
music—loud, unintelligible lyrics wrapped in
discordant, jagged rhythms.

He thought of his own daughter, from his first
marriage. Just like the girl he was watching
now. Always ready to argue, so righteously indignant of his opinions, and ready to sleep with
the first guy who had tattoos and no future.

He lit another cigarette. The headlights of an
approaching car caught his attention. It was
halfway down the block, moving slowly. It was
a newer vehicle—he could tell by the shape and
the glow of the halogen headlamps. When it
passed beneath a streetlight, he saw that it was
a late-model BMW. Meigs straightened up. The
car was out of place in this neighborhood. Despite his laziness, twenty-five years on the street
had honed his intuition to a fine edge. He tossed
his cigarette into the bushes below him and
stepped into the shadows. The car stopped directly in front of the house, motor running,
double-parked. The passenger door popped
open. A medium-size Hispanic male in jeans
and a sweatshirt jumped out and headed toward
the house. With one quick hop, he was over the
yellow barrier tape, moving quickly toward
where Meigs stood.

"Hold it right there!" Meigs ordered, his right
hand unsnapping the safety strap of his holster.

He was ready to draw his 9mm semiautomatic pistol.

"Oh, hey, man, whoa," came the quick response to Meigs's actions. "I'm one of the good guys. Look." The stranger flipped open a wallet badge. "Detective Rodriguez, Narcotics. My partner and I saw you standing here and we're kinda lost. We're looking for an address that's somewhere around here."

Meigs relaxed. At roll call, they'd been advised there might be some drug operations in his sector during the next few days. He resnapped his holster and stepped forward. "Where ya looking for?"

"Hey, man, this rain is the shits, ain't it?" The detective approached Meigs. He stepped onto the porch, wiping his face. Meigs could see the butt of a large-bore semiauto protruding from the detective's waistband. *What a cowboy*, Meigs thought. He had a low opinion of the Narco-boys. To him, they walked around the department like they owned the place. Always acting like they were undercover, living on the edge and looking like shit. They weren't cops; they were a bunch of teenagers looking for thrills just like the dirtbags they were arresting.

The detective thrust his hand into a pocket and pulled out a scrap of paper. "I know we're close, but I get lost up in this neck of the woods. I've always worked out of South Precinct. Let's see, the address is on La . . . La . . . shit! Christ,

I can barely read this. The ink's run in this god-damned rain. Here, can you make it out?"

He thrust the damp piece of paper at Meigs. The writing was indecipherable. Meigs shrugged his shoulders and handed it back. Frustrated, the detective bit his lower lip. "I know we're close, if I could just remember the name of the street. I know it starts with an L—it's 'La' something."

"Latona?"

"Yeah, that's the ticket, forty-two-hundred block of Latona, a tan and green house. Do you know it?"

Meigs nodded and pointed westward. "Eight blocks over. On the other side of the freeway. Take Forty-fifth."

"Hey, man, thanks. Say, you gotta like our new ride—the Beamer's a beauty, isn't she? We just got her out of the pool. Came from that bust on Queen Anne, the doctor doing all that coke."

Meigs didn't bother to respond. It was one more straw on his *Narcos are cowboys* pile. Suspects' cars, seized during drug arrests, were placed in a motor pool for the Narcotics detectives to use, especially if they were late models. BMWs, Cadillacs, Porsches, or Corvettes, that's what they always picked for themselves.

The younger man grinned, sensing Meigs's irritation. He had accomplished his goal. "Have a nice night, man," he said slyly, and headed down the stairs.

"Little prick," Meigs swore under his breath.

But his vexation was instantly forgotten. Above the sound of the rain and overflowing gutters came the unmistakable sound of someone stepping onto the rotting back steps behind the home.

The detective, too, stopped in his tracks. He understood the significance of the noise. Meigs motioned to him with hand signs. *I'll go left; you go right.*

Rodriguez signaled his understanding. He pulled out his .45, pushed the safety off, crept to the side of the house, and began to edge around the corner.

Meigs stepped silently down onto the wet grass, keeping his flashlight off. If someone was back there, trying to get in, he didn't want to give them any warning.

He felt his way forward in the dark, until his eyes adjusted enough for him make out a path through the overgrown shrubs that ran the length of the property. He strained to hear any suspicious sounds, but the weather drowned out all other noise. Continuing, Meigs rubbed up against an unseen low branch, dumping a large quantity of collected rainwater down his collar. "Goddamn it! Son of . . ." His voice trailed off with the realization he might have just given himself away.

Onward he trudged until he reached the rear edge of the house. He listened, trying to sense if anyone was around the corner. Nothing. Maybe, he rationalized, the creaking had come from the tall firs across the way, their boughs groaning in the wind. Then his concentration switched to Rodriguez. Christ, that dick with his cannon was going to be coming around the other side any second. Meigs didn't relish the idea of being mistakenly shot by some hyper cowboy punk.

The old beat cop bent low and eased forward, until he had a good view of the backdoor and yard beyond. Nothing seemed amiss. *Okay,* he thought, *now where's that little Mexican asshole.* Meigs strained his eyes, but couldn't make him. *The little shit! Where in Christ's name is he?* He waited a few more moments, pondering what to do as the rain continued to pound down; his uniform was now thoroughly soaked. "Aw, the hell with it." He drew his pistol and stepped fully around the side. "Hey, Rodriguez," he called out. "I'm checking the back door. Don't fuckin' shoot me! Got that?"

Meigs quickly made his way to the steps. Rather than climb them, he reached up from the side and rattled the doorknob. It was still locked. Suddenly a car started close by. Instinctively Meigs spun around, then moved quickly toward the sound that was emanating from behind the detached garage. It was less than fifty feet away. He slowed as he reached the outbuilding, not wanting to expose himself, but he was too late. The unseen driver punched the gas and sped away down the alley. Meigs rounded the corner in time to see brake lights flash as

the car reached the end of the narrow access
and entered the cross street. It turned right and
disappeared.

Who the hell was that? he wondered. He reholstered his weapon and trotted back to the scene.
He scanned the yard, his flashlight held at
shoulder height. "Rodriguez, where the hell are
you?" Still no reply. Meigs made his way up
along the side of the house the detective had
supposedly traversed. Seeing nothing, he
headed across the front yard and checked the
street. The BMW was gone. Meigs shook his
head. "That little fucker left me. Goddamned
Narcs. You can't trust them for anything!"

Disgusted, he trod back to his station on the
front porch, poured himself another cup of coffee, and lit a damp cigarette. The sergeant
would probably be by in the next half hour to
check up on him. Maybe he could be relieved
long enough to go back to the precinct and
change. Until then, it'd be a cold wait, kept
warm only by his seething anger over the detective who had deserted him. He'd figure some
way to get him back. Nothing official, just some
street justice.

Another car passed in front of the house. He
studied the taillights. They were not like the
ones he had just seen in the alley, but they did
jog his memory. He remembered stopping a car
a week prior, and writing a hefty speeding ticket
because the bastard had mouthed off to him. It
had the same kind of taillights. "Let's see, that

was a Honda, or a Toyota. Naw, it wasn't that, it was nicer. But what?"

Meigs slumped against one of the porch pillars. "Ah, who gives a shit anyway." And he folded his arms and hunkered down. It was going to be yet another long, cold night.

Twenty-six

"Miller."

"You paged? It's Milkovich."

"Frank, where are you?"

"About ten from the office. What's up?"

"Hey, I hate to dump this on you, but I just got a call from an attorney a couple of minutes ago. She says that she represents Sgt. Paula Anderson, up at North Precinct, and she's demanding we cease the IA on her client based on God-knows-what dumb-ass legal precedent. What gives? I hadn't heard you were doing an internal on her. I certainly didn't authorize one."

As he listened, Milkovich glanced over at the blue Ford. Harris had her phone pressed to her ear. Still on hold, he figured. She looked impatient. Another car's headlights flickered across her windshield. Suddenly the image of Harris's green eyes occupied his consciousness. It was only momentary, however.

"Frank?"

Milkovich's mind changed gears. "Chief, it's not really an investigation yet. I'm just looking at the initial complaint."

"Well, this attorney sure doesn't seem to think so." There was irritation in his voice.

"Listen, boss, there is no internal at this point. I'm just at the preliminary review stage. You'll obviously know when and if I move to the formal internal stage."

"How close are you?"

Milkovich sighed. "Darby is the priority right now, correct?"

"You bet your ass he is!"

"Then at this point I'm just trying to keep everyone satisfied in this thing with Anderson. I spoke briefly with the alleged victim just a little while ago, but it can take a back burner until I make some headway with Darby."

"So why is this attorney so hot to trot? Is there something I need to know, and now?"

"Yeah, there is, but I don't think I should discuss it with you over a cell phone. It's not something scanner-land needs to hear about."

"Christ almighty, now what? The press is snapping like a bunch of piranhas because I'm being so tight-lipped on last night's knifing. They know something is up; they can smell it. They're like a pack of dogs and I'm the son of a bitch that's in heat! I don't want any surprises. Understand?"

"I do, but Anderson can wait. I'm going to need another day on Darby."

"Okay, but I want a briefing on this other thing A-SAP. I've got a dinner engagement I need to go to right now. I can be free about twenty-one-hundred hours—I want to talk then, both Anderson and Darby. And do me a favor."

"Sure."

"You got a pencil ready?"

"Yep."

"Call that bitch of an attorney for me and try to calm her down. She's expecting a response, pronto."

Milkovich jotted down the phone number and hung up. He glanced again at Harris. Her continuing blank, now slightly irritated expression told him she must still be on hold. He smiled in sympathy, but she didn't respond.

He felt relieved that he was going to have a chance to meet with Miller before the night was out. Something was screwy with the Darby case, and it was time to lay his cards on the table—good chance to check the chief's reaction.

With the phone still in his hand, he punched in the number Miller had just recited as a powerful sense of foreboding engulfed him. The Griggs-Anderson problem was not going to be something that would keep on the back burner for very long, despite his promises. He knew the bottom line, and from his perspective, it ironically had the potential to be far more explosive than Darby. It was one thing for a cop to kill his girlfriend. You could even toss in drugs. The public expected a few rogues in the department.

But what Griggs was alleging, although it was a simple case of sexual harassment, had all the elements of ripping a wide swath through the organization. Heads would roll and the newspapers and TV cameras would be there to record every agonizing execution.

Midway through the first ring, the phone receiver was snatched up. "Stephanie Chang, may I help you?" Her voice was stiletto sharp.

"Chief Miller asked me to give you a call regarding—"

"Sgt. Paula Anderson." The attorney cut him off. "You must be Sergeant Milkovich. Am I correct?"

"Yes."

"Very good," Chang pronounced. "I represent Sergeant Anderson and must insist, per your department policies and labor contract, that you cease your investigation of her immediately. It's outrageous, your conduct in this affair. You're in violation of your own procedures. My client has not received any notice of an internal investigation, yet you are conducting one. This is a direct violation of labor law and will result in a civil suit, which I am prepared to file on Monday, if you don't stop this moment and turn over copies to me of all documents in your possession relating to this situation. Have I made myself perfectly clear?"

Milkovich sighed. Typical legal spittle.

"Well?"

"Well, what? I haven't the slightest idea what

you're talking about. There is no official internal investigation being conducted regarding Sergeant Anderson."

"Then you mean it's unofficial?"

"I didn't say that."

"Then just what is the nature of this improper conduct?"

"Now wait a second, miss. What'd you say your name was?"

"Ms. Chang," she hissed.

Milkovich grimaced. The attorney on the other end of the line was baiting the traps that would be used later to win an action on her client's behalf. So far he hadn't tripped on any of her land mines. He continued to follow his usual strategy in dealing with lawyers—stay calm and say as little as possible.

"Ms. Chang," he proceeded. "If you read our department manual, specifically page two-twenty, paragraph three, you will note that upon initial receipt of a complaint pertaining to an employee of this department, that, and I quote: *'Initially, the complaint shall be screened to determine reasonable validity, before any further action is taken.'* End-quote."

"But Sergeant Milkovich, you have gone beyond that. I believe you're well into the investigative stage. I have evidence of this, which is *prima facie* for the initiation of legal recourse."

Milkovich grinned. This was a bluff. He knew it. She was prodding him to unthinkingly reveal what he knew. He decided to try to reverse the game. "Legal recourse, Ms. Chang? I don't understand. What evidence do you have?"

"You have met with my client's accuser. You have interviewed her, which is a violation, and since you've been so haphazard with our state's employment laws and shown such disregard for my client's civil rights, I shall see to it that I have your badge when I get done with you."

Milkovich shrugged off the threat and zeroed in on what she had just said about his meeting with Griggs. Was it a guess, or had Anderson seen them? Was she stalking Griggs, as the younger woman believed?

"Sergeant Milkovich. Sergeant, are you listening to me?"

At that moment, Milkovich had begun to view Griggs's complaint in a new light, and decided that Anderson's alleged misbehavior had likely crossed the line from the civil arena, to criminal. With that, the manner in which he could handle the case radically changed. Employee rights under the department manual became moot. Criminal behavior was treated just the same as if the perpetrator were any other citizen. A slight smile formed on his face. He knew that there was no longer any requirement to deal with the suspect's attorney in regard to providing information. Not until the investigation was done and submitted to the prosecutor for the filing of charges.

"Ms. Chang," Milkovich said with some relish. "This may be a criminal inquiry; in fact, for your information, at this moment it is."

There was a period of silence. "I see." The lawyer's tone was decidedly constrained.

Milkovich remained mute. Silence was now the perfect tactic.

Finally, a long, reflective sigh emanated from Chang's end of the line. Her voice softened, as she modulated persuasively, "I do think it's imperative that you interview my client as soon as possible. She has in her possession evidence that will not only exonerate her, but will show that the accuser is a pathological liar. I realize that there is a holiday tomorrow, and you are probably on overtime right now, but would it be at all possible for you to meet with us in, say, an hour?"

Now this was interesting, Milkovich thought. An attorney who wanted her client to talk. That was worth a meeting anytime, even at midnight. He glanced at his watch. It was 1730. As he looked up, he saw Harris speaking rapidly into the phone. She seemed agitated, her free hand waving wildly in the air. Now what? he wondered. He returned to his caller. "How about 1900—ah, seven p.m. Where would you like to meet?"

"We'll have to do it at Sergeant Anderson's precinct. She's just gone on duty. She'd be available there."

"That'll work."

Milkovich hung up. Exiting his car, he dashed through the now heavy rain to Harris's vehicle. He slid in and immediately saw that something was wrong. Harris sat stone-faced, her phone resting in her lap. At first he said nothing. He could see her eyes beginning to water. He felt uncomfortable, and looked away, resisting his desire to immediately probe. He waited. As he did, he watched the rain droplets form into streaks on the windshield and run down its width in ever-changing patterns. At last, Harris spoke. "He really is a bastard." Her voice was sullen. "A goddamned lying bastard."

Milkovich waited for more.

"You know, up to this point, in the back of my mind, I kept telling myself that he had nothing to do with any of this. That it was all just a really weird set of circumstances, and that when he got back from his reserve duty, everything would make sense." Harris paused, groping for the Kleenex box on the floor, and blew her nose. She then turned to Milkovich. "Damn it, Frank. I trusted that asshole. I really did. I thought that just maybe I had at last met the one who'd— Boy, what a rookie mistake." She blew her nose again, gave a ragged sigh, then seemed to muster her resolve. "Frank, he's going to be our man. I know it now."

Milkovich's ears perked.

"There is no John Francis Darby, age thirty-seven, in the navy, at least not in the reserves on the West Coast. And that message number he gave me—it doesn't exist either. At least, not in the navy. The agent traced that for me too, and it belongs to a company out of La Jolla, California, called H and L Enterprises."

"Are you sure about this?" Milkovich could barely contain his satisfaction.

"He checked twice. Not only that, but he did a search on the name associated with the personal data I knew about, and went back twenty years. Guess what—there was a John Francis Darby fifteen years ago in San Diego, an ensign. The college he graduated from was San Diego State, just like our boy. But . . ."

"But what?"

"He was killed that year. A training accident."

"So what you're saying is . . ."

"Yeah, Frank—who the hell is our John Francis Darby?"

Twenty-seven

Jane Fenton had closed her purse, stood up from her desk, and started for the door when the phone rang. Obediently, she returned and picked up the receiver. "Lab."

"Jane? It's Dr. Reid. Glad I caught you. I've just received a couple of pieces of information that might be helpful for your investigation, and thought I'd better get hold of someone before the long weekend."

Fenton looked at the large clock on her wall. It was nearly 1800. "You caught me as I was heading out the door. I was calling it a day."

"Well, I'm glad I got you. Doesn't look like either one of us got the early start we talked about. Now, as per the new protocols, I had certain blood workups done immediately."

Jane listened respectfully. There was no rushing the doctor. Besides, Fenton wasn't so much in a hurry as she was stymied. She had reached a stopping point, and had actually hoped the caller was Harris, finally responding to Fenton's repeated attempts to reach her. They needed to discuss the direction she and Roy should take. Fenton had tried Harris's cell phone for the last half-hour, but it had automatically flipped over to voice mail. She had paged twice with alpha messages and left several unanswered messages. With no further recourse, she had decided to leave and make the next call from her apartment. Roy was long gone and probably halfway through his first fifth of bourbon. The case was cooling; chances of a lucky break were diminishing by the minute. It would take a while to get an arrest now. Good fortune, when it happened, almost always occurred in the first twenty-four hours of the crime, and Christina Herrera's murder was close to fading out of the red zone.

The pathologist finally finished describing the tests, and began to tick off the results. Fenton perfunctorily wrote down the information, placing little significance on the list—until Reid read the last item. Jane felt her heart jump. "Are you sure? There's no possibility of a mistake?"

"Positive. There's no mistake."

Jane blindly hung up, missing the receiver. She stood there in shock as the frenzied tone, signaling that the phone was off its hook, went unnoticed. *My God*, she wondered, *how am I going to tell Leah Harris about this?*

Twenty-eight

Detective Gilroy pulled away from the drive-through, and eased into the creeping traffic, steering with only one hand. In his other he held a large hamburger with all the trimmings. The smell made his mouth water. As he bit into the triple-decker, a portion of tomato, covered in catsup and mustard, flopped out and onto his pants leg. "Aw, son of a bitch. And I just had this goddamned suit cleaned!"

The car behind him honked. He hadn't noticed the stoplight turn green as he tried to wipe up the mess. Without thinking, he flipped the guy off with his free hand, and began to move forward slowly—on purpose. "Son of a bitch," he muttered again in disgust. He set the burger down on the seat beside him and began paying more attention to his driving. He glanced into his rearview mirror. The car that had honked was changing lanes and speeding up to pass.

Embarrassed at what he had done, Gilroy kept his eyes forward, but as the other vehicle passed, he caught a glimpse of the driver—a middle-aged Hispanic male, driving a dark green Lexus. Gilroy squinted to catch the plate number. "One-two-three P-T-G."

Oh, shit, he thought. *It's Herrera's car!* A few hours prior, he had routinely obtained a computer printout of all cars registered to the banker. There had been only one, the Lexus.

Gilroy remained calm, deciding to follow discreetly rather than give away his position. Traffic was heavy and the detective knew he could tail him easily, using the other cars as blinds. He grinned widely and whistled. "You're supposed to be on your way to California, you bastard."

The three lanes of traffic reached another red light. Gilroy was six cars back. He reached down and jabbed *recall* on his cell phone. "Okay, Harris, where the hell are you?" There was a short pause, then two rings and a transfer to her voice mail. "Get off your goddamned phone, Sarge! We got work to do."

Gilroy disconnected.

The light seemed to stay red forever. The detective reached for his burger, took another bite, then set it back down. His eyes still fixed on the Lexus, he fumbled on the floor for his milkshake. The light turned green. Gilroy straightened up empty-handed. His concentration now shifted wholly to keeping a benign distance between himself and his quarry. It was easy. The holiday rush had choked the streets. No one was going anywhere fast.

Twenty-nine

"I'm hungry. How 'bout you? Do you want something to eat?"

Harris forced a smile. She had been seething in silence, ignoring her pager and not noticing she hadn't disconnected from her last phone call. The line was still live. Suddenly she reached over and gently slapped Milkovich on his knee. "Damn it, let's get to work. I know where Darby lives; I can get a telephonic warrant, and we can toss the place good. With a little luck, we'll get something we can use."

Not a bad idea, Milkovich thought, but his stomach was beginning to ache. "A sandwich and a cup of coffee first. It looks like we could have a long night."

"I suppose you're right. Let me check my voice mail and then let's get something." Harris glanced down at her cell phone. "Ahh, shit."

"What's the matter?"

She pointed toward the receiver and rolled her eyes. Milkovich understood and chuckled.

Harris pressed *end* and entered a new number. Milkovich looked on, admiring the silhouette of her face outlined by the dashlight.

Messages started replaying; he could hear the beep as each began, but Harris held the receiver too tightly to her ear for him to hear what was being said. The third message had Harris rolling her eyes. From the side of her mouth she said, "You won't believe this, Frank. This one's from Darby! He says he's riding as an observer on a navy flight to Panama and won't be able to call until Sunday. Boy, what an imagination. Ha! His apartment will be real interesting to look through, won't it?"

Milkovich nodded.

Another beep.

"Say, here's another interesting one. It's from Herrera. Says, after breaking the news to his aunt, she's decided to come up rather than him flying down, so he'll be around if we need him."

"Hmmm."

"And one other call. Jennings got the warrant signed for the victim's house."

"Good."

"So what do you want to do about the money there? We can't sit on this much longer."

Milkovich thought for a moment. His feet were hurting, and he knew that was a bad sign.

Trying to do it all usually meant nothing got done right. Still, if it was Colombian drug money and it was linked to someone in the department, and furthermore, if someone had been murdered over it—well, he'd have to forge on, hurting feet or not. He drew a deep breath and replied, "At this point, I don't have a bloody idea what we're going to do with the money. I suppose we can leave it as bait, with the house under twenty-four-hour surveillance and see what bites. Or we can be up-front with it and just go in and seize it under your new warrant. What do you think?"

The lack of food and sleep were beginning to dull Harris's reactions too. "You know, I've never seen a million dollars. Let's just seize it. If Darby's prints are on any of the bills, my case is made. So's yours. Then anything that looks like a tie to your Colombian connection theory can be shipped off to the Feds. I've got a murder to solve."

"All right then, we do Darby's apartment, we do the victim's house and . . . Aw shit, I almost forgot—I have to meet with an attorney in an hour about another case."

"You gotta be kidding!"

"Sorry, I'm not. It's something I've just got to do. And I still have to meet with the chief, give him a briefing—which is going to be very interesting. I haven't told you this, but . . . something is screwy on that angle too."

Milkovich paused. He was violating depart-

mental policy on IA confidentiality if he told
Harris anything. His impeccable ethics were
one of the reasons he had been given his current assignment, and also the reason he was
so alienated from the rest of his fellow employees. Pieces of information on coworkers
were traded like baseball cards among the officers and other employees. It was a game that,
if you didn't play, marked you as an outsider
and a target for misinformation, especially by
the big collectors. For them, coming to work
had nothing to do with their job; their gratifi-
cation came from learning the latest dirt, then
trying to find someone who hadn't heard
about it, so they could twist it further and pass
it on.

"I think . . ." Milkovich hesitated. Could he
trust her? Could he ever trust anyone? He
looked squarely at Harris. She gave a slight
smile. Nothing was said; nothing needed to be.
Without a single word being exchanged, both
instantly sensed a commonality of purpose that
evaporated the normal barriers between people.
Milkovich smiled back and proceeded, "I think
that the chief knows something about this. In
fact, I think he knows a lot."

Milkovich proceeded to detail his suspicions,
including how Miller had been overly lavish
with his praise and the fact that Darby's personnel folder contained no preemployment documents. Then there was Milkovich's desk—had
the chief rifled it?

Harris listened, her jaw dropping with each new revelation. "Well, I'll be damned," she whispered, and for a moment sank into deep thought. Then suddenly she turned, a wry grin now on her face. "What if . . ." She paused to weigh the consequences of expressing her theory. Would Milkovich think she was crazy?

"What if what?" Milkovich fired back.

"Promise you won't call me insane? This is going to be a lulu."

"I promise, but what?"

"Well, just suppose," Harris started slowly, "just suppose we invert the scenario on John. Reverse our direction a hundred and eighty degrees and start with an opposite premise. John is not John; we know that now. But *why* is John not John? That's really the question we need to ask."

Milkovich nodded.

"So, now, where does this lead us? What are the facts?" Harris began to list them one by one. Summing up, she asked, "Anything else you can think of?"

Milkovich peeked at his watch. It was 1810. Not enough time to get something to eat before meeting with Anderson's attorney. Food would have to wait. He looked at Harris, his forehead creased. "I guess you've covered everything."

"Okay, here goes, Frank. What's the possibility that John Darby is a plant? An undercover officer, a Fed—DEA, or maybe FBI. Think about it. The faked identity—classic FBI trick, using someone who was real but is now dead. Then there's your Colombian drug connection. Suppose that Darby was planted here to portray an officer gone bad, in order to work his way into the organization. The cover they created for him would work exceedingly well for that. His reserve navy duty supposedly took him to San Diego at least one weekend every month, and that made him an excellent courier for illicit purposes. Cash south, drugs north." Harris paused. She studied Milkovich's face. It was emotionless, like a parish priest listening to a confession. *What is he thinking?* she wondered.

She drew a breath and continued, "Don't you see, Frank, the personnel file with no preemployment history and your suspicions of Chief Miller. He'd be in on it; he'd have to be. He's probably the only one in the department who knows."

There was a long silence while they considered Harris's theory. *It's possible*, Milkovich thought. He remembered hearing stories of the DEA doing just that in several departments in the South. But that was because the departments themselves were so corrupt. Here, in Seattle, it seemed a little farfetched. This was a clean department and had been for as long as he had been on the force. Still, though . . . He heard a duck quacking in his brain. It just might be.

He turned to Harris and looked her straight on. "If what you're proposing is correct," Milkovich said in a hushed tone, "then you and I are in the middle of something that—oh man!— is going to blow up big-time, and when it does . . ."

There was another long pause. Milkovich suddenly wondered if Harris might have once again shifted her allegiance back to her lover. With some hesitation he said, "We still have to do the search warrant on Darby's place. I think it will tell us a lot."

Harris glared. "You bet your goddamned life we're going to do it! He's still my prime suspect until proven otherwise." Then she winked. "I don't like being taken for a fool, and I am not going to talk myself out of anything for anybody right now."

Milkovich was relieved at Harris's determination to obtain the truth. He admired her grit, but he didn't have time to dwell too deeply, for although he wanted to discuss the flaws in Harris's new theory, it'd have to wait. His thoughts were having to shift yet again to his rapidly approaching meeting with Anderson and Chang. He looked at his watch one more time. "I've got to get moving, Leah. Listen, I shouldn't be tied up for more than half an hour, max. Do you think you could get the warrant and your team together to do Darby's place by twenty-hundred? I'd sure like to see what's inside before I have to meet with Miller. For once, I'd like to be ahead of the game.''

Harris nodded and grinned. She was of precisely the same mind.

Thirty

"Damn." Gilroy scowled. Although certain it was Enrique Herrera at the wheel, he still hadn't gotten close enough to make an absolute confirmation. The Lexus made another right turn; he followed, sure he had been made. But how? he wondered. The rain was still pouring down and the traffic was still heavy. It didn't make any sense. To Gilroy's thinking, there was no way Herrera could have known he had a tail, except . . . The Lexus made a left, continued for three blocks, and slowed. Gilroy gambled. He went right, guessed a parallel route, and drove it for several blocks. Then, hoping that his intuition was right, he veered back to the main artery and pulled to the curb at the intersection to wait.

It didn't take long. Herrera's Lexus flashed by moments later, just as the light changed. A BMW followed, going against a red light and nearly impacting an older Buick that had already started across. Gilroy's scowl turned to a chuckle. Now he knew. There was someone else following Herrera.

He eased back into the clogged traffic, staying a distance behind the other two cars. They proceeded straight for about a mile, but then the BMW abruptly pulled off the roadway, into a convenience store parking lot. As Gilroy passed by, he attempted to get a license number and identify the occupant. He failed at both. The windows on the car were tinted dark, the plate too far away to make. The detective continued on, realizing that with all the turns, Herrera had made one big circle; they were nearly back where they had started. They continued over another hill, then down past the University of Washington football stadium. As they approached a small shopping mall adjacent to the northeast corner of the campus, Gilroy saw Herrera's left turn signal come on. It was the first time he had used the indicator. Now Gilroy was certain Herrera was unaware of his tail.

The Lexus pulled into the turn lane, waited for an opening in traffic, and drove into the large parking area. Gilroy went on past and whipped into the lot at the next entrance. As he did, he slowed to watch as the Lexus parked in a slot in front of the Safeway. Herrera exited slowly, hunched his shoulders, and headed toward the brightly lit grocery store. At first Gilroy eased into a spot a dozen rows away, but as Herrera passed through the store's front doors, the detective decided to reposition himself. He backed out and proceeded to the side of the building, coming to a stop in the shadows. From there he had a clear view of the Lexus, unobstructed by the other cars. In the dark, he reached for the wrapper that still contained his half-eaten hamburger. Though it was now cold, he took another bite. Years of experience had taught him that it might be a long while before he'd get another chance to eat.

Thirty-one

Stephanie Chang sat alone in the same interview room where Milkovich had first met Harris. Chang was tall and slender, with long, straight hair that flowed over her shoulders. Though she possessed mainly Asian features, a parent or grandparent must have been European. Her height likely came from that side of the family. She was wearing a black silk skirt, offset by a tangerine blouse in raw silk and a coordinated tweed jacket. She looked the image of a successful thirty-something professional. Only ten years out of Stanford Law, she had already established herself as the leading tort attorney in the arena of sexual harassment and other employment discrimination claims.

Milkovich entered. By any standard, Chang was a beautiful woman. But her face was hardened, and her unemotional gaze left an ill feeling in the pit of his stomach. Milkovich knew he was tiring, and to begin an intellectual battle at this hour, with this woman, meant he'd probably be the losing contender. He'd have to try a different tactic; a frontal assault would never work.

He stepped forward cautiously, as though approaching a large, growling dog. Chang rose and formally extended her hand. "Sergeant Milkovich, I presume?"

Milkovich reached for and took her hand. He squeezed it firmly, feeling how icy cold it was. "Where is Sergeant Anderson?" He forced a smile and waited to see if Chang would return it.

Chang let go of Milkovich's hand, and pointed to the empty chair across from her. "Have a seat. Paula will be here in a moment. I wanted to speak to you alone first."

Oh, God, Milkovich thought, bracing for a stern lecture on employee rights. He decided to try to avert it. "Ms. Chang, I've heard about your work. You've won some important decisions in the courts lately; if I remember correctly, it seems you never lose."

Stephanie Chang's expression changed slightly. A fleeting, self-satisfied grin appeared. "Discrimination, especially against women, is rampant. I really don't have to work very hard. I just expose the facts, and when they are exposed there is little need for argument; it's usually just a matter of setting the award. The facts always speak for themselves. My success has simply been due to that."

Milkovich pondered. So far he could see no weakness in her armor, except perhaps vanity. While he sorted his thoughts for what to say next, Chang stepped into the void.

"Tell me, Sergeant Milkovich, what are your observations regarding sexual harassment in your department? Do you personally feel there is a problem?"

Milkovich saw the trap. He knew in litigation of this type, his personal feelings regarding the issue could be used by Chang to obtain a finding that a hostile work environment existed for minority employees, and especially women. If he said there wasn't a problem, then Chang could portray management as oblivious to a problem, and hence negligent. If he said there was, then it proved her point that a hostile environment existed, and worse, management not only knew about it, but did nothing to correct the wrongs. Either answer was going to get him dragged into court and interrogated.

He pretended to be on the verge of saying something to keep Chang from pressing any further. The silence crackled. Then, like a boxer knocked down in the first round but saved by the bell, he came out for round two ready to block any blows. "Whoa! Hold on a second, Ms. Chang. I can't make a comment on that, at least not in a conversation with you at this time. Any opinion I might have on the climate in our department would be based on internal investigations that I have conducted. And because those investigations are confidential, my opinions about them should be regarded likewise. It would be both unethical and unprofessional to discuss this with you."

"But in court," Chang cut in, "I could subpoena you and—"

"That's a different story," Milkovich shot back. "There I would be under oath and obliged to provide the information. Of course, that's provided our legal counsel didn't object, and then the judge would have to make a ruling on relevancy. Only then might you get to hear what I have to say."

Milkovich watched Chang's body language. Her arms were folded in a tight knot and grew tighter with his last words. Now it was time for his own right hook. He let it fly. "You know, Stephanie, you make me nervous, and I mean *real* nervous. I can see why you win so often. You're like a badger that will take on a grizzly bear. No fear, none at all. I like that."

"Sergeant Milkovich, your opinions about me are inappropriate." Yet as she said this, her arms slackened and, to Milkovich's surprise, her stony expression changed to a wry look, and ended with a low chuckle.

Milkovich relaxed. Now he knew that she knew that he was not going to be an easy quarry. The game would be much more complex, but there would be time-outs when their facades could be dropped like opposing attorneys outside the courtroom. Round three would come later.

Thirty-two

"Herrera hasn't come out yet, boss," Detective Gilroy said into his cellular. He had finally connected with Harris. "It's only been a few minutes. So you think he's up to something? He was supposed to be long gone, wasn't he?"

"Sorry to let you down, Phil, but he called and left me a message that his plans had changed."

"Ah, damn it, I thought I might have caught him in a lie. So what do you want me to do now? Bug out?"

Harris thought for a moment. "Go ahead and sit on him. Let's see where he goes and what he does. This guy is really interesting."

"Roger that. Say, what are you up to?"

"A search warrant for Darby's apartment. Almost got it cranked out."

As Gilroy continued to talk with Harris, he looked up to see a pair of headlights slowly approaching. The brightness instinctively forced him to look away, but as the vehicle passed, he could see that it was a police car. He watched in his rearview mirror, trying to recognize the driver, but he was too late. The prowler car disappeared behind the rear corner of the building.

"Hey, Sarge, looks like I got help," Gilroy said jokingly. "A patrol unit just went by. Looks like he's doing the ol' check for Dumpster divers."

"Anybody we know?"

"Couldn't tell. He went by too fast. Probably just had to take a leak." Gilroy was still laughing as he hung up the phone.

He rechecked Herrera's car and finished his cold burger.

Thirty-three

Stephanie Chang reached into the black leather briefcase that lay beside her on a chair, and withdrew a legal-size folder. Milkovich could see that it contained a number of documents, although Chang kept the file open only to herself, holding it like a poker player with a straight flush. Moments passed before she closed it and folded her hands on top.

Milkovich waited patiently, letting the silence be his crowbar to pry out the information that Chang possessed. Anderson's attorney exhaled through pursed lips. *Here it comes*, he thought, and he watched as Chang reopened the folder and pulled out several pages of typed text.

"As you can expect, Sergeant," Chang began, "it is my duty to always act in the best interest of my client. Sometimes, however, that duty can be difficult to articulate clearly. A client may have conflicting, or even competing, interests which cannot both be served. A course of action in one direction will negatively impact the other. To be honest, before I could recommend what course my client should take, I needed to assess the individual who was going to be in the position of making key decisions in this matter. So often, you see, a legal right may be successfully defended, but because of a breach in confidentiality, the success of that defense is really a moot issue in the client's day-to-day situation. Information that becomes known to peers, supervisors, or friends can alter and even destroy those relationships. Thus a legal victory can become strikingly hollow."

Milkovich grinned. "Then I passed your test?"

"So far," she said, pausing for another moment to glance at the sheaf of papers, then up to the clock on the wall. "It's getting late. I do not wish to keep you too long. In fact, it would probably be best if instead you first read this. Then, perhaps, we can get together—say, on Friday."

Chang set the document down on the table and slowly slid it across to Milkovich.

He left it sitting before him. "And this is?"

"Let's just say it's my client's record of what has occurred. I think you will find it enlightening." Chang's expression softened even further.

It unsettled Milkovich. He sensed that his meeting in the park with Griggs, as well as the contents of her diary, were not as closely held as he had been led to believe. Milkovich reached for the papers. "Maybe, for the sake of time, you could give me the condensed version."

"Very well. The truth of the matter is quite simple. Sergeant Anderson is the victim of unwanted advances and affections by Officer Deborah Griggs. Plain and simple. Over the last several months, this woman has made repeated attempts to engage Sergeant Anderson in a personal relationship which the Sergeant has, without exception, declined."

"Were these so-called attempts made on or off duty?"

Chang sighed. She cleared her throat, then sat forward while staring directly into Milkovich's eyes. "My client, Sergeant Anderson, is a lesbian. That is no secret. Her superiors and her coworkers are well aware of her sexual orientation. She has truly been a leader in breaking down old stereotypes, and this has benefited your department greatly in obtaining a diversified employment pool."

Milkovich leaned forward also. Their faces were now only a foot apart. "On or off duty?" he pressed.

"You must understand, Sergeant Milkovich, Paula does not wish this young officer any grief. She believes that she can handle it herself, but will be unable to do anything if there's an official internal investigation going on. Let's be frank. If you proceed any further, eventually, and probably quite soon, the department gossip mill will be chewing up these two officers. Great strides have been made in gaining acceptance for alternative lifestyles in the public service sector. But this . . . This will bring out all the bigots from their hiding places and give them fuel for their hatreds. We just can't allow this to happen."

Milkovich thought for a moment. He now knew what the document contained: a one-hundred-and-eighty-degree version of what Griggs had told him. In this one, Griggs would be the aggressor. And, given that Anderson had been around the block a few times, she would have independent sources to corroborate her claim.

Milkovich sat back in his chair. Another pissing match, he ruminated. Yet, comparing his earlier meeting with Griggs, the contrast between then and now struck him as atypical. Griggs had shown up with her puppy; Anderson, with a high-priced attorney. Milkovich had a saying for that. He called it 'Milkovich's First Law of Lawyers.' He repeated it silently to himself as he sat there: *The more expensive the lawyer, the guiltier the person they represent.*

Thirty-four

Bam! The sound of a large-bore pistol round being fired somewhere behind him startled Gilroy. The milkshake he had been sipping slipped from his hand. For a fraction of a second he sat perplexed, then swore out loud: "Christ Almighty!" He yanked out his service revolver, grabbed for his portable radio, and bolted from his car. Splashing through mud puddles, he dashed along the side of the building toward the rear, from where the sound of the shot had come.

He skidded to a stop just shy of the edge of the corner. He jammed his radio into his coat pocket and raised his revolver to the ready, using both hands. He paused. He had been in the business long enough to know not to rush into a shooting. It was a good way to get killed.

His ears strained for a sound, any sound that might indicate what he could expect to meet on his next step. He drew a deep breath and held it. Still he could hear nothing above the pounding rain and the beat of his own heart pumping wildly. Overflow from a broken gutter spattered his backside. Removing one hand from the gun, he cupped his ear and leaned as close to the edge as he dared. Seconds ticked by. Then faintly, over the din, came the drone of an idling car engine. He judged it to be maybe fifty feet away. Gilroy took another breath. It was time; he couldn't wait any longer. With his grip tight on his gun butt, he cautiously peered around the corner.

Ahead of him was the police prowler that had passed by only moments earlier; its engine was idling, exhaust fumes drifting horizontally across the ground like a London fog. Beyond it, lit by a lone light above the loading dock, Gilroy could see a row of Dumpsters and several jumbled stacks of wood pallets. There was no movement. All was still. Nothing seemed out of place.

Gilroy started forward slowly, hugging the shadowed wall, his eyes scanning for anything out of the ordinary. Step-by-step he advanced, all thoughts focused on what might lie ahead. Then, as he neared the car, he stopped again.

From behind, it looked empty. Gilroy visualized the possibility of finding the officer lying wounded behind one of the large refuse bins. *Not tonight*, he prayed. *Please, not tonight.*

Inching forward, he reached the right rear quarter-panel. He thought he heard something from behind. He whirled and dropped to one knee. Again he listened, straining his eyes to see into the dim, wet void, but there was nothing. *Damn,* he thought. Something was wrong, very wrong. His heart pounded faster. Beads of sweat mixed with rain rolled off his brow and salted his eyes. He winced and moved into a low crouch.

Slowly he made his way along the passenger side of the car, his head just below the window line. As he reached the front wheel well, he stared ahead toward the first Dumpster. Still nothing. *Where the hell are ya?* he wondered.

He rose cautiously. Almost as an afterthought, he turned and peered into the empty car. What he saw made his heart skip, and a shudder ran though his entire being. Through the rain-streaked glass he could make out the body of a young female police officer lying askew on the front seat. She was limp, her arms twisted in a deathly grasp.

Gilroy instantly dropped down to his knees for better cover, and grabbed for his radio. His immediate desire to help the fallen officer was tempered by instinct and training. There could still be a bullet waiting for him. He listened for any sound, anything that would give him a clue to what had happened. He needed help, and fast.

He punched the *on* button to his radio. There was no sound. Angrily, he flicked the switch again and again. *Lousy piece of crap!* He had forgotten to recharge it from the previous day's use.

Okay, he considered, *what the hell am I going to do now?* Sucking a deep breath, he cautiously made his way back toward the front passenger door. Slowly he reached up and tried the handle. It was unlocked. He inched it open. As he did, the fallen officer's 9mm semiautomatic pistol fell to the asphalt with a thud. There was blood on it. Gilroy barely noticed. What he saw told him instantly what had happened. He groaned, looked away, then climbed to his feet. He jammed his revolver back into its holster, wiped his eyes, and bent inside the patrol car, being careful not to touch anything.

Her mouth was agape and slowly oozing blood. Her blue eyes stared upward, a look of shock upon them. She was dead, Gilroy was certain. The large exit wound at the right rear of her skull made that obvious; half her brain was now spattered about the car's interior, mixed with bone chips and mats of scalp. He had seen this type of wound dozens of times before: self-inflicted, a gun barrel placed into a mouth, a trigger pulled.

The smell of the spent round still hung heavily inside the vehicle. Gilroy leaned farther in. Just to be certain, he estimated the direction from where the bullet might have come. If from the outside, there would be damage to the exterior of the vehicle, but there was none.

Slowly he pulled back, noting a piece of paper with typing on it stuffed in the center console. It was too dark to try to read without better lighting—and without gloves, Gilroy did not want to disturb the evidence. He sensed it would be a suicide note.

With his head hung low, Gilroy retraced his steps back to his car, got in, and picked up his telephone. In minutes, he knew, the scene would be crowded with other officers. News would spread fast. Soon the media vans with their large satellite dishes would arrive, and the circus would begin. He dreaded it. A young woman had just taken her life, a fellow officer, a brother in arms. He fought back his tears as he dialed the number. Gilroy failed to notice that Herrera's car was no longer in the lot.

Thirty-five

" 'And therefore,' " Sergeant Harris read aloud to the judge on the other end of the telephone line, " 'your affiant has probable cause to believe that evidence related to the homicide as previously described will be found at residence number C11, a condominium apartment complex, commonly referred to as the Greenlake Terrace.' " She paused to let the judge render her decision. It came quickly.

"Sergeant Harris, I find that you have probable cause to enter the residence as so described and to execute a search for evidence as listed in your narrative. Please affix my name to your document now."

Harris did as she was directed, signing in her own hand *Judge Helen P. Winters* to the bottom of the form she had prepared. "I have signed it," Harris said.

"Very well, this ends these proceedings. You may stop your tape recorder."

Harris looked at her watch, and said for the record, "This concludes the request for a telephonic search warrant, case number C01-85421. The time is now nineteen-twenty hours." Harris pushed the *off* button to her microcassette recorder and thanked the judge for her time.

"Good hunting," came the reply. They both hung up.

From behind the closed door of the office she had borrowed, Harris could hear loud voices suddenly erupt. Officers were running down the precinct hallway, shouting. It struck Harris as odd; she rose from the desk and pulled open the door. The watch commander was rushing by, but he halted when he recognized Harris. Making a noticeable effort to control his voice he said, "We've got an officer down at the U-Mall, behind Safeway. I think it's a fatality. She's been shot—it may be self-inflicted."

Officer down rang like explosions in Harris's ears. She braced herself against the doorjamb. "Who?" she asked in a low voice, fearing the answer.

"It's a rookie; I'm not sure of her name, I hate to say. Do you want to ride out there with me?"

Harris shook her head. "I'll only be in the way. Another HIT unit will get the case. Dave's next, I think. By the way, Frank Milkovich is here somewhere right now—IA will have to get involved; I'll warn him."

The lieutenant nodded and dashed away.

Thirty-six

The rain slowed slightly as Enrique Herrera turned in to the gas station. Traffic was thinning. He had driven the five miles from Safeway in under ten minutes. He pulled up to a premium pump. Steam from the hood of his Lexus wafted in the bright fluorescent light. The station was empty, save for a battered pickup at another fuel island, where a pair of teenage males were peering under the hood. One of them was emptying a quart of oil into the rocker manifold. They were oblivious to his presence.

Herrera checked his watch, then craned his neck to better see inside the small ministore. Behind the plate-glass window, an individual was seated at the check stand; images flickered on a video screen mounted high above the coolers. Herrera glanced again at the teenagers. They still hadn't looked up. The place seemed otherwise devoid of customers. He reached for the handle, gently opened his door, and eased out onto the pavement. The scene remained unchanged. Satisfied he had not been observed, he turned up his raincoat collar and hastened toward the store.

Inside, the cashier was entranced by the TV program. Herrera approached the door, but stopped short of opening it. Gently he tapped at the window. The attendant looked up with a start, nodded, and reached beneath the counter. Herrera eyed him intently, then raised his gaze to the security camera behind the clerk. He saw the small red light go off. The cashier straightened and motioned Herrera inside.

"*Buenas noches, Señor Herrera,*" the cashier said bashfully.

Herrera raised his index finger to his lips to signal silence.

"*Sí,*" the man replied, understanding his error. He inclined his head slightly.

Herrera turned his attention again to the pickup. The youths had closed the hood and were now climbing inside the cab. No one else was about. He unbuttoned the top of his coat and reached inside the breast pocket of his suit jacket. He withdrew an inch-thick, sealed business envelope. Grasping it in one hand, he tore the envelope open, exposing a tight bundle of used one hundred dollar–bills. The cashier stared hungrily at the money.

"Tonight?" Herrera breathed softly.

"*Sí,* tonight," the attendant replied, and extended his right hand, palm up, anticipating the envelope. Herrera did not oblige; instead he turned the envelope upside down. Without touching the money, he allowed the bundled bills to slip out and fall onto the counter. The cashier grabbed the wad and quickly stashed it in a black leather jacket draped over the back of his stool. Herrera neatly folded the empty envelope and placed it in his coat pocket. He was a careful man. There would not be any trace evidence. He left without saying another word.

Thirty-seven

There was a knock at the door. "That must be Sergeant Anderson," Stephanie Chang said.

Milkovich swung around to see. His conversation with Chang had taken a different tone over the last few minutes. Beyond the grudging realization that they faced their intellectual equal, a commonality had been established—and with it, walls lowered, allowing them to relax in each other's presence.

The door opened slowly, but instead of Sergeant Anderson, Leah Harris looked gravely into the room, one hand on the knob. Her face was pale, her posture sagging. "I'm sorry to interrupt."

Milkovich glanced at Chang, then Harris. His first thought was that Darby had been located. He was about to ask that, when Harris resumed. "We've got an officer down behind the U district Safeway. Head shot . . . She's dead."

The words drifted through the room like a

cloud of suffocating gas. Milkovich rose from his chair to join Harris. "Who?" he asked in a hushed tone. His feelings were more of disgust than sadness. Through his career, nearly a dozen officers had been killed while on duty in this department, and neighboring jurisdictions. He had known some of the fallen officers, one very closely. News of another death simply evoked a sense of tragic waste.

"Who?" he asked again. Harris seemed near tears. Her vulnerability affected Milkovich deeply. He closed the distance between them, took her by the shoulders, and enveloped her in a comforting embrace. He felt the warmth of her body; remnants of her perfume remained despite the long day. The odor was intoxicating.

Beep, beep, beep. The moment was lost. Milkovich cursed his pager as he fumbled for it. After several attempts, he got the readout. It was a number he knew well; it was the chief's. He glanced back to Harris. She had stepped out into the busy hallway, looking purposely in another direction.

With a start, Milkovich remembered Chang. She sat rigidly erect at the table, her hands neatly folded. She had doubtless observed everything. Milkovich winced inwardly. He cleared his throat and gestured with his pager. "I've got to make a phone call right away. I'm sure it's going to be about the shooting."

Chang nodded her acknowledgment. "I understand," she replied cordially, "and I suspect that, due to the circumstances, Sergeant Anderson isn't going to be available either."

"Probably not," Milkovich agreed. "Everyone on duty right now is either at the shooting scene or en route, whether they're needed or not. Police are a family of sorts. When one is hurt, the others draw close."

Chang grasped the file she had coyly displayed at the start of their meeting, and stood up with her briefcase. Transferring both to her left hand, she walked around to Milkovich and extended her free hand. He took it, shaking it firmly.

"I'll be in touch." She passed by Milkovich, then Harris, and disappeared down the hallway.

From his point of view, the meeting had been successful. He knew he had been able to convey to Chang his sincerity, integrity, and open-mindedness. He was relieved. This would buy him sorely needed time. Further, in their future encounters, she would not be as likely to challenge his every word. They shared a mutual respect for each other's position, and the underlying complexities.

Milkovich glanced at Harris. The welling in her eyes was gone. She was now massaging the back of her neck, a professionally distant manner affixed upon her being. She said soberly, "I don't know the officer who got shot. It's possibly self-inflicted. I overheard one of the guys passing by say it's a rookie named Griggs, something like that—"

The name hit Milkovich like a sucker punch.

"Son of a bitch!" He slammed his right fist into the palm of his other hand. "Damn! I don't believe this!"

Milkovich's strong reaction caught Harris off guard. "You know her?"

"You're damned right I know her; she's the officer I met in the park this afternoon before you arrived!" Milkovich's demeanor shifted. "Christ, there's no way she was suicidal then. Something isn't right here, Leah. Something isn't right at all. She had problems, big problems, but she certainly wasn't depressed, and that was . . ." He stopped to check the clock on the wall. "Christ, that was only three hours ago!"

"Are you going to the scene?"

Beep, beep, beep.

"The chief," Milkovich fumed. He didn't bother to look at the number on the pager's display. He went directly to the wall phone behind the table and dialed one of the few numbers he had ever committed to memory. It rang once.

"That you, Frank? Where are you? We've got a cop down!"

"I just heard," Milkovich answered calmly. "And I'm already at the North Precinct."

"Good. Here's what I want you to do; get down to that scene right away and find out what the hell is going on. I'm hearing it's a suicide, a female rookie. Christ, if she's left a note, find out what's in it and get back to me right away. This could be murder for our department. I need damage control, and now!"

As Miller spoke, Milkovich weighed whether to reveal what he already had learned about Griggs. He knew he should, but decided against it. He feinted. "What about the Darby case? I've still got work to do on it tonight."

"Drop it," the chief ordered. "This is more important. In fact, you can forget about Darby. He called me just a little while ago. He heard about that girl being murdered, and he's got a legitimate explanation for his picture being in her house. So don't worry about it; I'll fill you in on Friday. Just get over to that shooting scene right away and get me the info. . . . Got it?"

Milkovich didn't get a chance to reply. There was a click and the chief was gone. Milkovich stood silently, holding the receiver. Slowly he replaced it on the hook.

"What?" Harris came forward into the room as Milkovich sagged heavily against the wall.

A peculiar smile broke across his face. He chuckled, his eyes taking in Harris's concern. "Are you ready for this? The chief just told me that he had had a phone call from Darby a little while ago."

Harris froze in disbelief. "You're shitting me. From where—and why? What's going on here?"

"There's more," Milkovich continued. His smile was cynical. "According to the chief, Darby's got a legit explanation for his picture being in the victim's bedroom."

"Which is?"

"The bastard wouldn't say. Only that he'd fill me in later."

"And you believe him?"

"Not on a rat's ass! We're onto something. The drugs, the money, the dead girl in the house. Someone's dirty here and I smell cover-up."

"The chief?" Harris looked stunned, as the enormity of the situation took hold.

Milkovich nodded gravely. His wry amusement had vanished, replaced with steely-eyed determination.

Harris reached into her coat pocket and pulled out a neatly folded sheet of paper. She handed it to Milkovich with a sly smile on her face.

"What's this?"

"A search warrant, Frank. For Darby's place. I got it just a bit ago. It's signed, sealed, and ready for our delivery."

Milkovich frowned. He handed the warrant back to Harris, and shook his head disapprovingly.

"There's a problem?"

"Of course there is, Leah. The chief just told me that Darby is not criminally involved in this case. Whether I believe him or not, it depreciates any probable cause you may have had in obtaining your warrant. Unless, of course, you're ready to go on the stand under oath and testify that you have reason to believe that the boss is lying through his teeth."

Harris winced. She knew Milkovich was right, but resisted immediate surrender. "But I . . . Ah, shit." Her words came out as jumbled as her emotions.

Milkovich remained stoic. He had had much more practice in burying deeply personal feelings—although the desire to reach for Harris again and take her in his arms kept leaping to the forefront of his mind like a tune stuck on replay.

Finally, Harris spoke. "Frank, I never came in here. Do you understand?"

Milkovich looked away from Harris and pondered her words. He knew what she was asking him to do. Could he genuinely accept that the ends justified the means? He raised his head and stared at the ceiling. Then, as though talking aloud to himself, he said, "I've got to get to Safeway now, and I'd better remember to tell Sergeant Harris when I see her again what the chief said about Darby. I'd better not forget." With that, Milkovich walked past Harris and out of the room, turning only once at the doorway to caution, "If you find something, you sure as hell had better call me!" He winked and was gone.

Thirty-eight

Detective Gilroy stood beneath an overhang that sheltered the loading dock doorway from the intermittent rain. From his position, he could look down and into the patrol car still containing the slumped body of Officer Griggs.

Medic 1 had arrived; paramedics performed a cursory check for signs of life. Gilroy had requested that they use the least intrusive means. They had complied, leaving the body and the vehicle in the same condition as they had found it.

Several other patrol units had also arrived. Gilroy directed them to seal off the alleyway at both ends and sent an officer to find the store manager, to open the doors to the dock. It would be warmer and drier if they could set up inside, and there'd likely be a coffeepot nearby.

In a short while, from the same direction he had come, more officers appeared. Gilroy recognized the shift lieutenant and a sergeant. Grim-faced, they walked toward the car and peered briefly through the driver's side. The lieutenant turned to join Gilroy. The sergeant, though, grabbed the door handle and pulled it open. She peered inside. Gilroy had to resist the urge to chastise her. Touching anything could contaminate the scene; but he knew from his past dealings that his warnings would fall on deaf ears. Even the lieutenant wouldn't say anything.

Sgt. Paula Anderson was a strongly built, determined woman, quick with a smile or a leer. She was highly decorated, a cop's cop who could run faster, shoot better, and gain a confession quicker than any of her male coworkers. She also had a well-earned reputation for a fierce, overpowering temper directed toward anyone who might challenge her decisions. Flare-ups were increasingly routine and monumental.

"Glad you made it," Gilroy said as the lieutenant reached his side. And Gilroy wasn't lying. Now he could turn the scene over to the supervisor, give a statement to whomever was assigned lead detective, and get out of there. The press would be swarming on them in moments, wanting details. The chief and every administrator would be right behind them, as would the Internal people, and all because, at least to his way of thinking, an officer couldn't deal with the stress of the job and decided to eat her gun.

"This is the shits," the lieutenant said glumly.

Gilroy nodded halfheartedly.

"I think she would have been a fine officer," he continued. "I wonder what devils inside drove her to do this?"

Gilroy shrugged his damp shoulders. His eyes were fixed on Anderson. She was halfway inside the patrol car and seemed to be searching for something. Again he resisted the urge to caution her about disturbing anything. He had done so a couple of years prior at another death investigation and the woman had exploded right in his face, shoving her stripes right to his nose, then screaming at him like an army drill sergeant humiliating a new recruit. He had taken it then with gritted teeth. She was connected in the department, and any protest by him up the chain of command would have been ignored as whining by higher-ups.

"So what happened? Did you see or hear anything?"

"Just the shot," Gilroy replied. He was still focused on Anderson.

The lieutenant saw his concern. "She's just trying to help. I think she and Griggs were, ah, friends."

Gilroy caught the lieutenant's inflection on the word *friends*. He knew that Anderson was a lesbian—it was common knowledge in the rank and file. But if . . .

Gilroy turned directly to the lieutenant and said softly. "You think Griggs and Anderson were . . . ?"

The lieutenant nodded slightly. "There's been some talk." He kept his voice low. "But what the hell, that's their business."

Gilroy's honed senses were setting off alarm bells in his mind; he wondered why the lieutenant wasn't on the same page. "Lieutenant, you've got to get her out of that car. The IA boys will scald you alive if it turns out something's out of whack here. Hell, you've got the butter bars there on your collar—do something!"

The lieutenant continued to hesitate. Gilroy watched with disgust. It was clear that the man was afraid of Anderson, and if he was going to do anything, it would require more pushing. Gilroy wasn't so inclined; it wasn't his place.

The lieutenant repeated his feeble excuse for Anderson's behavior. Then they both saw her step away from the vehicle. "There now, here she comes." His relief was apparent. He'd been able to avoid the confrontation.

Muffled voices sounded behind them, and a lock was turned. Moments later, the door rolled up and they were joined by several of the store's staff and the uniformed officer who'd sought their help.

"Holy shit!" An employee caught a glimpse of the dead body. The man turned and gagged while another stared wide-eyed, unable to break away. From behind this group stepped Milkovich. He had driven directly to the shooting, his radio scanning the tactical frequencies so he could listen in on the off-color, off-the-record comments the other officers were making between themselves as news of the suicide spread amongst them. It gave him a sense of the possible undercurrents that may have been at work in the precinct.

Gilroy saw him first. Their eyes met. Both nodded in recognition; then Milkovich came forward as Sergeant Anderson slowly climbed up to the dock. Her face was flushed and she appeared stunned.

The lieutenant's cell phone buzzed. He flipped it open and moved several paces away.

"We meet again," Gilroy commented as Milkovich drew near.

Milkovich frowned. The irony was not lost on him. About to reply, he was interrupted by Anderson.

"What a goddamned waste!" She sighed, her voice cracking. "What the hell was she thinking of?" She drew a deep breath and shook her head in profound disgust. Milkovich remained silent. He had never met Anderson face-to-face, and it seemed to him that she didn't know who he was.

She turned to Gilroy. "You were the one who found her, right?"

Gilroy nodded. "I heard the shot."

Anderson grimaced.

"It scared the shit out of me," he added.

Anderson's demeanor suddenly shifted. "What were you doing here? Were you on a case or something?"

"Yeah, that knifing from last night. I was sitting on a suspect vehicle out in the front parking lot when she—" Gilroy stopped and pointed to the patrol car below them. He continued, ". . . when she came whizzing by me. Funny, at the time, I didn't give it a second thought. Back when I was on patrol, if I needed to take a leak, I'd always cruise behind a store like this. At night, it's nice and private and . . ." Gilroy went silent. Anderson's curled lip told him he had misspoken.

He sought to change the subject, but Milkovich interceded. "Wasn't Officer Griggs in your squad?"

Anderson turned on Milkovich. She flashed an unspoken challenge, as if saying, *Who the hell are you?*

Their eyes met and locked. "She was, wasn't she?" Milkovich pressed.

The stare-down continued in silence, each measuring the other, neither willing to be the first to look away.

Several plainclothes officers appeared from down the alleyway. The sound of their steps and the crackle of their portable radios caught everyone's attention. Both Milkovich and Anderson blinked simultaneously. She grinned, and flashed a look of comprehension at Gilroy. "He's IA, isn't he?"

Gilroy slowly nodded. He secretly hoped that this revelation would cause Anderson some discomfort, but she displayed none.

Looking back to Milkovich, Anderson swiped her damp brow with her shirtsleeve. "Yeah, Debbie was in my squad. She was a good kid, and this . . . man, I gotta tell you, this is the shits!"

"What do you mean by that?" Milkovich inquired gently.

"What the hell do you think I mean?" Anderson shot back. Her blood pressure was on the rise.

"Whoa, slow down. No one is blaming you for anything."

"The hell you aren't! I've been around here long enough to know that someone's going to take the rap for this, and it is *not* going to be anyone upstairs. Naw, I know what's going to happen. By morning, even though she's the one who stuck a gun up her nose and blew her brains out, she'll be the victim of something, something that—"

Anderson stopped midsentence. Slowly the high tension melted from her face, replaced with wariness. She glanced at Gilroy, then back to Milkovich. "You know what, I don't think I should be talking to you. I think, ah, I think I'd rather have my attorney present."

"You think you need one?" Milkovich shot back.

Anderson bristled.

Milkovich saw that he had hit a nerve. "Why

an attorney, Sergeant? No one has blamed you for anything—yet."

Anderson breathed in deeply. "Say, what the hell is your name, anyway?

"Milkovich," he replied "Frank Milkovich."

Recognition dawned on Anderson's face. She proceeded cagily. "Okay, Milkovich, I want to cooperate as much as possible. I certainly don't want to hinder your job; but, damn it, like I said before, in situations like this, someone gets left holding the bag and I don't intend to be that one. See?"

"Understood Sergeant, and believe me, no one is blaming anyone for anything," Milkovich lied. Anderson may not have pulled the trigger, but in his mind, she played a major role in what had just happened. Their conversation stalled and both turned their attention elsewhere.

Down below, two of the detectives donned rubber gloves and began peering into the patrol car. A third circled the vehicle, his eyes focused on the ground. Gilroy joined them, showing how he had approached the car, explaining what he had heard and seen. Milkovich watched and waited, although his mind occasionally wandered to thoughts of Leah Harris and the smell of her perfume. The moments were fleeting, reality rapidly intruding at every lapse.

Milkovich sighed. He knew video and photographs would have to be taken before the body was removed. Chances of finding a suicide note and removing it for inspection before the detectives were ready were slim. He looked at his watch. It was 2046. By now, Harris would be reaching Darby's apartment.

A sudden shudder passed over his body. Things were going from bad to truly awful.

Thirty-nine

Leah Harris sat in her idling car, in the far corner of a Burger King parking lot. She was five blocks north of her destination, waiting for several other officers to join her in the execution of her warrant. She absently watched as a steady stream of customers flowed in and out of the establishment. Her mind was elsewhere. Thoughts of Darby, of her career, and strangely of Milkovich mingled with one another in a confused, fragmented way.

She remembered their brief embrace. She had felt . . . what—perhaps an attraction. She couldn't put a description to it. It was simply there. Maybe it was her exhaustion, she quickly reasoned. Maybe the stresses of the day. She didn't know, but there was a connection. Unfortunately, it violated all her professional sensibilities. A growing depression had begun to envelop her. She fought back the encroaching dark mood. Then she remembered that there was a pint of double-chocolate-swirl ice cream in her freezer at home. It was a pleasant diversion, and she promised herself that she could have all of it when she finished with this night. It was a devil's bargain to keep her mind and body going.

She closed her eyes and leaned back in her seat. "God, I'm tired. . . ." She yawned loudly. Then, like a marathoner with only a few more miles to go, she rallied herself. Another cup of coffee? she mused. The thought sent a dissenting rumble through her stomach, but her brain overruled. She climbed out and crossed lethargically toward the brightly lit entrance, breathing deeply of the damp night air. It was perfumed with the aroma of grilled hamburgers, french fries, and onion rings. The smell sparked a long-forgotten teenage memory. A night like this, a date with a high school football player, and a trip to a drive-in. He was gorgeous, she recalled. Tall, muscular, with gentle eyes. Oh, those eyes—they had driven her wild, as she lay in bed at night, walked the halls by day, or sat at the dinner table with her mother and stepfather. It was those eyes. For two weeks that was all she could think about. She had been in love.

Harris paused to look upward. Even with the city lights, she saw a full moon break through the clouds. Just like before, she remembered . . . just like a night twenty-odd years ago. She sighed softly. A sense of loss fell upon her as she continued through the doors and got in line at the counter. Where had those years gone?

Ahead of her were two young families, both with small children; one mother was pregnant. Trying not to stare, Harris studied the woman's bulging abdomen. Again her mind drifted. What would her life have been if she too had had children?

Her depression resurfaced and took hold more tightly. She scanned the rest of the patrons. They seemed oblivious to the world in which she lived. Happily ignorant of the constant pain and cruelty she witnessed every day. What did they know? Nothing, nothing at all about what life and death truly were. They all took their existence for granted.

Food arrived for the first family. One of the children grabbed a drink from the loaded tray. The second, not wanting to be outdone, lunged at his brother. The drink went flying. It crashed to the tile floor, its contents spattering in a wide arc. Several chunks of ice struck Harris's right foot.

"Oh, Jeffrey!" the mother placated, as the father looked with resignation at the server.

Trying not to overreact, Harris stepped farther to her left to avoid the advancing puddle of orange soda, and watched in amazement as the family walked unconcernedly past their mess and seated themselves at an open table. The other family ahead of her also had no reaction.

They simply moved forward, placed their order, then took their food to a far booth. Harris felt indignant. Wasn't anyone going to do something about the spillage, let alone the child's misbehavior?

The pimple-faced, overweight clerk cheerily greeted her. Harris briefly studied the menu. Though hungry, she resisted the urge to purchase any food. It would violate her bargain with the ice cream.

"Coffee, please, just some coffee; and make it tall and black."

The counter person filled the request.

Harris took her steaming cup and delicately tiptoed past the spilled soda, making her way back outside. As she did, she observed the white Chevy van belonging to Jane and Roy pull into the parking lot, stop for a moment, then head to a spot alongside her Ford.

Harris stayed on the curb. She folded back the tab on the lid, and lifted her cup of coffee in salute. Taking a sip, she was surprised to find that it tasted good. The warmth was soothing and suddenly she felt revived. "Just what the doctor ordered," she pronounced to herself. She took one more sip, then went to join her waiting team. Only it looked as if just Jane would be working with her. If Roy was along, he'd never have let Jane drive.

Forty

Enrique Herrera sat quietly, staring out at Puget Sound from the thickly cushioned chair in the study of his penthouse. There wasn't much to see. Low clouds, intermittent drizzle, and darkness had obscured any shipping traffic. Only the running lights of an occasional tug or adventurous pleasure craft passing near to shore actually punctured the mist.

For half an hour, Herrera had remained in this position. At last, he stood and stretched, went over to a small antique butler's table, and poured a shot of single-malt scotch from the crystal decanter atop the marble surface. With one gulp, he downed the drink and quickly poured another. Grasping the glass tightly, he walked back to his chair, yet remained standing. He moved closer to the large picture window.

His impatience was growing. It was past the time it should have taken, and doubts began to creep into his mind. Was his information wrong? Was this too personal for his involvement? He sipped at his drink, feeling the bite of the liquor as it trickled down his throat. From a room away, a clock tolled. He counted cadence—one . . . two . . . three—and continued to the end. It was nine o'clock. Moments later, the call came. Herrera jumped for the phone and gripped the receiver. He said only one word: "Yes?"

Herrera listened to the voice at the other end. What he heard caused the glass he held to slip from his fingers and crash to the hardwood floor. There was a click and the line went dead. Herrera remained frozen for several seconds, then slowly set the receiver back in its place. *What now?*

He crossed back over to the butler's table and opened a small drawer. Inside lay a Glock .40-caliber semiautomatic pistol and several loaded magazines. He picked up the gun and shoved a clip into the butt, then pulled the slide back. He saw the sheen of the silver-tipped hollow point at the ready. He let go, and with a loud metallic snap, the bullet was seated in the chamber. For a moment Herrera just stood there, gun in hand, his finger caressing the trigger. The day had come, one that Herrera knew was inevitable. He sighed once.

The thought evaporated as his sense of mission took hold. Time was critical. There were things to be done. He shoved the pistol into his waistband at the small of his back, and dropped two magazines into his coat pocket.

He checked his watch, then looked one last time out the window. He wished it weren't raining. The view on a clear night, with a full moon near to setting, was the loveliest sight he had ever known. He was sure he would miss it.

Forty-one

By now, Griggs's death scene seethed with police officers. Many were standing by silently, their eyes on the body soon to be removed. A few others, not part of the investigation team, moved about in confused, random patterns, talking in low, self-conscious voices; they offered to do the most menial tasks, as if they needed to feel they were of some help. Photos were quickly taken, rough sketches made, and a few triangulated measurements recorded. Through all of this, Milkovich remained in the shadows, watching and listening.

"Anyone see a bullet exit?" a detective sergeant dolefully queried.

"Not on the right side," an unseen detective replied.

"How about you, Ron? What about the left?"

"Nothing here either, Sarge."

"Okay guys, then it's time to pull 'er out.

Where're the guys from the ME's office, and who's got the body bag?"

A detective yelled for them. Moments later, two white-clad attendants came down the alley trundling an ambulance gurney. One wheel was loose and it rattled loudly. Twenty feet from the car they stopped, pulled out extra-thick latex gloves, and put them on.

"You ready?" the sergeant asked.

Both nodded.

"Good, bring the bag up to here." The sergeant pointed at a spot on the wet pavement, parallel to the driver's side of the door, about six feet away. "And when we get her out, we'll set her on the bag for a bit. We'll need more photos." The sergeant paused for a moment, then began cautionary instructions. "We gotta be careful with how we handle her. There's a lot of body fluids spattered all over the headliner and Plexiglas partition. If at all possible, I don't want it smudged, understand?"

Again they nodded, then moved forward. It was at this point that Milkovich stepped to the edge of the platform to get a better view. The lieutenant hung up from his fifth phone call and joined him, followed by Gilroy and Anderson. There was an unnatural silence; even the nervous banter had dropped to a hush.

"All right," the detective sergeant said quietly. "Let's get this done." He grabbed the car door handle and pulled.

The first attendant immediately poked his head

through the opening and briefly studied the position of the twisted body. "We'll probably lose what's left of her brain when we move her," he deadpanned. "Everything's going to fall out that big gap in the back of her head."

The sergeant nodded in agreement. He knew that, but there wasn't much he could do about it. He then turned to a nearby detective. "We need an extra set of hands here, c'mon."

The detective hesitated. He had just pulled off his gloves and tossed them into the trash collection bag. He fumbled in his jacket pockets, as if looking for another pair. Seeing his turmoil, the detective sergeant called out sarcastically, "Hey, does someone have an extra pair of gloves for Smitty?"

Before anyone could answer, Sergeant Anderson lunged off the four-foot-high platform, landed with a bounce, and pushed her way through to the vehicle. "I'll do it," she offered, pulling a pair of gloves from her back pocket. She added derisively, "You dicks always leave the shitty jobs to us patrol guys anyway."

The detective sergeant frowned. He, too, had had more than one run-in with Anderson over the years. Her caustic jabs were a constant source of irritation, and he had never found a satisfactory means of dealing with them. Today it seemed simpler to acquiesce to her offer.

They began their grisly task.

"We'll go feet-first," he suggested. "I'll grab the left leg; Anderson, you take the right, and you guys grab the arms as we begin to slide 'er out. And why don't you try to cup your free hand over the back of her head?" He nodded to one of the lab crew. "Let's try to keep her as intact as possible. Everyone got that?"

They all nodded.

"Good, we'll do it on the count of three."

They all moved into position, surrounding the driver's door. There was a momentary pause as each drew in a breath to steady their nerves. Then the detective sergeant bent down and clenched Griggs's ankle. Through his rubber gloves, he could feel that she was still warm. "Ready?"

There was no reply. There didn't need to be. "Okay," he resumed. "One, two, and—"

With the three count, the detective sergeant pulled and, in one fluid motion, each in turn grasped his or her assigned area and gently extricated the body from the vehicle. Straightening, the four then moved the five short steps to the body bag in unison.

"All right," the detective sergeant encouraged, "down to the ground slowly." And Officer Deborah Griggs was laid gently upon the plastic body bag as delicately as a piece of fragile crystal.

"Done." One of the attendants sighed. The other attendant, the one who had held onto the back of Griggs's head, looked at his gloved hand. It was bathed in blood and speckled with small chunks of bone and brain. He made a face as though he were bothered by it. He wasn't.

"Good job," the detective sergeant commented. He looked around for the photographer. "Hey," he called out. "Come over here when you get a sec and take some close-ups of the entry wound and the rest of her body. Left, right, top, you know the routine."

Meanwhile, the attendants and Anderson stepped aside, clearing a view for Milkovich. He could now look straight down into what was left of Officer Griggs's mouth. Both her lips were torn and tattooed by the blast from her gun. A trail of blood still trickled down her right cheek while her eyes bulged wide and open. They looked surprised.

Milkovich studied the wound, then glanced at Anderson. She had joined another group of officers and appeared oblivious to the body on the ground. "She seems like she really cares," Milkovich said in a sarcastic voice, just loud enough for Detective Gilroy to hear.

"She can be one mean bitch," he replied. "Thank God I don't have to supervise her. The brass is so goddamned scared of her because of her tantrums and her direct line to the ACLU."

Milkovich thought for a moment, then asked, "Who does she hang with in the department? Anyone at all?"

"You mean friends?"

"Sure, anyone." His eyes were still on Anderson. She was thirty feet away, her back turned to him.

Suddenly Gilroy turned and faced him. His expression had changed. His eyes narrowed and his lips tightened. "Are we going on the record? I mean—hell, you know what I mean. What I personally think about Sergeant Anderson is my business. She's still a cop. Granted, she's a . . . But, Christ, half the goddamned department is either gay, a cross-dresser, or a victim of something or another. Who am I to give a diddly-shit about that anyway?"

Milkovich let him say his piece. It was the same thin blue line ethic that he always encountered. It was all right to talk behind someone's back, but to say anything negative in an official capacity about a brother—or sister—officer was taboo. Doing so meant ostracism. Quick, brutal, and permanent until the day you were forced to resign.

No words were spoken for a moment; then Milkovich said, "I'll be honest. I haven't the slightest idea where I'm going with this. Hell, the only reason I'm here is because the chief is afraid we'll find a suicide note that will make the department look bad. Beyond that, I just don't know. . . ."

The expression on Gilroy's face altered slightly. Milkovich caught the change. He knew he had said something that had cracked the wall, but what? He waited without further comment, counting on his silence to pry open the door to Gilroy's trust.

Below them, the photographer began snapping pictures in rapid succession. The light of the strobe ricocheted off the concrete walls, like small flashes of lightning. The effect reminded Milkovich of being in a disco in the mid-seventies. The vapors from everyone's breath mingled with the darting light, creating the illusion of a smoke-filled party atmosphere. All that was missing was a massive sound system pumping out throbbing dance tunes, and a roomful of sweaty bodies in bell bottoms and miniskirts.

The thought faded as Anderson abruptly turned. Her eyes briefly met Milkovich's and he knew that she knew he had been staring at her. He casually returned his attention to Gilroy in a makeshift attempt to belay her suspicions.

"Just being around her gives me the willies," Gilroy began again. "Look at her, over there; she's pissing and moaning about something. God, I . . ." Gilroy's words faded.

Milkovich waited another moment, then decided it was time to press. "Listen, Phil, you've got something to say, I know it. That stuff about covering for your fellow officers may have worked for us when I was a rookie, but that was a long time ago. Times have changed. People have changed. Now there's a lawyer on every block just looking for a way to find us liable for something. And when that happens, careers go down the tubes like turds down a toilet. You think—"

"Cut the preaching," Gilroy broke in. "Jesus, you'd think I was covering for a mass murderer or something. She's just a loudmouth bitch with friends in high places."

"What do you mean by that?"

"What, the high places?"

"Yeah, that's exactly what I mean."

"Well . . ."

"Well what, Phil? Hell, we know she didn't sleep her way to where she is, now, did she?"

Gilroy grinned. "You're a funny man, Milkovich. You're making me laugh."

"I want to make you talk."

"Aw, what the hell." Gilroy sighed. He cleared his throat. "It's really no big deal. It's just that being on the HIT squad has caused me to be out and about at all hours of the night. I see things. Lots of things. And one of the things I've seen is the chief, late at night, pulled car to car with her, shooting the shit."

"Miller?"

"Of course Miller. Who did you think?"

Milkovich raised an eyebrow.

"At first I didn't think much of it. In fact, I thought it was kind'a nice to see the boss out rubbing shoulders with us grunts, but I've never seen him talking to anyone else like that."

"How many times have you seen this?"

Gilroy exhaled through his teeth. "I dunno,

maybe a half dozen times, maybe more, over the last couple of years. I haven't been exactly counting."

"Where were they doing this?"

"Just around. Nothing special. It didn't look to me like they were trying to hide or anything."

"What do you think they were doing, playing footsie?"

Gilroy laughed. "You've got to be kidding! You said it yourself, she's as dykey as they come. Hell, you're enough of a detective to figure out what she was doing."

"Dirt collecting?"

"Bingo! Give the man a prize."

Milkovich smirked. "So you think she was feeding the boss information on who was screwing up and getting their hands dirty?"

"You got it. And that's why she's an untouchable. She's got a direct line to the throne room."

"Hmmm." Milkovich pondered. "Sounds logical, and it would explain a few things. When was the last time you saw them together?"

"Well you know, that's kind of interesting."

"Why's that?"

" 'Cuz it was just last night, when I got paged for the Herrera girl."

Milkovich's eyes narrowed. "Where were they?"

"Actually, it was pretty close to where I live. My place is on East Thirty-sixth, just off McKinley. You know, by the park up there."

Milkovich quickly nodded. It was the same

park where he had talked to Griggs only hours before.

"It was about one-thirty in the morning when I got the call and I was probably out and into my car in about ten minutes. Anyway, as I'm driving by the park, I see a patrol car sitting in a corner of the parking lot, in the shadows. I take a quick look to see who it is—sure enough, it's Anderson. The chief's car is parked right next to hers. Like I've seen before."

"Are you sure it was them?"

"Hell, yes, it was them. The chief lit up a cigarette just as I passed by. The light from his match was enough to tell."

"And you say it was at one-thirty or thereabouts?"

"About that, give or take a few minutes."

"Did you have your radio on?"

"Sure."

"Had they put the homicide out over the air?"

"Oh, yeah. There were guys walking all over each other with it."

"Then anyone with a radio on would have known what was going on."

"Of course."

Milkovich's thoughts retraced their way to earlier in the day. What Gilroy had just said seemed to contradict what the chief had told him this morning. But what was it that he had said, exactly?

"Hey, what's going on—you know something?"

Milkovich didn't hear the question. He was attempting to recall the chief's words, or at least their context. They seemed so trivial at the time, but now he remembered . . . Miller had told him, *"I was trying to get a good night's sleep and I get a call like this."* Now he knew for certain that the chief had lied to him. But why?

"There was someone else with them last night," Gilroy added innocently.

"Someone else?"

"Yeah. God, I can't remember his name. . . ."

"Another cop?" Milkovich prompted.

"Right, works Narcotics, kind'a Indian-looking—er, Native American. God, for the life of me, I can't think of his name. Hell, he helped out on a drug homicide just this last summer."

Milkovich's heart jumped. The coincidences were mounting up too fast. One more and his paranoia meter would be pegged in the red. He tried to pace himself. "Tall guy, dresses nice?"

"Yeah."

"A weight-lifter type?"

"Uh-huh."

"Does the name Cummins do anything for you?"

"Yeah, that's him. Jerry Cummins. He's slick. Knows his shit real well."

Milkovich shook his head. Cummins had also lied to him. He, like the chief, would have to have known about Christina Herrera's murder right after it happened. Yet Cummins had played dumb when he had talked to him at Starbucks. Too many connections, Milkovich thought, and no reason for any of them. There had to be a common thread, a relationship that bound together all the players.

Suddenly Milkovich felt a tap on his shoulder. Turning, he found himself face-to-face with Anderson. She scowled at him and jabbed his breastbone with her index finger. "Okay, *Internal* man," she growled. "What the hell are you talking about behind my back?"

Milkovich glanced sideways. From the corner of his eye, he saw Gilroy slip from the loading dock and into the store. *Chicken*, he thought.

He faced Anderson down. "Getting cold out here, isn't it?"

Anderson's scowl deepened. She had grown used to men recoiling when she charged. She bit her lip. "Listen, if that asshole detective was bad-mouthing me, I want to know about it, and now. I'm not about to wait until you've collected enough bullshit hearsay and lies so I can be lynched nice and legal!"

Milkovich's smile widened. He did this on purpose. He sensed it would irritate her further. "What makes you think we were talking about you?"

"Oh, cut the fucking games. You're here to do me. That's the only reason. Look, I don't give a shit if my attorney is here or not. I'm goddamned tired of all this crap!" Then abruptly, Anderson's face softened, spooling down like a jet engine at flight's end. Her eyes clouded.

"You want to know about harassment, I'll tell you about harassment."

Milkovich shifted the weight on his feet.

"For almost four years, when I was first hired, I was the only female working patrol. No one will ever know what that was like. A day didn't go by that one of you assholes didn't try to fuck me or screw me behind my back. Do you know how many times I've been grabbed on the ass or had one of your righteous boys in blue try to cop a feel, then brag about it to his buddies? I've had shit stuffed into my shoes, I've had blanks stuck into my gun, I've called for backup and had the crap beat out of me 'cause the guys—my fellow brothers in arms—were moving kind of slow that day. Well, I've survived. I showed them that women can do the job, and do it better than most of you dickheads; and I've got the scars and broken bones to prove it."

Anderson sniffled. The chinks in her tough veneer had crumbled enough that Milkovich was suddenly seeing another facet to the woman. Was all the loudmouth bluster just an act; was it only a means of coping in a truly hostile environment?

"I remember when you started," Milkovich reminisced. "A lot of media attention back then. It must have been tough."

Anderson nodded.

"I hate to admit it, but I remember that at the time, I too had my doubts about a woman being able to do the job."

246   *Michael A. Hawley*

"You and everyone else," Anderson replied. "Oh, yeah, we were good little meter maids and records clerks. Nice to have around the office, nice to get in the sack with, but not to do this job. Look, Sergeant, I'm a lesbian. It's no secret and I'm not sorry for it. I am what I have to be around here. I'm tougher, smarter, and I've got more guts than practically anyone else. I do the job, I do it well, and if it pisses you guys off that I'm a dyke and I don't fall down and worship your dick anytime you try to whip it out, well, so be it. But I love this job, I love this department and no one is going to take it away from me without one hell of a fight!"

Milkovich listened intently. He was beginning to get a better understanding of the woman before him. In a curious way, he appreciated her blatant honesty. It was then that he decided on a more direct approach. "Were you sleeping with Griggs?"

"Sure," Anderson said without hesitation. "A couple of times, a month or so ago. Then she turned into this *Fatal Attraction* bitch. She wouldn't leave me alone. God, she was crazy. She was constantly fantasizing about us, following me, sending me notes, showing up at my door at all hours. You know, I tried to help her, I tried everything, but . . ."

"But what?"

Suddenly Anderson's eyes began to water. Embarrassed, she quickly wiped them with her shirtsleeve, and shook her head in disgust. "For the record, I guess I am pretty much responsible for this." She paused and pointed to Griggs's body. "After she went and talked with you this afternoon, she called me. She told me everything she had told you. I guess I lost it when I heard all the lies she had made up about me. Well, I lit into her with everything I had. I tried to make her feel like the sleaziest fucking bitch that ever walked the face of this planet. I guess I succeeded, 'cause look at her now—just look at her, damn it."

Again there was silence. Anderson had vented. It had all come out. She turned to leave. Milkovich allowed her to take a step away; then, when she was no longer facing him, quietly asked, "You and Chief Miller are pals, aren't you?"

Like a tornado, Anderson whipped back around. Dr. Jekyll was now Mr. Hyde. "What do you mean by that?"

"You're friends, right?"

A puzzled look formed on her face. "I don't know what you're driving at. I've only met him a couple of times at the precinct. Friends! That's rich!"

With that she turned and left the loading dock, taking the steps two at a time to rejoin the group of officers milling about the scene.

Forty-two

Harris checked her watch. It was 2110, and still no sign of the two patrol units that she had arranged to accompany them for the search of Darby's apartment. She yawned wide.

"Cut that out!" Fenton groaned. She sat on the driver's side of the evidence van, Harris next to her. They were still in the Burger King parking lot, engine idling to ward off the cold.

Before she could apologize, Harris yawned yet again. "God, I'm tired."

"Ain't this fun." Fenton deadpanned. "Just another romantic evening with my pal Leah. You're a great date!"

"I said I'd buy you a burger, or whatever you want. Doesn't bribery count for anything?"

Fenton grinned and reached between the seats for a stainless thermos. "Want some of this? Double espresso. I brewed it just before I left. One cup will keep you up all night."

Harris opened her door and dumped out the

remaining contents of her cup. "I'll try anything to stay awake."

Both savored their coffee and stared absently ahead. The effects of the caffeine soon took hold. Harris stretched. "Can you think of anything else of interest at the autopsy this afternoon?"

Jane's reverie evaporated. She hastily set her cup down in the dashboard holder and busied herself with a minor spill. Anything to avoid looking at Harris. She did have something to say, but now didn't seem the right time. So she lied. "There was nothing too unusual. Doc Reid doesn't think there was a rape involved, although the victim did have sex a few hours before she died. I guess you already know that it was, ah, consensual. The wounds were consistent with being caused by a fillet knife, like the one we recovered at the house. When and if I ever get some time back at the lab, I'm sure I'll be able to show that it was the murder weapon. What else? She hadn't consumed much alcohol. I didn't smell any when Reid split her open. I usually can, if the blood alcohol is above a point-one-five. Also, there was no overt evidence of drug use. The little gal was probably stone-cold sober when she got it."

As she listened, Harris mentally calculated the time that Darby had arrived at her apartment the night before, compared to what Jane had just said about the victim having intercourse before the murder. Was there a chance that it had been with Darby? By now she felt certain there was.

She sighed. "Do you ever get tired of all this crap?"

"How do you mean?"

"You know . . . Hell, look at us; in three hours it will be Thanksgiving Day. If we were normal, we'd be getting the last few things ready for roasting a turkey. Then maybe a little cuddling in front of the fire with some guy who has a normal job, and—"

"And lots of money."

"Sure, lots of money, why not."

"And no pagers going off."

"Right."

"And pres-to-Logs instead of wood burning in the fireplace."

"Pres-to-Logs?"

"Yeah," Jane said with enthusiasm. "I love the smell of pres-to-Logs. I wish they made pres-to-Log perfume!"

"You're weird."

"We're both weird, Leah. Haven't you figured that out? Look around us. We're the ones who are different. If we were normal, we'd both be married, have a house in the 'burbs, and be raising two-point-five children."

Harris laughed. "That's not even normal anymore. It seems like everyone gets married, has a couple of kids, gets divorced, then gets married to someone else who also has a couple of kids; then they have kids of their own. God, how can they keep track of the presents on

Christmas Day—and whose grandparents are whose!"

"Y'know, sometimes when I'm lying awake at night, I wonder what it would have been like to have had a few kids. When I was younger, my mom pressured me all the time, even though she knew that Pete and I were barely making it. It didn't matter to her; she just wanted a granddaughter in the worst way. I finally had to lie, to stop the harassment. I actually told her that I was infertile, that there was no hope. Boy, that was a mistake. She went to her grave blaming her own genetics."

"You actually told your mother that you couldn't have children because of a medical problem?"

"Yep. Pretty sick, huh?"

Harris sat with her feet up, cradling her bent legs. She balanced her cup on one kneecap. "My mom is the same way. She just can't understand why I value my job over having a family. Sometimes I wonder that myself. All my friends that I went to school with have all been married, most have kids, several have already divorced. I don't know what my problem is."

"Have you ever been close?"

"To what, getting married?"

"Yeah, you know, Mr. Right and all? I bet there've been a few guys who've worked up the courage to propose."

Harris inclined her head.

"Aha! So what screwed it up. Was the guy a jerk, or were you?"

Harris reflected. "I dated one guy during college pretty steadily. Everyone kind of assumed we were going to get married when we graduated. But it didn't work out."

"Did you love him?"

"Sort of."

"Whoa, that's commitment!"

"We were very close, but when the time came, we'd graduated, our college days were over, and it just didn't seem right. There wasn't the spark I was looking for. We just mutually drifted apart. I don't think either one of us ever said to the other that it was over. It kind of just faded like a sunset."

"Okay, that was puppy love. Who was next?"

Harris briefly closed her eyes, then stared into the distance. She was surprised at her reaction, and struggled to regain her composure. The rain had started back up, the drops running like tears down the windshield. "There was a time . . . I could have married the guy in a heartbeat. But"—Harris slowly rocked back and forth—"I just blew it, that's all. I just really blew it."

"Tell me the details. We've got nothing else to keep us entertained."

Harris took another sip. "His name was Ronald Patrick Stromberg."

"A cop?"

"No way! He's a dentist. He's got a big practice in Tacoma now."

"A doctor, ooohh!" She regretted the girlish humor the minute she said it. "I'm sorry, I was just trying to get you to lighten up."

Harris nodded, and made a conscious effort to shed her moodiness. "I met him when I had been on the force for about five years. I was in Detectives, working Vice. I was stuck being the bait for the weenie wavers."

"You had to do that? With the fishnet stockings and high heels?" They both chuckled at the image.

"I had done well on the sergeant's exam. I was number two on the list, so I knew that it was just a matter of time before I would be out of that detail. Wouldn't you know it, that's when I met Ron."

"While you were working?"

"You know, a lot of the guys we hooked were lawyers and doctors looking for a little quickie during lunch. Boy, did I ruin their day!"

"So how did you meet?"

"Nothing special. A friend from college called and asked if I was interested in a blind date—an old schoolmate of her fiancé's. I don't know what possessed me, but I accepted. The four of us were going to double, dinner and a concert. When I walked into their apartment, Ron was coming out of the kitchen. Our eyes met and it was *wham!*—instant connection. For the next month or so we were inseparable. Then came my promotion. I took it, went back to patrol, and on to graveyard. I'll tell you, nothing kills a relationship faster than having a screwball schedule like that. I even thought about quitting. I came that close, but—"

Fenton raised her hands in mock reverence. "Ah, the big *but.* I know it well. You just couldn't tear yourself away from all this!"

"You're right, of course. I don't know what it is. Sometimes it feels like an addiction. I find myself looking and longing for the next high I get from cracking a case and slamming some jerk into jail. God, I love that, but the price . . . Is it too steep?"

"Depends."

"What do you mean by that?"

"Simple, Leah. It all boils down to one thing in this job. You either believe that you were normal before you started the job, and the job has turned you into a rogue. Or—and this is what I believe—you were really a rogue to begin with and this job, being a cop, was simply the best fit for your personality. Given the latter, you've no choice other than to do what you do. You wouldn't make it any other place."

"And if I think the job did this to me?"

"Then you're screwed 'cause you'll blame the job for every little personal problem you have, from ingrown toenails to divorce, because you can't accept the fact that you are different."

Harris sighed. Maybe what Fenton was saying

made sense, but she had no time to weigh the thought. A patrol car was pulling into the parking lot.

It was 2135.

Forty-three

Herrera drummed his fingers impatiently, waiting for the cross traffic to clear and the light to change. His mind raced with the details he needed to complete before the night was through. The light turned green and the Lexus surged forward.

He drove north, then circled back for several blocks, keeping one eye on his rearview mirror. Satisfied that he was not being followed, he headed toward the university district and his office. As he neared his destination, he lifted the cover to the center console and felt for the security card that would allow him into the parking garage after hours. He slowed to turn in, waiting for a young couple to stroll past the entrance. Again, he checked his mirrors. The streets were now clear of traffic.

He remained wary, despite confidence that his plans were known only to himself. He proceeded to the key lock, inserted his card, and activated the gate. Quickly he passed through, then waited for the gate to lower before driving down to the first level.

Several cars were still there, interspersed among the empty spaces. Herrera recognized them as belonging to other late-working executives. He chose a slot second from the elevator. A black Cadillac was in the first.

Exiting, he stood beside the Lexus for a moment, briefcase in hand, and surveyed the area. Everything seemed normal, but Herrera's sixth sense said otherwise. With his free hand, he pulled open his coat slightly, in case he needed to draw his weapon. He then headed toward the bank of elevators, his footsteps echoing loudly off the concrete.

As he reached the portal, his eyes were drawn to the deep shadows to his right, where he knew there was a stairwell. He thumbed the up button, then whirled about, sure he had heard a footfall. Nothing. The lighting where he stood obscured his ability to see beyond, into the remote corners of the dimly lit garage.

"Who's there?" he called out authoritatively.

The elevator car arrived with a chime. Suddenly, from out of the darkness stepped a bulky figure.

"Oh, it's you," Herrera said. "What the hell are you doing here?"

There was an ironic chuckle and, "Ricky boy, something's not going right, is it?"

"What do you mean by that?" Herrera slowly eased his hand toward his gun grip.

"Ooooh, not so fast, Ricky. We've got business here. Leave the piece where it's at, *comprende?*"

Herrera shifted his hand back.

"That's better—much better."

Herrera tensed as the figure stepped forward. They were but ten paces apart, and Herrera could clearly see that one hand was shoved deep within the trench coat, and wrapped around an ominous bulge. Herrera harbored no doubts that the bulge was a gun, pointed directly at him.

"So what's up?" The banker tried to keep the pitch of his voice calm. "I received your message; everything can be corrected. It's just going to take a little time."

"A little time? Things are going all to hell and you think it's going to be all right in a little while. Shit, Ricky! You're a smart man; in fact, I think you're a little too smart."

Herrera studied his opponent's eyes. They seemed glazed and tired. He caught the odor of alcohol. Drunk, he judged, or close to it.

Herrera quickly reckoned the odds were reasonable that he could land a blow to the forehead with his briefcase, before his aggressor could pull out the gun. But he decided to prolong the impasse awhile longer. Maybe he could get closer.

"Why'd Darby have to kill Christina?" Herrera asked bluntly.

"Darby?" The surprise seemed genuine. "Darby didn't kill anyone. That idiot may have been screwing her, but he didn't kill the bitch. Hell, I figured you did it when you—"

Herrera raised an inquiring eyebrow. "Darby didn't do it?"

"Naw, but my money is still on you, ya cold-blooded bastard. I thought she was family."

A sheepish smile crept onto Herrera's face.

"What's so funny?" The bluster in the voice suggested incaution.

Herrera played his gambit. "You!"

"Me?" A slight stagger, a step closer.

Herrera imperceptibly shifted his stance to create a better trajectory. "Correct. I didn't have a thing to do with it."

"But the money . . . where's the goddamned money?"

It always comes down to money, Herrera reflected with disdain. He could see the thick neck beginning to quiver as adrenaline surged through bulging veins. The trigger would soon be pulled. And yet, he needed to find out; if Darby hadn't killed Christina, who had?

He asked, "How do you know that Darby didn't kill her?"

"Why should he? This is kinda funny. I know I didn't kill her, and Darby didn't do it. Now if I am to believe you, which I'm not saying I do, it certainly provides an interesting conundrum."

"A third party?"

"Christ, there'd better not be. It'll just piss everyone off!"

Herrera saw his chance. In one swift motion,

he swung his briefcase and dove for the cover of the nearby Cadillac. A shot rang out, but it was too late. Herrera had already rolled behind the car, drawn his weapon, and brought it to the ready. He took aim, but his target was gone. Chief Miller had already stepped back into the shadows.

Forty-four

"*Victor two-thirteen to Ocean twelve,*" The radio crackled in Harris's car. She reached for her mike and keyed it. "Go ahead, Victor two-thirteen."

"Yeah, this warrant we're serving . . . we gonna have any problems?"

They were in a caravan, proceeding on the street that ran parallel to Darby's place. She was in the lead, followed by the marked patrol unit, then Jane's van. Harris had briefed the young officer that it would be a low-risk search, that the suspect was not there. She just needed a uniform to stand at the front door, to ward off any curious neighbors who might come wandering by. While she would have preferred two units, only the one was available. Harris reassured herself it would be no big deal.

She keyed her mike again, recognizing that the officer probably hadn't done many search warrants before. "Hey two-thirteen, this will be a piece of cake. Just do like I told you."

A single click crackled back over the air, the signal that he understood.

Darby's residence was situated in a complex adjacent to a large city park with a zoo and a lake; a favorite place for joggers and kite flyers. There were twenty-four units in all, staggered in groups of six that formed a slight arc to match the shoreline. They were large town houses, well detailed and expensive. The tenants' second cars, parked under cover, were mostly Mercedes and BMWs.

Harris flipped on the turn signal and slowed. "I forgot to tell you. . . . The unit we're searching is at the far end, I think. Just follow me."

The radio clicked in response.

Harris drove through the entrance and down the sloping drive, dropping about ten feet below street level. The others followed her past several of the residential clusters, and pulled into any available slot—ignoring the discreet RESERVED PARKING signs. Harris walked over to Jane's van.

She rolled down her window and said, "I'll just wait here, until you're sure that there's no one around."

Harris pointed to the last unit. "He's not here. No lights, and his car's gone."

The officer joined them. "Which place?"

Harris glanced at his name badge. His name was Meeker. She turned and pointed again to the one on the end.

"So how are we going to get in?" Fenton

asked. "I hope you're not planning on kicking the door down."

"There should be a key."

"Where?"

"Under the mat."

Jane rolled her eyes in disbelief. "You're kidding me. He keeps a key under the mat?"

Harris nodded. "That's what he's told me. Of course, I've only been here the once and I never went in." Harris paused and gazed about. *Nice place,* she thought. She hadn't taken notice on the previous occasion.

"Oh, hell, I'll go with you. You may need some moral support."

Fenton exited the van, zipped her coat tight, and pulled Harris to the side so that Meeker couldn't hear what she had to say. "I've been thinking. . . . Are you sure you want to do this? What if you do find something in there? You're going to be too pissed to do a decent job, I can tell. Why don't we get someone else?"

Harris cut her off. "Let's just get it done. We can call it a day, go home, and get some sleep. I've had it. I'm sure you have too."

"Sergeant Harris!" The two women turned toward Meeker. "I think I saw the curtain move in the last window, upper left. You sure no one's in there?"

Harris whirled toward Darby's place. She instinctively grabbed Jane by the arm and pulled her into the shadows of the van.

Meeker was already crouching there. "Sarge, it moved, I'm sure of it. Does this guy have a cat, maybe?"

Harris peered around the edge of the vehicle and studied the residences in Darby's building. The first unit was only thirty yards away. It was occupied; a television flickered behind a window on the second floor. The next unit had a small porch light on, but no other. The rest were all dark inside and out, with no signs of life. Harris looked back at Meeker. "How in the hell did you see a curtain move from here? Christ, I can't even see his front door, it's so dark."

"Honest, I did. A car passed by on the street up above and the headlights lit up the building for a sec. It happened. I'm sure of it."

Harris crept over to her Taurus and opened the passenger door. From beneath the seat she pulled out her pistol, then snapped the slide back to inject a round into the firing chamber, and stuffed the gun into her coat pocket. She grabbed her flashlight and eyed Meeker. "Come on. Let's just get this done."

Meeker hesitated. "Sergeant, is this really proper procedure? . . . Aren't we—"

Harris cut him off. "Follow me." She moved out briskly. Meeker dutifully followed, his hand firmly on his still-holstered sidearm.

They reached the first unit and stepped onto the concrete walkway that paralleled the building in a gently meandering lane. Separate paths led up to each front door, bracketed by small landscaped plots of evergreens and cedar chips.

Harris slowed to reassure Meeker with a final precaution. "Look, no one should be home. If there is, I know the person inside and there won't be a problem—okay? But just in case, stay about ten feet behind me. I'll knock and announce. If there's no response, I'll find the key."

"But what if it's not there?"

Harris didn't answer. She started forward just as a car drove by on the street above, its headlights briefly sweeping across Darby's apartment like the pulse from a lighthouse beacon. Harris froze. In that millisecond of illumination, she had seen enough to place her on guard.

"You saw it, didn't you, Sergeant! I was right, wasn't I?"

Harris whipped around, finger to lips. In sign language, she tried to explain what she had seen. Meeker watched her pantomime without comprehension. He gawked over her shoulder, trying to see what she meant, then shrugged.

Frustrated, Harris blurted in a stage whisper, "The goddamned door is open!"

Meeker craned his head to see what Harris was describing. "So what do we do now?"

An open door, by procedure, required a building search with at least three officers and preferably a K-9 unit. Harris knew that with the current circumstances, it might take an hour to assemble the proscribed manpower. Until then, they would have to sit and wait, keeping the door under observation.

Conflicting emotions welled up in Harris. She was tired, drained, worn to a point where rules, policies, and procedures seemed to be needless roadblocks keeping her from the truth. Her caution was fading, her vision tunneling to a point where immediate entry was all that mattered. "Aw, screw it!" She took a stealthy step forward, then another, and another, until she could discern the outline of the porch step.

Her eyes had become accustomed to the dimness. From where she stood, she could clearly see the front door, pushed a third of the way in. Another car passed by, its headlamps backlighting her furtive form. If someone was looking outside, they certainly knew she was here now.

Disregarding her intuition, she stepped closer. Suddenly a chilling scream shattered the night air. It came from somewhere inside the apartment. Harris lowered her crouch, as the sound of scrambling footsteps raced near.

Harris's attention remained riveted on the door.

Bam! It flew wide open, striking the inside wall. Simultaneously, a shadowy figure bolted out, charging directly at her.

Without forethought, Harris let go of her still-pocketed gun, gripped her flashlight with both hands, and swung with all her might. She felt the blow land hard, but it was too late. Her assailant's momentum sent her cartwheeling, her forehead striking the pavement with a dull, sickening thud.

Sights, sounds, and smells swirled in jumbled fragments, unconnected and unfocused. No pain, no sensation; yet somewhere in her mind, an inner voice called out, *fight the darkness.* But the voice faded to a groan and Harris's consciousness flickered out.

Forty-five

Milkovich looked at his watch. He hadn't heard from Harris yet. It was nearly 2215. More than enough time to get to Darby's and see what might be inside. His impatience was growing by the second.

The scene before him was changing. He was still at his observation post on the loading dock. Griggs's body was now gone, removed to the morgue by the medical examiner's personnel. The crowd of officers, including Anderson, had dispersed. Left behind were several detectives and evidence technicians. One of them called over to him, "I think we've got a suicide note . . . You want a look-see?"

Milkovich took the steps in one leap, and moved quickly to the open front passenger door. Another detective was headlong inside the compartment. Milkovich got as close as he could. "That it?"

"Yeah, right there, halfway under her logbook. Looks like a personal note of some kind. I can only see the first lines . . . says something about ending it all."

Milkovich observed the bloodstained piece of paper, but was too distant to discern the writing.

"Excuse me, Frank."

It was the photographer.

He stepped aside, and the technician bent to take stills of the note's location. That done, the detective leaned back in and grabbed the paper. Straightening, he held the sheet up to the dim light and studied it. Milkovich leaned over his shoulder.

The note looked to have been composed on a computer. Milkovich recognized the font and style, and suspected it had been prepared on a department PC. The detective read it silently, then handed it to Milkovich. "Standard crap. Life just ain't worth livin'." He shook his head and continued on with his duties.

Milkovich studied the message left behind by the girl who had seemed so alive to him just hours before. It didn't make sense. He knew people. He liked to think he could read them the way others read magazines. But had he been wrong? Had he completely misjudged Deborah Griggs's well-being?

With note in hand, he moved back toward the loading dock and the brighter lights that came through the open doors. He raised the piece of paper up so that it was clearly illuminated. It read:

I am sinful, bad, and worthless. No one understands. No one knows me. Life is only pain and
suffering. That is what I can no longer bear. No one
hears me. I don't belong here. I want to leave. Death
seems so comfortable, so peaceful. I want to go
there now. Mom, I'm sorry, but it's got to be this
way. Don't cry. Please don't. When you find this, I
will be happy. I know it. I love you all. . . .

DEBBIE

Milkovich gazed once more toward the patrol
car. "Bullshit!" He stalked over to the lead detective and thrust the paper at him. "Here, you
can have it back."

The detective took note of Milkovich's face.
"Frank? What's the matter? What's eating you?"

"I'm pissed, pissed at this whole setup."

"What do you mean, *setup*? You see something in this I don't?"

Milkovich stood silent for a moment. He knew
what he wanted to say, but the question was,
should he? He had no proof, no evidence, nothing concrete, only his years of experience and
what he had learned from them. Things were
not as they seemed. The red flags were everywhere, but only he seemed to see them.

"Come on, Frank," the detective pushed.
"What's up?"

Milkovich scratched his head, looking once
more at the patrol car. "I can't prove anything,
not a thing, but I'll bet my pension that this was
a setup."

The detective's eyes bugged. "This is as black-and-white as they come! Cases don't come any cleaner than this!"

"I know, everything is perfect. The head shot, the suicide note, the stressed rookie who just couldn't cut it. Means, motive, and opportunity— Investigation One-oh-one. Textbook in every aspect, except for a couple of things."

"And what might they be?"

"Let's start with the suicide note. How many notes have you ever found that were typed, right down to and including the signature? I know this is the age of computers, but really, doesn't this seem screwy?"

"She's young. These rookies nowadays can't even write their own names, much less a note. Everything has to be on a computer."

"Okay—but look at the content. It's all bull-shit—every word of it."

The detective shrugged. "I've seen better. So what you're telling me is that someone else wrote it?"

"What do you think? Look at it. If you were going to kill yourself, wouldn't you say something a little more profound than this load of horseshit?"

The detective raised the page up to reread the entire contents. As he did, Milkovich continued. "That note says nothing, but to me it screams out. It's like a road sign designed to point your investigation down a street you're already traveling. And because it's got everyone so focused on what they assume happened, you're missing the right exit."

The detective lowered the paper. "Well, you're right about one thing, Frank. I've sure as hell seen better notes, but that doesn't prove anything. Jeez, Frank, this gal ate her gun. I got a close look at the wound. It's a classic contact shot, no stippling, no nothing. If you're saying that someone else pulled the trigger, I just don't see how. When the trigger was pulled, the barrel had to have been pressed right up against her lips. She hasn't been moved, that's a certainty. The blood spatter and lividity show that. If we are to theorize that she didn't shoot herself, that someone else did, then that someone else had to have been sitting in the car right next to her, and shoved Griggs's own gun into her face and blew her head open. And all of this, without Griggs raising a fuss?" The detective paused for a moment and raised a questioning eyebrow. "Frank, I checked her hands; there were no resistance scratches, no gouges or marks. They were clean. Nothing, *nada*. You got that?"

"And the gun? You're sure that it was her duty weapon that was used? Where was it?"

"Right about where it should have been, if she pointed it at herself and pulled the trigger. At the bullet's impact, her hand flung back, launching the gun. It hit the front passenger door at the armrest, and fell into the space between the seat and the door. When Gilroy popped the door open, the gun tumbled onto the pavement. Which is where we found it. All textbook."

"Blow-back?"

"Yep, there's the usual bits of bone, blood, and flesh on it, and right where they should be. Now, Frank, you still haven't made me think for one moment that this gal didn't do herself. Come on, there must be something else; and for God's sake, don't tell me you're into voodoo or channeling!"

Milkovich ignored the chiding. "The gun, was it standard department issue?"

"Of course." The detective was becoming irritated. "Take a look yourself. It's over in the ID van, all bagged and tagged."

"I may. What about serial numbers, do they match up?"

"Yep. Gary called the precinct and had them check the armorer's database. The gun we recovered was Griggs's. There's no doubt in my mind about that. Everything matches. Now of course, Frank, you're well aware that we won't know for certain until the autopsy and the lab tests whether the gun was the one that fired the shot, but I'll tell you right now, it was."

"There's still something that isn't adding up, Andy." Milkovich sighed. "I met with Griggs about five hours ago. She had a beef with another employee. She was mad, maybe a little vulnerable, but depressed or suicidal? No goddamned way."

"Well, Frank, word is that she was a lesbo, a

queer, a dyke. You know how they all are. She could have left you, met up with a lesbo pal and had a little spat that tipped her over the edge."

Milkovich grimaced at the stereotyping. So much for the department's efforts at diversity training. He recognized the smug expression on the detective's face. It would be useless to challenge him. "Okay. The chief just wanted me down here to make sure that if there was a suicide note, there wasn't anything in it that might stain our department's pearly white reputation. From the looks of it, the chief's got nothing to worry about."

"I'd say so."

"And there were no resistance wounds on Griggs's hands?"

"Like I told you, Frank, clean—not a mark on them. There's just no way someone could have gotten into her car, pulled her gun, and shoved it into her face without her putting up some kind of fight. I don't care how green she was."

Milkovich nodded his head in resignation. As the detective returned to his work, Milkovich began to make a careful survey of the scene, meticulously traversing the area, weighing the facts. There had to be something concrete, he reasoned. Some facet that had been overlooked, but what?

He made a complete circle, pausing near where he had started. He overheard one of the detectives speak into a portable radio. "We're about done. Why don't you get the tow truck up to where we are. The car's ready to be pulled." The radio crackled a response as Milkovich's eyes were again drawn to the wet pavement.

Next to him stood one of the garbage bags set up by the investigators to deposit used gloves and other garbage generated by the investigation. The bag was half-full. When there was a lot of blood, multiple sets of gloves were used up in a hurry. Milkovich eyed the pile and had a sudden inspiration. "I'll be damned, that's got to be it!"

With renewed vigor, Milkovich went to the Dumpster beside the dock. There, lying in plain view among the flattened cardboard boxes and rotted produce, were what he knew could be the key. The elusive piece of the puzzle that could tie the shreds of evidence together into a unified whole.

Nervously, he reached in and grabbed one of the gloves that he had seen Anderson toss into the bin. Bringing the open end to his nose, he sniffed. Nothing. It contained only the smell of latex with a hint of talcum. He set it aside and picked up the other glove.

"Well, I'll be." Unlike the first glove, this one held an additional odor, an acidic, burned aroma that Milkovich had no trouble identifying.

He stepped from the shadowy area of the garbage receptacle to look at the glove in better light. His suspicions were confirmed. The faint speckling inside the glove, combined with the smell of spent gunpowder, meant only one thing to Milkovich: Sergeant Anderson had fired a gun, and very recently. So recently, in fact, that she hadn't had time to wash her hands before putting on the gloves to help move Griggs's body.

Milkovich smiled. The picture was beginning to come into focus. The connections were there, but he knew he needed more, much more. He walked casually over to the evidence van, grabbed a small brown paper bag from within, and placed the gloves into it. He then folded the bag tight and slipped it into his back pocket. As he did, he heard the tow truck rumbling toward him. He stepped back as it passed by, then strode up the alley, disappearing into the darkness.

He now knew for certain that Griggs hadn't shot herself. Anderson had pulled the trigger. That was the *what*. It was the *how* and the *why* that still remained fuzzy. Milkovich rounded the corner. He was completely alone. Drawing a deep breath, he looked skyward and mouthed, "You sons of bitches . . . I'm going to get your asses. Just watch me!"

Milkovich grinned a Cheshire-cat smile and continued quickly to his car.

Forty-six

Harris felt a hand shaking her shoulder. "Leah, you okay?" It was Jane Fenton. Harris struggled to sit upright, her mind unclear. Slowly she focused on her friend.

"We'd better get some ice on that bump on your head. You hit the concrete pretty hard. In fact, we'd better get the medics here to check you out."

Harris tentatively touched the injured area, now ruefully remembering how she had come to be knocked to the ground. She turned her head in a searching arc. "Where's the . . ."

"You coldcocked the little puke with your flashlight. See?" Fenton showed her the dented black tube and shattered lens. "Don't worry, Meeker slapped some cuffs on him and stuffed his groggy little ass into the patrol car. You caught him right when he was trying to rip the place off."

Harris drew a tremulous breath. She felt like a train had hit her. "Help me up."

"Jeez, Leah, really, we ought to get the medics here to check you out."

"I'm fine," Harris snapped. "There's no time."

Fenton shrugged her shoulders in resignation and asked, "Then are we going to go in now?"

"In just a minute." She straightened her clothes, brushing off debris. "First I want to see who this kid is." Harris crossed back to where they had left their vehicles. She found Meeker standing next to his car, jotting something in his logbook. Inside the caged portion of his patrol car, illuminated by an interior red light, was a teenage male with a bloody forehead. He was listing heavily against one of the doors and whimpering, "I didn't do it . . . I didn't do it . . . believe me, I didn't do nothin'."

"Nice lump," Meeker said as he eyed Harris's approach. "But the one you gave this kid is even better! Good aim!"

Harris ignored the comment. She stepped closer to the side of the vehicle where the burglar sat. He was young, fifteen or sixteen. Short and wiry with a scraggly mustache. With his wrists cuffed behind his back, and sitting askew, his hands were exposed to Harris's view. She could see several cryptic letters tattooed on each knuckle. A gangbanger. He had the look, and the tattoos confirmed it. "Open the door," she told Meeker. "I want to ask him some questions."

Meeker retrieved the key from his duty belt and unlocked the driver's-side door. He reached inside to press a button on the electronic control panel; with a metallic thud, the rest of the door locks popped up. "There, Sergeant, he's all yours." The officer stepped to the rear door and pulled it open. Harris moved in closer, and was about to say something, when Meeker leaned past her. "Listen, you little asshole," he said in a grunt. "The nice sergeant here wants to ask you a couple of questions. You'd better answer them or I'll beat your fucking head to a pulp. You got that?"

Now that, Harris thought, *is going to make him real cooperative.* She bent forward so that her head was just inside the car. The kid was still whimpering, saying the same thing over and over. "I didn't do it, man, I didn't do nothing. . . ."

"What didn't you do?" She kept her voice nonthreatening, trying to override the effect of Meeker's bombast. The boy had a large gash across his forehead. Blood was still seeping from beneath a temporary compress. "You can talk to me. Come on, what's the matter?"

Suddenly the young man's mantra ceased. He turned wide-eyed toward Harris. "Ah . . . ah . . . ah . . ." He tried to speak, but no words came out. He resumed his stammer.

"What is it? What are you trying to tell me?"

The suspect clamped his mouth shut, jaw muscles twitching. He looked at her, and without warning, spat a large wad of saliva and blood square into Harris's face.

"Son of a bitch!" She reared back as though bitten by a cobra.

Meeker leaped into the void with his nightstick drawn, and shoved it with ramrod force into the suspect's body. "How do you like this, you little dirtbag? Feel good, punk, huh?"

Harris wiped the sputum from her face while yanking on Meeker's gun belt. "That's enough! Stop it!"

Meeker shoved the stick one more time into the juvenile's midsection before complying with her directive. He threaded his baton back into its holder. "Ha, I showed that little jerk something."

Harris didn't acknowledge his bluster. She made for her car and opened the trunk. Reaching in, she unzipped a first-aid kit and withdrew several packets of alcohol swabs to cleanse the affected area.

"You ought to go to the hospital," Meeker said. He had ambled over to her side. "With that lump and all . . . and shit, with that asshole's slimy spit all over you. Christ, I'd be puking! It's probably crawling with germs."

Harris didn't need the reminder. Even though she had just scrubbed it clean, her skin felt alive, burning with infection from the filth. She shuddered. It required all her mental discipline to force the irrational fears back into hiding.

"Really, Sergeant, get someone else to do the warrant. Go get yourself checked."

"I will, I will—later." Harris closed the trunk. "But first"—she glanced over to Darby's apartment, then back to Meeker—"Take our little misfit here down to Juvenile Hall. Book him on something. Someone else can interview him later. Just get him out of here." She lowered her voice. "By the way, if I ever see or hear about you spooling up a suspect like you just did, especially a kid, I'll personally see you get days off. You got me?"

Meeker nodded sheepishly, bit his lower lip, then hurriedly changed the subject. "But the warrant, what about it? Are you going to get some other unit here? There could be more of these fine specimens of humanity inside."

"With the noise we've made? If there was, they're long gone by now!"

Meeker shrugged naively, and headed toward his patrol car. Moments later, his engine started and he pulled away, leaving Harris standing alone. She looked at her watch, then about for her partner. "Hey Jane?"

"Over here." Fenton was against her van, where she had watched events transpire. "That jerk was right about one thing, Leah. You should get that bump looked at."

"After we search the apartment."

"No backup?"

Harris groaned in exasperation.

"Okay, okay, I get the picture." She gestured. "Let's just get it done so I can go home and get in my nice, warm, dry bed and sleep for twelve hours with my phone off the hook." Fenton handed Harris a spare flashlight.

Slowly the pair approached the entry. There were no sounds from the dark interior. At the landing, Harris whispered for Jane to hold up. She proceeded on alone and gently knocked at the doorway. She counted to three, then called out, sotto voce, "Police, we have a search warrant. Anyone home?"

Fenton giggled at the absurdity. "Was that really necessary?"

"Hey, rules are rules."

"And like you've been following them to the letter tonight? Yeah, right!"

Harris ignored the ribbing. She aimed her flashlight inside, found the light panel, and lit up the foyer.

Fenton looked along the length of the hall, then to the stairway leading to the second floor. "The kid was upstairs. Look at the mud on the risers."

Harris nodded, but her attention was on the keypad for the home's security system. A small green light glowed steadily. "Not armed . . . strange."

Fenton peered up at the device. "Probably in a hurry."

"But Darby told me he was a fanatic about

activating the system when he's gone. He's got a sizable gun collection."

"Well, thank God that kid didn't find it." She tugged on Harris's jacket. "Come on, let's get this done so I can go home. Where do you want to start?"

"Let's do a cursory walk-through of the entire place. What grabs our attention, we'll go back to take a second look. Who knows, maybe we'll get lucky, and . . ." Harris's voice trailed off. Lucky for what? However the night ended, she knew things would never be the same for her.

They started down the hallway. The first door on their right was a small bathroom for guests. It held nothing of interest. Further along, also on the right, double doors opened onto a comfortable study. Harris turned on a table lamp, and they quickly scanned the interior. Everything looked in showroom condition. Not even the pencils lying atop the desk seemed out of place.

Hanging above a Remington bronze was a large painting that caught Fenton's eye. "I'll be damned, it's an original. Must have cost a small fortune."

They backed out and continued on. The kitchen was equally undisturbed. It was situated across from the great room. There, the vaulted ceiling and greenhouse windows provided a panoramic view of the lake and city lights beyond. Jane was awestruck. "Nice . . . very, very nice!"

In one corner was a baby grand piano. Jane

walked over to admire the instrument. She called to Leah, but Harris didn't turn her head. She was studying a group of framed photos atop an antique sideboard. All the subjects were girls, young, vibrant, beautiful. "Look at this piano. It's a Steinway. They're thirty thousand dollars. And this place, look around us. Everything in here costs bucks—real big bucks."

Harris rotated, sweeping an appraising eye about the room, coming to a stop at Fenton. "You thinking what I'm thinking?"

Fenton nodded.

"Just where does a guy who makes sixty thousand a year get the kind of money to afford a place like this?"

Fenton glanced up to the ceiling, then back to Harris. "This condo alone probably cost close to half a mil. Can you imagine what the taxes on a place like this must be?"

"Come on; let's go upstairs. I don't think we're going to find anything more down here without a good toss."

"Say, maybe his folks were rich and he inherited a bundle."

Harris answered with a hollow laugh. "He told me he was an orphan."

They began their ascent to the darkened upper floor. "Why am I not surprised that our housebreaker didn't even wipe his feet?"

Harris raised an eyebrow. "Were his feet muddy? I couldn't see his shoes while he was sitting in the patrol car."

"You know," Fenton pondered. "It was dark out there. I'm not sure. But if he didn't make this mess, who did?"

Harris reached for the gun in her pocket. It was still there, cold, hard, comforting. She brought it to her side, finger on the trigger. "Stay back and low." She spoke in quiet tones, then continued alone to the landing, where she stopped. Straight ahead was another bathroom. The door was wide open; nothing looked amiss in the dim rays from below. On her right was a short hallway. On her left, behind double French doors, was what looked to be an entertainment room; she could make out the shape of a wide-screen television and weight-lifting equipment. To the right of these doors, another hallway jogged off at a ninety-degree angle. Where it led, Harris couldn't tell, but she assumed the master bedroom lay beyond.

She gestured again for Fenton to remain where she crouched on the stairs. Harris peered around the corner to her right. Two doors opened onto the hall, slightly ajar. She surmised they were both bedrooms. She crept quietly to the first, gun at the ready. In one practiced move, she swung open the door, spun around the jamb, and hit the light. Nothing.

She repeated the same process with the next room, then went back in the direction she'd come, to the French doors. Bent low, she gently touched the brass door latch. The well-oiled hinges easily gave way without a sound. Harris eased into the room and to one side, to avoid being backlit. She waited breathlessly, listening for any sound. Nothing. She reached to turn on a lamp, felt something touch her shoulder, and spun around so fast she knocked the light askew. Her heart surged with adrenaline, but there was no one there. Suddenly a slender Siamese cat sidled out from behind the armchair and leaped gracefully to the headrest, obviously a favorite perch. He meowed and bumped Harris's arm, seeking attention. She lowered her gun and drew a shaky breath. She had almost let a round go.

"You okay?" Jane called apprehensively.

Harris paused a moment to reply. Her heart was still beating rapidly and she wanted her answer to be reassuring. "Hey, you know what? That Meeker was right. There is a cat in here. It just found me."

"Anything else?"

"Naw, it looks clear." Harris made another quick scan of the room, setting the lampshade straight before switching off the light and withdrawing. The cat scurried past her and raced down the hall. *Just like Alice in Wonderland,* she thought, *except I'm following a cat instead of a rabbit!*

Despite the frazzled nerves, Harris projected a relaxed image to Jane when she popped back out of the room. She rolled her eyes in mockery. *What a job!* they said.

Now Harris slowly stepped her way to the

last door, beyond which her feline guide had disappeared. She stepped to one side and nudged the door open further with her foot. Although rays from the stairwell were faint, from where Harris stood, she could see a partial layout of the suite. Ahead was the main room. Along the far wall, a king-size bed extended out from between wall units. To the right was a short hallway leading to the master bath. To the left, a pair of double doors opened to a sitting room that overlooked the lake.

Harris edged herself inside, staying to the shadows. She allowed a moment for her eyes to adjust to the dimness, then looked from left to right. There was no sign of life; however, the bed had been slept in, and there was loose clothing piled on a chair. There were also two empty beer bottles: one stood on a dresser; the other lay haphazardly on the carpet. That struck Harris as odd.

She moved farther into the room. As she did, a faint but familiar smell reached her nostrils: a sickly-sour aroma that instantly heightened Harris's readiness. She sniffed again—she was certain this time. Gritting her teeth, she continued toward the sitting room, the apparent source of the odor.

She drew close, her hand tightening on the trigger. Her senses were scanning at maximum—her peripheral vision expanding, her hearing acutely aware of the residence's groans and creaks. But it was the smell, the slaughterhouse odor of ground flesh, bones, feces, and urine that she homed in on like a beacon to a lost flier. She reached the double doors set with patterned glass. One side was half-open, but only a small portion of the interior was visible from where she stood. Her gaze turned downward to where the bedroom carpeting abutted quarry tile. An unmistakable trickle of blood, the origin of which lay somewhere beyond, had snaked its way to the doorsill. Harris rocked her head back and prepared to go in.

It was 2235.

Forty-seven

Gilroy glanced up from his writing pad, did a quick check for any immediate threats, then resumed his report. It was a habit ingrained from his early years on patrol, and was so automatic that he was no longer conscious of the continual motion. It was also a survival technique. Sitting alone in a patrol car in the dimness of night made an officer an easy target for anyone with a grudge against a cop. That kind of threat, whether real or imagined, made quick completion of paperwork a difficult and nervous chore.

Gilroy yawned, then set his pen down. He had moved his car from the alleyway's entrance to a distant corner of the shopping mall parking lot. For forty minutes he had labored to record precisely each moment and detail that led to his discovery of Griggs's body. His five pages of scrawl were nearly complete. It was time to go home. He had had enough.

The detective stretched and looked outward,

toward the grocery store. It was quiet now. Gone were the media trucks, the curious officers and investigators working the case. Griggs's car had been towed, the litter removed, and everyday life resumed as though nothing had happened. The parking lot itself had thinned to a small cluster of vehicles; the comings and goings of patrons were now down to a trickle.

Gilroy watched absently. His right hand was sore from writing and he massaged it with his left. On his periphery he noticed yet another patrol car enter the lot from the street and proceed solemnly past the store, then down the alley. Another gawker, Gilroy thought. Over the next twenty-four hours, morbid curiosity would draw dozens of other officers, all with a thirdhand theory of what *really* happened.

He resumed his task and in a few minutes clicked his pen closed and was done. "There," he mumbled, "now I can stay home tomorrow."

Without hearing any further word from Sergeant Harris, he had decided to call it a night right after he dropped off his report.

Gilroy started his car and let it warm up while he stowed his paperwork. Suddenly the same patrol car reappeared from behind the store, turned left, and headed toward the vicinity of his darkened, unmarked vehicle. It was moving fast.

Gilroy studied it as it came closer. His tired eyes attempted to identify the driver, but it wasn't until the vehicle sped past him that he recognized a grim-faced Sergeant Anderson at the wheel. Gilroy sensed something amiss—but what?

He spun his head to see where she was heading and followed her movements as she made her way out of the lot and onto the city street, her rear tires squealing on the damp pavement. Without thinking, Gilroy shoved his car into drive, but kept his foot off the brake. He didn't want his red lights to attract her notice.

His car lunged forward.

With Anderson's taillights rapidly fading, Gilroy hastened to the roadway and fell in behind her now-distant vehicle. The traffic was light and Gilroy figured he would have no trouble maintaining a several-block separation. "But heaven help me if she figures out I'm tracking her." He groaned. "I'll be dead meat for sure." He crossed himself in mock reverence and discreetly popped his low beams on.

Forty-eight

Milkovich had been motoring aimlessly since departing the death scene, his thoughts about Anderson, Griggs, Miller, Darby, and the Herreras all swirling about his mind like shadows beyond a flickering campfire. Drugs, money, and murder, a very simple recipe, yet he knew he was still missing the essential ingredient.

A car horn honked.

For the first time since he'd slid in behind the wheel, he became conscious of his driving—and his lane straddling. He veered back over the white line and braked for an upcoming stoplight. Just then his cell phone rang. Startled, he fumbled for the receiver, taking several attempts to get it to his ear. "Milkovich."

"It's Leah; where are you?" Her voice was agitated.

"I'm on Ravenna just passing University Way."

"I need you as soon as possible. . . ."

"At Darby's?"

"Yes, and hurry. It's . . . Oh, Christ, I can't tell you on the phone."

Her anguish set off alarms.

"Have you got backup? Do you need backup?"

"No, that's not it. Look, I've got to go; another call's coming in. Just get here. It's the lakeside condos just off Corliss. You're less than two miles away. Just hurry." The line went abruptly dead.

The signal was still red. Milkovich ran it.

He turned north and wove his way through traffic, nearing Harris's location in under four minutes. A block away he slowed to a normal speed and proceeded to the driveway.

Easing down it, he immediately recognized the silhouette of the evidence van and proceeded to pull in beside. Exiting, he heard a voice call out, "Over here." His eyes darted about the dim area until he spotted Harris and Fenton, huddled beneath the eaves of Darby's residence. He dashed to their side.

Even in the poor light, he could see that they looked shell-shocked. Further, Harris had been injured. She was wincing and holding the side of her head. "Are you all right?" His concern had notched close to panic.

Harris gently patted the wound. "It's nothing—the least of our worries." She drew a deep breath and became brisk. "It's Darby—he's dead. We found him in his bedroom."

"Dead!"

Harris nodded gravely.

Milkovich kicked the ground in anger. "What the hell is going on here?"

"Don't know," Jane broke in, "but he's been that way for at least a couple of hours. The blood is half-dry and there's definite rigor setting in. That takes at least two clicks on the clock."

Milkovich's thoughts raced back to the last conversation he had had with Chief Miller. When had the bastard told him that he had just spoken to Darby? He glanced at his watch. To his surprise it was 2302. He hadn't realized how late it was getting. He quickly calculated the time differential and concluded it still was possible for Miller to be telling the truth. He reassessed the state of his companions, then asked in a clinical tone, "How'd he get it?"

"A meat cleaver," Harris replied. She used her right arm to mimic the death blow, making one swift chopping motion. "Split the back of his head wide open. He never knew what hit him. Whoever did it must have come up from behind." Milkovich grimaced at the image of a large blade crashing through a skull and severing the brain in two.

The trio stood silent.

The rain had stopped, and the clouds parted to reveal the moon, near cresting. Milkovich watched the night sky as his thoughts churned. Suddenly his eyes were drawn to Harris. The moonlight had caught her at a side angle, touching her sad face in such a way that she looked like a pouting artist's model. *My God*, Milkovich realized, his morbid thoughts displaced. *She's beautiful, bump and all. . . .*

Fenton saw his look, and sensed its meaning. Her body tensed.

Harris, too, felt Milkovich's stare. She turned her head just enough so that their eyes met. Her heart shuddered and she had to look away. Everything seemed so ethereal, the events and emotions of the past twenty-four hours. One day, that was all it had been. And now, ninety feet away, upstairs in his bedroom, John Darby lay dead. Twenty-four hours prior, she'd been making love to him, planning on his being a focal point in her life. Yet here she was, in the midst of a murder scene, standing beside someone she barely knew, and feeling herself drawn to him by an affinity she couldn't understand.

Guilt set in. Shouldn't she be mourning Darby? Shouldn't she at least feel that? But for all her efforts to muster a sense of loss, she couldn't. When she had entered the sitting room where Darby lay, she hadn't felt any shock or pain; instead, she'd reacted reflexively, making an analytical survey of the wounds, the condition of the body, and the state of the room. It was all so businesslike. It could have been a mannequin lying on the floor for all it mattered to her at that point.

Harris felt close to tears. But her sorrow was

not for Darby, nor for Milkovich, but for a sense
of loss in herself. A sense that her own humanity had been stolen by the job she so loved. She
cast her eyes to the asphalt.

Milkovich interpreted this as grief over Darby.
He felt compelled to reach out to comfort her,
but Fenton's presence held him back. Instead he
asked, "Are you sure you'll be all right?"

Harris's brow creased in despair. "What the
hell do we do now, Frank? I just don't know.
God, have you got any brilliant ideas, anything
at all?"

Milkovich shook his head, and shot a glance
at Fenton. She shrugged in despair and said,
"Don't look at me! At the point where I'm at, I
could care less if the president of the United
States was dead in there. I've had enough for
one day. I just want to sink myself into a nice,
hot tub, then crawl into bed."

"Hey, Jane." Harris sighed. "You can bug out
if you want to. Another team will have to do
this scene anyway. There's no sense in your having to be stranded here; go on home. You can
do the paperwork on Friday."

Harris forced a reassuring smile.

Jane considered for a moment, then reached
over and took her friend by the shoulders. "I
couldn't leave now, even if I wanted to. We're
a team, right? You're stuck with me whether
you like it or not. It's fourth quarter and we're
at the two-minute warning. I'm not going to the

locker room, even if we are behind by thirty points."

Harris's spirits were bolstered by Fenton's corny words. She mustered her resolve, drew another deep breath, and straightened. "Okay, then, let's figure this out. There's got to be a connection to what's been happening. It's got to be there." Harris looked at Milkovich. "What do you think? Where's the hub? The focal point that everything else is being driven by? Is it Christina Herrera? The dope? Darby? The money?"

Fenton's ears perked. "Hey, what's this about dope and money? Have you been holding out on me?"

Harris eyed Milkovich. He too shrugged his shoulders. In a matter of hours there would be no secrets. "Go ahead and tell her."

Fenton crossed her arms suspiciously. "Okay you two, what's really going on?"

Harris sighed and proceeded to bring Fenton up-to-date. With each new disclosure, the lab tech's eyes bugged further. When she had finished, there was a long silence. Fenton looked from one to the other, hoping to see a glimmer of enlightenment, but was met only with grim faces. Finally she blurted, "So what the hell is the key to all of this? You're the high-paid experts. . . . What gives?"

"I think," Milkovich mulled, "I think it's everything."

"Everything?" Harris cried.

"Yeah," Milkovich replied. He turned and looked directly at her. "The challenge is to find a commonality that will explain all the facts."

Milkovich paused pensively, as though his entire thought process had been suddenly derailed by a fresh notion. He rubbed his chin and continued. "Then again, it could be that events are linked only by their proximity in time."

Harris leaned close. "What are you driving at, Frank? You're telling me that you don't think there's a connection between everything that's been happening? I don't buy that."

"No, it's not that events are not related; it's perhaps that more than one thread binds them together. Trying to find the single link is obscuring all the others."

"I see what you're driving at." Harris paused and stared directly into his eyes. She felt the affinity again, but this time the connection was intellectual, rather than emotional, as if she could sense what he was thinking. "You believe Griggs is somehow involved in all this now. You do, don't you?"

Milkovich nodded his head slowly.

"Was it a suicide, Frank? I heard a lot of radio chatter on the way over here. Everyone seemed to think so."

Milkovich scowled. "I'm not sure how I can prove it beyond a reasonable doubt. But I'm certain she didn't kill herself. What's worse, I know who did pull the trigger. It was Sergeant Anderson."

"Anderson! Christ, Frank, do you know what you're saying? Cops don't kill other cops. Besides, I think she was at the precinct when the call came in about the shooting."

"I'm still working on that part; but trust me, Leah, she did it. Let me go a little further. You want links, I'll tell you about links. Griggs was murdered by Anderson. The sergeant had motivation, means, and . . . well, like I said, it's the opportunity part that I'm a little weak on. Anyway, Anderson is linked to Chief Miller—"

"How do you know that?"

"Your Detective Gilroy provided that information. He's seen them meeting in odd places at odd hours."

"Why?"

"That I'm not sure of, either. But let me finish. Just follow the links. Like I said, Anderson is linked to Miller. Miller is linked to Darby, and Darby is linked to Christina Herrera, which leads us to her uncle. What I see is a trail of money and drugs all the way. This whole thing stinks of dirty cops."

"And Darby—you believe he was dirty?"

"What do you think, Leah?"

Harris looked to Jane. "You think so too, don't you?"

Fenton uncrossed herself. "It's beginning to add up that way. Look at his place. Unless he inherited a bundle from somewhere, he sure must have worked a load of overtime to afford the stuff we just saw."

Milkovich interposed, "Tell me something. The scene in there—what does it say to you, I mean taken in isolation from the other? What does the evidence say?"

"There isn't much evidence, aside from the weapon, if that's what you mean. Nothing that's obvious."

"Signs of a struggle?"

"No."

"Forced entry?"

"No."

"Blood spatter, footprints, resistance wounds?"

"Oh, yeah, plenty of blood. There are some footprints, but probably from a young punk intruder—I'll tell you about that later. Resistance wounds, though—not a one."

"Which means?"

"He was probably killed by someone he knew, who could get close without arousing suspicion."

"Another cop?"

"Or the drug connection."

Harris pondered the logic. "And how the hell are we going to prove any of this?"

"Through intensive investigation, or"—Milkovich gave a deprecatory laugh—"what usually happens—we get lucky."

Suddenly Harris's pager went off. "Now what?" She didn't recognize the number displayed. The pager beeped again. It was the same number, but this time it was followed by 911. She walked over to her car and removed her notebook. Setting it on the hood, she flipped the pages until she came to a business card she had recently slipped inside. "Well, I'll be damned. Hey, Frank, look at this." He ambled over and Harris thrust her pager and the card at Milkovich. "Of all people—Enrique Herrera is paging me. At least that's the number I'm getting. What do you think?"

Milkovich grinned. "This could be it. Call him and see what he wants."

Harris rolled her eyes and activated her cell phone. Nervously she punched in the numbers and waited as the connection went through. It rang once. From the other end came Herrera's voice. "Sergeant Harris. Good of you to so quickly return my call."

Milkovich moved closer so he too could hear the conversation. Harris winked at him, her hand covering the mouthpiece. "It's Herrera, all right!" she whispered excitedly, then shifted her attention to the call. "What can I do for you?"

"Many things." There was irony in his inflection. "Many things that need to be known before the bluff comes undone . . ."

"What bluff?"

He chuckled. "It is a private joke."

Harris listened carefully to his words. Something was wrong. His voice was strained, the cadence labored—was he drunk? No, that wasn't it.

"What I need is to meet with you and the other officer—Milkovich, I believe is his name."

"Meet? When?"

Herrera coughed. "As soon as possible."

"But why Sergeant Milkovich?"

"Not over the phone . . . It needs to be told in person. How soon can you come to my office?"

"Twenty minutes," Harris offered without hesitation.

"That'll do."

"Are you all right?"

"Don't worry about me; just come now."

The phone line went abruptly dead. Harris looked questioningly at Milkovich. "For some reason he wants to see you, too. How the hell would he know you by name?"

"One of the threads," Milkovich replied. "I, ah . . ." He stopped.

"What?"

"Come on; let's just get going. We'll take your car."

"And Darby?" Fenton entreated. "What the hell do you want me to do with him?"

Harris gave an embarrassed laugh. She spat out instructions for Jane to report the death and explain that another team would have to be activated for the investigation. "Let the captain know that I'm in hot pursuit—but don't tell him any more than that. Promise him that I'll get back to him as soon as possible. Okay?"

"I don't like this, Leah."

"That makes two of us."

Fenton threw her hands up in despair, but acquiesced to her friend's request. As she watched Harris and Milkovich drive back out onto the city streets, a sudden ominous chill overcame her exhausted body. Would she ever see them alive again?

It was now 2346.

Forty-nine

Parking streetside was easy at this time of night. Harris pulled into a spot only a hundred feet up from the main entrance to Herrera's office building. As she twisted off the ignition, Milkovich warned, "I think we're expected." He pointed to an elderly security guard standing just inside the well-lit lobby, his nose pressed to the glass, his eyes cemented on a patch of concrete just beyond the front door.

Harris noted the man, then turned to her colleague. "So are we just going to walk in or what? At this point, he's a hell of a suspect. What's your gut feeling?"

Milkovich didn't reply immediately. Instead, he parted his coat and withdrew his service revolver. Checking the action, he placed the gun back in its waistband holster.

"And what about backup?"

Milkovich shrugged his shoulders. Then,

without thinking, Milkovich shifted in his seat and gently patted Leah's knee. "Screw it. Let's just get this over with. Whatever happens is going to happen. Besides, this game has its own set of rules, and I'll be damned if they're in any policy manual I've ever read!"

Leah Harris felt the warm reassurance of Frank's hand. It made her blush. Embarrassed, she averted her eyes, but only for a moment. An awkward silence fell. Neither spoke. Slowly, though, Harris looked back up and met Milkovich's caring gaze. Their eyes locked in a desperate yearning for the close companionship of another human being. The silence grew louder. Then, despite years of training, professionalism, and commitment, they drew close, their lips touching for one brief instant. But in that twinkling both felt the vacuum in their personal lives suddenly flood with new possibilities.

Harris straightened, flustered.

Milkovich did too, but smiled gently and said, "Don't say anything. Just don't—not right now. We're tired, at wit's end—just don't say anything, please."

"But—"

Milkovich thumped his forehead. "Of all the times I pick to make a move."

"You made the move? It was me."

"Oh, is that right."

Harris's playfulness suddenly vanished. "Ah, shit, look, Frank."

Milkovich whirled around and saw that the security guard had opened the door and seemed to be motioning to them.

"Frank—"

"Skip it. We'll talk later."

Harris nodded reluctantly, drew a deep breath and put her game face back on.

The pair quickly exited and walked toward the stooped official. As they drew near, Milkovich whispered, "He's a retired cop, I'm pretty sure of it. He went out just a few years after I came on the force. God, he must be seventy-five or eighty."

Harris didn't reply. Her eyes were scanning the area, looking for anything that might alert them to a trap. However, the street was empty of traffic; the few parked cars were unoccupied. The only sound that filtered out of the dull hum of a city at rest came from several blocks away: a driver racing his engine in anticipation of a light change.

An eerie feeling descended over Harris, and she slowed her pace. She sensed that someone else was observing them. But where? Instinctively, she crouched slightly while pivoting and slowly scanning from left to right and back again. She sighed and straightened. "There's someone out there watching; I can feel it. Don't you?"

"At this point, does it really matter?"

"Here, you two," the uniformed guard called out gruffly. "Are you coming in or not? I haven't got all night to be holding the door like some hotel valet."

They picked up their pace, stopping just inside the lobby. The guard pulled the door shut and twisted the locking mechanism. "There, now I can get back to work."

"Just a second." Milkovich smiled. "How'd you know we were coming?"

"You're cops, right?"

Milkovich and Harris nodded in unison.

"Heck, I did twenty-nine years on the force." The codger grinned. "I came on in 'forty-eight. I did Traffic just about all those years. So when the boss calls down and says to watch for two detectives—why, I still know my cars, and I know cops. Easy, huh?" His eyes twinkled. "It's just like that Mustang parked way down toward the other end of the block. That's your backup, right?"

"What Mustang?" Both Milkovich and Harris stared out, but the brightness of the interior impacted their night vision.

The guard stepped between them and pressed his face against the glass again. "It was right down . . ." The guard shook his head in disbelief. "That's the damnedest thing. He was there not more than a couple of seconds ago. I'm sure of it."

"I'm sure you did see it," Milkovich said.

"But why'd you think it was another cop? Isn't that what you said? You thought it was our backup."

The guard frowned. "Hey, I may be an old fart, but I still know a thing or two, and the guy in the Mustang, he was a cop."

Harris and Milkovich traded looks.

"That Mustang passed by just like I said. He gave the entrance a once-over, then circled the block and pulled in way up at the corner. I saw him kind of crouch down, then . . ." The guard paused. His voice turned quizzical. "I think I don't want to know what's going on, do I?"

Milkovich slowly shook his head.

The guard mulled over the response, then winked and said, "Come this way. The boss said to take the express. Follow me."

He led them to the bank of elevators that Harris had ridden earlier in the day. At the farthest one, the guard pressed the up button and stepped back. "This is as far as I go." He began to walk away, then turned. "Hey, if the Mustang returns, I'll get the plate number. I still got twenty-twenty eyes." Not waiting for a reply, he quietly shuffled down the corridor and disappeared, his rubber-soled shoes absorbing the sound of his fading footfalls.

Harris turned to Milkovich. "So we're being followed?" The tension sounded in her voice.

"Yep."

She frowned. "You don't seem too concerned. Why the hell is another cop following us?"

The elevator chimed. The doors whooshed open. Both hesitated; then Milkovich stepped forward, grabbing Harris's hand. He pulled her in with him and stood silently in the compartment, watching the doors glide shut. "It's too complicated to explain now," Milkovich said softly. "Trust me and just follow my lead, all right? I—"

He stopped and looked deeply into Leah Harris's eyes. The pupils were wide and her eyes were watery. He felt as though he could see right into her soul. He bent his face toward hers, but suddenly his attention was drawn to the floor. Harris followed the direction of his look. She stepped back, dropped to one knee, and dabbed at a dime-sized spot on the carpet. She nodded confirmation to Milkovich. It was blood.

With a slight jolt, the elevator began its swift ascent. Harris grabbed the railing and rose to her feet, swaying slightly. "It's fresh. . . ."

Milkovich motioned to remain quiet. With a slight gesture, he noted the upper left corner of the car's ceiling and whispered, "We're being watched."

She winked her understanding, breaking their forced silence with a nonchalant remark. "Hungry, Frank?"

Milkovich chuckled. "Weren't we talking about food nearly five hours ago?"

"Yeah, I guess we were. I just had this sudden urge to have a turkey sandwich. Lots of white meat, smoky cheese, lettuce, with mayo and spicy mustard. Boy, that would hit the spot about now."

"Well, your timing's good." He tapped his wristwatch. "It is after midnight."

Harris looked blankly at him.

"It's Thanksgiving."

The elevator began to decelerate, and stopped with a slight bump. They moved to one side. Harris crossed her fingers for luck, then felt for her pistol.

"Ready?" Milkovich breathed softly.

"Ready."

They stepped into the darkened hallway and scanned left to right. Satisfied that no one was about, they moved toward the glassed-in foyer.

"His office is down the hall on the left. Just past the reception area."

Milkovich nodded, then motioned for her to halt. She looked at him questioningly while he stooped to touch another slight discoloration. Still crouching, he pointed to another spot ten feet away, in front of the door.

"Herrera's?"

Milkovich drew a deep breath and regained his feet. "I hope to hell it's not. But then, if it isn't . . . ?" A sick smile formed on Milkovich's face. "We've come this far. We've broken every goddamned rule in the book to get here. We might as well keep on going. If it's a trap, hell, we're already dead anyway."

Harris rolled her eyes and grabbed Milkovich by the jacket sleeve. She led him through the entry to the edge of the corridor and murmured, "Door's clear at the end."

Milkovich jabbed his head around the corner

and pulled back. "It's partly open, but there doesn't seem to be much light inside." He too was barely audible.

An overhead PA system suddenly crackled. "Please, just come on through."

Milkovich shot a glance at Harris.

"It's Herrera."

"No need to worry; I am alone. There's no one else here."

Milkovich spied another small camera mounted high on the far wall, but it was now immaterial. He grabbed Harris by the arm and the pair proceeded cautiously toward Herrera's location, pausing only at the inner office door. "Here goes. . . ." And Milkovich grasped the handle and pushed. The door gave way silently, and they stepped forward.

"Over here," Herrera called, his greeting cut short by a short spasm of coughing.

They started across the floor.

"Are you all right, Mr. Herrera?" she gently asked.

"I'm okay. Just come sit down, please. There're a number of things I need to talk to you about. . . ." His voice trailed off.

Harris and Milkovich came abreast of him. Despite the low light, their attention was immediately drawn to the dark stain centered on Herrera's lower abdomen. He clutched the area with his left hand and braced against another coughing bout. Instinctively, Harris bent down and reached toward the area of his wound.

Herrera waved her away. "No, don't be concerned about me. Please, just take a seat." He pointed to the couch next to him.

"But you need help. You're hurt."

Herrera forced a weak smile and said in John Wayne fashion, "The bullet only grazed me, ma'am; it's just a flesh wound." He paused, assessing the matted bloodstain on Harris's hair. "Looks like you've got a nasty little bump yourself."

Milkovich gently tugged the back of Harris's coat. He motioned with his head to sit, as directed. She complied unwillingly.

"Very good," Herrera said. He sank deeper into his chair. "What time is it? It seems I've lost track."

"A little after midnight," Milkovich said softly. "And we are here as you requested." He briefly studied the man, then continued. "Am I wrong in presuming that you know something more about your niece's murder—and John Darby's?"

An ironic smile broke over Herrera's pale face while Harris's head whipped around with a snap. "Darby? How would he even know that Darby is dead?"

Milkovich looked thoughtfully at the banker. "You know a lot of things, Mr. Herrera, don't you."

Herrera's sober smile widened. "Very good. They were right about you—it's a pity you couldn't be turned. I could have used a good man like you. I might have avoided this whole damn mess."

Harris's eyes ricocheted between the two men as she frantically leaned forward. "What the hell is going on here? Mr. Herrera, if you know something about these deaths, it's your duty to tell us. If you are in any way responsible, then I am going to have to advise you of your rights, as anything you say can and will be used against you in a court of law."

"I am well aware of that," Herrera retorted in measured tones, his smile fading. "Very well aware, indeed."

Milkovich nudged Harris's knee with his own, in an effort to calm her. Irritated, she jumped to her feet and circled the couch. "What the hell is going on here?" She stopped behind Milkovich and defiantly folded her arms. "Mr. Herrera, did you kill your niece last night?"

Herrera's face drooped. With his free hand, he wiped away the bead of sweat that had formed on his brow, and looked over to his desk area. "Would you please be so kind?" he said to Milkovich, ignoring Harris. "In the bottom drawer are some glasses and a bottle of scotch. Would you pour one for me? And, if you like, one for yourselves."

"You haven't answered my question," Harris reiterated.

As Milkovich rose he turned to Harris and said matter-of-factly, "I don't think he killed anyone. That's not why we're here."

Herrera coughed again. His whole body rocked forward, but he caught himself and gingerly settled back. "The scotch, please."

Milkovich moved quickly to the desk. He pulled out three glasses, glanced at Harris questioningly, then poured two drinks. Returning, he handed one to Herrera and retook his seat. Herrera cocked his head back and downed his drink in one swallow. He sighed.

Harris waited, her anger rising. She unfolded her arms and placed her hands on the back of the couch like a lioness ready to pounce. Meanwhile, Herrera began speaking in a quiet, introspective tone. "John Darby. Now there was a mistake of the largest magnitude. You say he is dead. I do know that, but it was not by my hand. Although I must admit I shed no pity for him. I curse him for my niece's death and hope he is burning in hell as we now speak. The man was a pig, a traitor, a man with no conscience."

Milkovich glanced back at Harris. Her anger seemed to have subsided as she now absorbed Herrera's every word.

He continued, the alcohol making his words more expansive. "It's ironic . . . quite laughable in fact, that you come here seeking the answers that I too seek. What a dangerous world we live in. Evil seems to lurk upon every doorstep. Everywhere we turn. And trust . . . Now there's a commodity in rare supply. It seems only family can be relied upon, and only if those relationships are constantly nurtured." Herrera paused, shifting to one side with a groan. He caught Harris's look. "I'll be all right," he reassured her. "There are things that need to be told. Please understand this."

Milkovich nodded reassuringly, but could see that Herrera was weakening. The injury, from where he sat, appeared to be more than just a flesh would. Blood was probably seeping internally. However, any intrusion by medical personnel would silence the man. Milkovich weighed the ethical dilemma. At what juncture did this man's life become more important than the information he could provide? An interesting point to ponder over a beer, but this was no classroom exercise. This was for real, and the decisions he made would be for life or death. At length he interjected, "You need a doctor, and you need one now. No matter what you have to tell us, it can wait." He turned and looked up to Harris. "Get the medics up here, Leah."

"Wait!" Herrera commanded. "Do that, and we shall all be dead within the hour. I know the hearts of the men I speak of."

Milkovich glanced at Harris and back to Herrera. "Five minutes, that's all I will give you."

Herrera grimaced. "Sergeant Milkovich, you're much too honest. Damn it, they were so very right about you."

Milkovich's jaw tightened.

Herrera's voice became emotional as he looked to Harris. "Christina truly was my niece.

Although I sensed when you were here this afternoon that you thought I was lying. But her death is very painful. In fact, I had every intention of avenging it, to find the bastard responsible and see that his fate was as painful as Christina's. . . . But no, I didn't kill Christina, nor that pig Darby. Someone beat me to him. What ironies . . . Someone with more pain? Someone with more to gain? What does it matter; he is dead, the question is moot."

"But why Darby?" Harris broke in. "Why your niece? Was it the drugs or money we found?"

"The drugs," Herrera replied philosophically. "Look around you—it's—"

"All from cocaine trafficking," Milkovich finished bluntly.

Herrera smirked. "I am a banker. Respectable, wealthy, a pillar of the community. How is what I have done different from what any other international corporation has done before me?"

There was no reply from either Milkovich or Harris.

Herrera continued. "I can tell you think otherwise, just like your friends said you would. No matter. It is this very trait that I can use right now."

"You keep talking about my *friends* and *they*," Milkovich said angrily. "You're talking about the guys in Narcotics, aren't you. *Friends*? Screw 'em. The bastards let me take a fall that was a setup from the word *go*. They all just stood there, mouths closed, eyes shut, while I got hauled onto the carpet for something I had nothing to do with."

"They had to."

Milkovich shot straight from his seat. "Then they're all dirty. The whole lot of them. That house your niece died in was a cell, wasn't it—a bank house—and somewhere in town is a drug house and in another part of town is a secure place where your records are stored, all without links to one another. That's how you've beaten us, by segmenting every aspect of your operation with fire walls. And, Christ, you kept it all secret by putting every drug cop in town on your leash. That's how you did it; that's how you've done it everywhere."

Herrera chuckled. "A leash, yes, but you've got the wrong master." He paused, looked to Harris, then back to Milkovich. "They're all Drug Enforcement agents, DEA. And so am I!"

The room went deathly silent.

Fifty

Jane Fenton slid into her van and struggled to shut the door. She'd answered as many questions as she could, held back a little on some, and played dumb on the others. She started her vehicle, slapped the gearshift into drive, and wearily zigzagged her way through the gathering crowd. As she reached the driveway that led up to the street, she was met by yet another patrol car coming in. She glanced at the driver as the vehicle sped past. *"Her!"* Fenton gasped. It was Sergeant Anderson. However, Fenton didn't bother to find out why she was there. She crested the hill, stopped for traffic, and turned right to begin a pensive journey home. She had barely begun when she spotted a familiar car parked discreetly off the thoroughfare on an adjacent side street. Curious, she slowed and turned. As she did, her headlights momentarily caught Gilroy in the act of ducking below his dash.

"Hmmm." Fenton drove by and, after a few moments, wheeled over and parked. Slipping out and staying to the shadows, she edged up to Gilroy's car and gently rapped on the passenger window. Startled, he whipped his head around, but sagged with relief when he recognized his coworker. Reaching over, he popped the door lock and waited for her to hop in, while at the same time he discreetly reholstered the gun he had nearly fully drawn.

Fenton eased in while Gilroy shot a quick glance back toward Darby's residence. "Small world, ain't it." There was a scowl on his face.

"Jesus, Phil, what the hell are you doing out here? Everybody and his brother is over there at those condos."

"Long story." He sighed. He reached up and rubbed the back of his neck while letting go a loud yawn. "Hell of a day, huh?"

Fenton nodded her head in agreement. "So what gives, though? What are you doing over here?"

Gilroy shrugged his shoulders. "I don't suppose you have any coffee?"

"In my van. If I get it, will you fill me in?"

Gilroy ruminated for a moment, checked his watch and nodded yes.

The time was 0019.

Fifty-one

"DEA!" Harris exclaimed, then noticed that Milkovich hadn't shared her utter surprise. Perplexed, she turned to him. "You're not buying this load of crap, are you, Frank? Christ, this is the biggest load of . . ." Her voice trailed off as she noted Milkovich's knowing smile.

"Your family," Milkovich began, "has been in the drug—er, export business—for a long time, haven't they?"

Herrera nodded. "It's a long story." He sighed. "Some might call it my misfortune, some treachery. I like to think that it was a good business decision."

"You were pinched," Milkovich said, smirking.

"Pinched? Now that's an apt description. I guess I was, though it didn't hurt too much. You see, the DEA focused on me from the onset. Other bosses, including my brother, got the headlines, but they knew I was the brains, and, coincidentally, the deputy director at the time was an old fraternity brother from Yale."

Harris's eyes narrowed. as she recalled the photo of Herrera and the vice president. She assumed the deputy director was not the only highly ranked fraternity brother in Herrera's acquaintance.

"I was pinched at a cocktail party in DC. It was a little affair for investment bankers like myself to do a little, ah, lobbying with Congress. You see, by this time my investment philosophy was shifting. I had decided to move most of our profits into legitimate ventures. Among them, banks—"

The telephone suddenly rang. It startled them all. Harris and Milkovich followed the sound with their eyes, but Herrera remained unmoved. There was a second half ring, then abrupt silence.

"That was an associate of mine, checking in," Herrera explained. "The person in the Mustang, keeping an eye on things when you entered the building."

"The party," Milkovich prodded. "What happened?"

Herrera became reflective. "The party . . . a pleasant evening, a wonderful networking opportunity, at least until my friend Don tapped me on the shoulder."

"Don?"

"The fraternity brother—the deputy director of the Drug Enforcement Agency. Initially we exchanged simple pleasantries. I was fairly certain he was familiar with my actual background. But this was business, and one must maintain appearances."

"Anyway, it was here that he made his offer. It was really quite simple—I go to work for the DEA or go to jail for the next two or three hundred years. Knowing that the best business opportunities occur when bankruptcy is at hand, I ordered a drink, and Don and I sat down in a quiet corner to discuss my options. They wanted information: who was who, and how and where the cartels were supplying drugs. Funny thing was, at this stage I really didn't know much about the day-to-day operations. It was pretty easy for me to convince him of my ignorance. But we then began to discuss assets, and how they could be seized. This was an area where I moved with caution. Issues of family loyalties were at stake; and again, you must realize that at the level we were operating, the adversaries are not engaged in trench warfare. Quite the contrary. This is business, and the mood is more that of collegial competition than anything else. In a very real sense, the drug cartels and the DEA are symbiotic. Both need each other for their respective existence. But I digress."

Herrera proffered his empty glass to Milkovich. Without hesitation, Milkovich rose, refilled the heavy crystal tumbler, and handed it back to Herrera. He quaffed half the contents and continued.

"Assets!" he pronounced as though he were onstage. "Now there's a subject that I was not about to speak openly about. I had to think fast, which in all modesty I am quite good at. I quickly formulated an idea that had a lot of appeal for both organizations, his and mine. This bank, the building you are in now, is a result of that idea."

Both Harris and Milkovich looked about.

"You see, I was a dead man if I actually revealed to the DEA any information that might hinder our operation, yet the idea of rotting in jail had its own dubious implications. From desperation is born genius: since I controlled the profits of ninety percent of the cocaine trade out of Colombia, it was very simple for me to cut the DEA in on some of it without anyone really knowing—not my partners, and not Congress. The billions I could siphon off would go unaudited into the DEA's budget for those special projects that operate best without applying certain meddlesome legalities or congressional oversight. And that, my friends, was what came to be known by the code name, 'the bluff.'"

"But," Harris spoke up, "our department's Narcotics detectives? Your niece? Why were they involved?"

"Patience, Sergeant Harris. Let me continue. When Don and I put this idea together, we needed a mechanism to channel these resources without attracting notice. If you study how we conduct our business on the street, then you will understand why this office is where it is. All our wholesale drop points are in California, Texas, and Florida. Look at a map. If the drugs are there, then I want the cash here."

"All the cash is brought in here?" Harris asked with surprise.

"Oh, no, that would be awfully cumbersome. No, that would not work. The cash is deposited all over the world and transferred here electronically. I finish the laundering at this site using a variety of methods. Call it the rinse cycle. Anyway, it's only the cash destined for the DEA that actually comes here in the form of paper, and that's where your compatriots came in. We needed a secure link for this. People who were trustworthy, yet able to operate in a hazy environment. About eight years ago, Don approached your Chief Miller with an interesting proposition. He obviously didn't tell him everything, but proposed to cross-commission a small number of your fellow officers to work dually as DEA agents in a long-term asset-seizure scam. There was nothing really new about the concept. Other federal agencies have been setting up this type of joint working relationship for years. U.S. Customs has a huge number of cross-commissioned agents working as local law enforcement. For the DEA, your officers would pose as money couriers, collect skimmed cash on a routine basis from drop points and safe houses, and deliver it to my bank, where it was diverted into a secret DEA account. The cartel never knew."

"And our department took a cut," Milkovich commented slyly. "Into our asset-seizure fund."

"Correct, Sergeant. And, of course, the officers who assisted us were also compensated for their extra trouble. It was just a little at first, but as the years went by, expensive habits did develop and the amounts tended to creep upward."

"That explains it," Harris mumbled.

"Explains what?"

"Darby's place; the money he seemed to have."

"Darby indeed!" Herrera scowled. "He was a DEA plant assigned to keep an eye on me. When I found out that he and Christina . . ." Herrera became rigid with anger. For a moment no one spoke. Then Herrera eased up and painfully readjusted himself, settling back into the cushions.

"Your niece," Harris asked. "Was she involved in any of this?"

"Oh, no, not at all. She was going to school and, God forgive me, I allowed her to stay in that house. It's all my fault!"

"Who do you think killed her?"

"Up until several hours ago, I would have said Darby. Now, I do not know."

"Could it have been drug-related? Sergeant Milkovich found a small amount of heroin in the house."

Herrera closed his eyes against the news.

"Again, such ironies." He shook his head. "No. No, Christina certainly wasn't a drug user. I am certain of this. Where that came from I can only guess, though probably—"

"One of the runners?" Milkovich offered.

"Most likely," Herrera surmised. "I have come to find that police officers, as a whole, are less dependable, more dysfunctional, and more sociopathic than any of my other associates. I suppose that was the flaw in the plan. I never foresaw this."

Herrera was growing paler, his breathing uneven. Milkovich moved close to the Colombian's side. "Get the ambulance."

"No, wait." Herrera forced himself up with his hands. "I must finish first. Sit down and listen or you will never make it back to your car."

"Mr. Herrera, you're bleeding to death right in front of us. You'll die if we don't get you to a hospital soon!"

"I'm dead anyway, unless . . . Just let me finish and you shall understand. Patience."

Herrera seemed to rally as Milkovich retook his seat. "Where was I? Oh, yes, Christina. You need to know this. The house . . . What a foolish mistake I made. I thought that a week or two in it, and she would be happy to take my offer to stay in a nice apartment right on the edge of the campus; but no, she would not hear of it. Once she moved in she would not leave."

"The money in the closet," Milkovich interjected. "The department's cut?"

"Yes," Herrera hissed. "Darby had stored it there on one of his runs, and there it sat while Christina occupied the house. For my part, it could have sat there forever. In the grand scheme of things, it was a trifling sum—but impatience grew. Your Chief Miller, Darby, and all the others were being denied their bonus money, all because of my inept attempts at trying to teach Christina a lesson. I've never been married, nor raised children, but I thought I knew best. Darby obviously befriended her for only one purpose."

Herrera's face turned grim. "If only I had known how hooked they all were. There was plenty of money. I could have taken care of the problem in twenty minutes, but I didn't see it clearly. Another mistake, I'm afraid . . ."

"What do you mean by *hooked*?" Harris asked. "Drugs?"

"Money," Milkovich answered. "They'd become dependent on the extra cash."

"Sergeant Milkovich, you are so very right. There is no stronger narcotic than money. People want it, they need it, and when they are deprived of it, they will kill for it. Now tell me, both of you, does any other drug produce such dangerous extremes in otherwise normal people?"

"Bullshit!" Milkovich growled.

Herrera's eyes narrowed. "You do not agree with me, Sergeant?

Milkovich jumped to his feet, took several steps away from the Colombian, then whirled around to face him. "It's bullshit, Herrera, because your values, your ethics and morals, occupy just a sliver of this world. Your notion of people is distorted. Darby, Miller, and the lot of them are not the majority, and to project their corruption on everyone else is a load of crap!"

"But I have corrupted them," Herrera argued forcefully. "I have taken average police officers and slowly and gently pulled them over that fine line between right and wrong. And I did so with very little effort. Sit down! Your righteous display is unnecessary."

Milkovich gritted his teeth and shot a glance at Harris. "Come on!" he spat. "Let the bastard bleed to death." And he started for the door.

Fifty-two

"It's Sergeant Anderson," Gilroy said without prompting as he took his first sip of the espresso Jane Fenton had just poured for him from her thermos. "I'm keeping tabs on her."

"Anderson? No shit! Milkovich has an interesting theory about her."

"Yeah, so do I . . ." Gilroy stopped midsentence as a car came speeding up out of the parking lot. "Damn! I thought that was her." He sagged slightly and turned to Fenton. "How's the boss? She around?"

Fenton shook her head. "You know that Darby's dead, don't you?"

"Yeah, I caught it on the tactical frequencies. What's the boss think?"

Fenton sat still for a moment. With a deep sigh, she twisted her body so that she could face Gilroy. He looked exhausted. His hair was tousled, his suit wrinkled, and the lines on his boyish face seemed especially deep in the dim light of the car. He looked old, much older than his thirty-two years. Suddenly a horrifying thought popped into her mind. What did she look like?

"Well?" Gilroy asked. He read her body language. "I've worked with you long enough to know something is on your mind. What's up?"

Fenton spoke tentatively. "Phil, I want to talk to you about something, but I need your promise that it will stay just between us. Okay?"

"Sure."

"No, I mean it. I'm dead serious about this. I found out something today that I'm not sure how to handle. It's been eating at me all night. I need your opinion. I just don't know what to do."

Another vehicle exited Darby's parking lot. Gilroy's eyes darted in that direction; he saw that it wasn't Anderson, and returned his attention to Fenton.

"Do you understand what I'm saying, Phil? This is really big."

Gilroy nodded emphatically.

"It's about Leah. I've tried a couple of times to talk to her about it tonight, but I just don't know how to broach it."

"So what gives?"

"Remember this morning, when Leah admitted to dating Darby?"

"Yeah, ain't that the irony of the century?"

"I kind of knew it was going on, but not who.

She let something of the sort slip a couple of weeks ago. And then, during our briefing—"

"Christ, and you were the ones who found his body."

"There's more."

"You gotta be kidding. What more could there be?"

Fenton paused, not so much for effect as to steady herself. "Our victim last night, the girl, she tested positive for HIV. The pathologist called me around 1800 with the news. I'd been at the autopsy this afternoon."

"Oh, shit, all that blood." Gilroy felt his body itching.

"Damn it, Phil, that's not it! What I'm talking about is Darby and Leah."

"They were sleeping together?"

"They're over twenty-one; what do you think?"

"So if Darby was involved with that gal from last night, like the picture suggests, there's a chance . . ." Gilroy bit his lip nervously, while from the corner of his eye he saw a patrol car exiting the parking lot. "There she goes again!"

Anderson's car turned right, and quickly sped up as Gilroy grabbed Fenton's shoulder and pulled her out of sight. Then, in quick succession, he started his engine, eyed Anderson's fading taillights, and slipped into gear.

"Sorry, no time to take you back to your van,

Jane." He picked up speed and from the side of his mouth he said, "Damn! What are we going to do about the boss?"

"I don't know, Phil. . . . I really don't know."

Fifty-three

"Wait!" Herrera called to Milkovich's retreating back. "You are just the man I need. Please sit down. You've passed the test."

Milkovich took another step, then turned and froze. For the longest moment there was silence as the two glared into each other's eyes. Suddenly Harris caught the faint outline of a smirk upon Milkovich's face, and then Herrera's. "Frank?" Her face contorted with confusion.

"It's a *double* bluff," Milkovich breathed. "A goddamned *double bluff*!"

Herrera's grin widened. "The double bluff indeed. You do understand. Honesty and intelligence. What a rare combination. Bravo, Sergeant!"

Milkovich turned to Harris. "It's all a lie, all one big lie. A double cross of the first magnitude. This cock-and-bull story we just sat through was a load of crap! Herrera may be working for the DEA, but he's a fraud. He's got that whole damned lousy organization screwed.

They may think he's working for them, but he's not. They're working for him!"

Herrera took note of Harris's blank expression. "If I may, your partner is absolutely correct. Though what I have described is fairly close to how things came about. The only difference is the real motivation of the parties involved. You see, things were going perfectly well for us in the late seventies, early eighties. We had little competition and huge demand, and law enforcement was generally inept. Profits were unbelievable.

"Then our position began to erode as competitors flooded the market with cheaper products. That's business. The difference here, though, was the plan I developed to prevent future losses. You see, I was able to convince my partners that more money could be made with a lot less effort by simply squeezing supply down below the demand. Prices and profits would then rise for those still in business. The key was elimination of the low-price start-up competitors.

"Now, there's nothing new with this solution. In my particular industry, tradition calls for rather crude means of elimination. But this hinders business and leaves the survivors nervous wrecks, always afraid that the next car they're getting into is going to explode. Hence, my simple plan." Herrera took another swallow of scotch. "Why not let the DEA unwittingly do the dirty work? For a fee, of course. Thus, I set up my friend at that cocktail party, leading him to believe that I was drawn into their web, when in fact, just the opposite was true.

"Over the years, I skimmed billions from the cartel's bank accounts, and it all flowed into the DEA's covert-operations fund. Another twist of irony—my bank administered that money as well. All this skulduggery really had but one simple purpose: by giving the DEA a cut of the action and providing select information on our competitors, supplies diminished, and demand skyrocketed. Our net profits doubled nearly overnight, even with the payoffs to the DEA."

"So, Mr. Herrera," Milkovich began, "what exactly is your purpose for telling us all this? It's pretty obvious you're not doing it to kill time."

"And what time is it, Sergeant?"

"Half past midnight."

"Good, I shall make it."

"Make what?"

"I must be quick about this. You are right; I have told you all of this for a reason. I need your help."

"Help!" Harris said incredulously.

"Leah is right," Milkovich growled. "What in the hell makes you think we'd help you?"

"Two reasons," Herrera said soberly. "First, if you don't, your lives are lost. But be warned— even if you do help, you must be ever wary. You have many enemies now."

"And the second reason?"

"Because, my friend, I am betting that you

will see the morality of this situation and settle upon the lesser of the two evils. Look at things from my perspective. I do what I do because it is my heritage. I am better at it than most because of my education. But all the same, I remain faithful to my roots. I have strong family ties and a moral code that I would never violate. If I had really been turned, become an agent of the DEA, I would have been killed—perhaps rightfully so—by my business partners. Compromising loyalties for personal gain is treachery and a mortal sin. This I have never done and would never do. Understand, in Colombia I would be a national hero, if the facts were known. To swindle the *Yanquí* is highly revered, and I have done so with efficiency and aplomb."

Milkovich and Harris remained skeptical.

"Now, Sergeant Milkovich, compare this to your fellow officers who work for me. Where are their loyalties? What are their motivations? I assert that they are the greater evil in this case. They have violated their own oaths; they have, for money, become traitors to their own cause. So I put this to you, in judgment before God: who shall be banished first to hell, me or them?"

Harris studied Milkovich. He seemed lost in thought. She turned to Herrera. "What is it exactly that you want us to do?"

"Let him go," Milkovich suddenly offered. "Let him slip into the night while we expose this story to the world."

"Ah, Sergeant," Herrera said with satisfaction. "You do understand. I knew you would."

Harris countered, "But an exposé—how, with what evidence? Without you, we'd be pissing into the wind. Besides, I'm still unconvinced that you're not involved in these murders."

"I can assure you I have never killed anyone, except . . ." Herrera checked his wound. The bleeding had stopped, and the edges of the stain were beginning to crust. "I had no choice. He shot first."

"Who?"

"Your Chief Miller."

Harris bolted upright. "Chief Miller! Where is he? What have you done with him?"

Milkovich grabbed her arm and pulled her to him. She whirled and angrily broke his grip. "Frank!" she hissed. "We can't walk out on this as if we had just caught a kid shoplifting. We're not in some goddamn twilight zone."

Milkovich's expression was inscrutable. He sensed that Herrera, although obviously acting in his own self-interest, was speaking truthfully about his lack of involvement in the murders. But Miller? No, that didn't surprise him at all. Everything seemed to be leading to this.

"Frank!" Harris pressed. "If you're not going to do something, I am."

"Wait," Milkovich said calmly. He turned to Herrera. "Miller—has his body already been disposed of?"

Herrera gave a curt nod. "I still have a number of nonpolice associates nearby who are good at such things. His remains will be lost to the ages."

An ironic smile crossed Milkovich's face. "Miller found out about the double bluff, didn't he? And when he did, he had no choice but to take you out, or chance being exposed as a corrupt cop."

"Your supposition is precisely right, Sergeant. Christina's death, and the link to Darby found at the scene, meant it was only a matter of time before this whole setup would be exposed. He couldn't let that happen. My silence was necessary for his own survival."

"But this whole scheme was bound to unravel at some time. It seems so obvious. God, for it to have gone on for these past years is amazing."

"But that was all I had hoped for in the first place," Herrera cut in. "As I said before, business climates shift. Environments change. What's a good strategy one year may be disastrous the next. The key to survival is two-pronged. You must recognize in advance where new opportunities lie, and you must have in place a good exit strategy that will maximize your investments, right up to the point where you shut down." Herrera paused for a moment, then added, "And you, my friends, whether you like it or not, are part and parcel of this."

"But—" Harris started, furious.

"No, wait, Sergeant Harris." Herrera raised

his hand. "Do not feel as though you are being used. Quite the contrary; if you do succeed, as I believe you will, your efforts may well result in winning the war on drugs in this country. Your exposure of the DEA will cripple the future effectiveness of that agency. Supply will smother the market, causing prices to crash and profits to tumble to the point where public policy will shift toward legalization. It will happen, and when it does, the crime and violence associated with the drug trade will disappear. Look at alcohol. How many homes are burglarized, how many people murdered, how many cars stolen, just for the sake of a fifth of fortified wine? Few, I tell you, because for a buck you can walk into the neighborhood market and take care of your addiction for the day."

Herrera's ears pricked, and he turned toward the window. Harris heard it too. "Your exit vehicle?" She perceived the faint *thud . . . thud . . . thud* of an approaching helicopter.

"Yes, in a few moments it will be landing on the roof of this building to take me back to the sanctuary of my family and legitimacy. With my departure, the transfer of the cartel's business interests will be complete. No more drugs; that market will crash. Just like any other multinational corporation, we will focus on our real estate ventures, new product development, and other opportunities. Right now we own an NFL team, the fourth-largest fast-food chain, and a significant percentage of numerous electronic and medical-technology companies. We also pour quite a bit of money into *both* political parties."

Herrera's eyes flashed. "Over there, on my desk, is the evidence you need. It's all on a computer disk—lists of documents, where they're located, bank account numbers and codes. That data, along with my signed declaration and powers of attorney, is all you need to expose this secret."

Herrera studied the two as the sound of the helicopter rose to a near-deafening level, then suddenly slacked, indicating a landing had been made. "You will do it," he pronounced. "I can tell. I know I can trust you to see justice done."

By the time those words had faded, Milkovich had moved to the desk. He snatched up the lone envelope, tore it open, and begun reading Herrera's statement.

"The disk?" Harris urgently asked. "Where is it?"

"Right top desk drawer."

Herrera added. "For obvious reasons, it's password protected."

Harris eyed Herrera suspiciously. "What's the password?"

"In due time. When I've lifted off and am safely on my way, I will have it e-mailed immediately to Sergeant Milkovich's office computer."

"How can we trust you?"

"The better question," Herrera posed, "is how

can I trust you? Now hurry, time is all but gone. And for God's sake—find out who killed Christina, and see that they pay dearly."

Milkovich could see the grief etched on the older man's face. He moved toward him and extended his hand. The Colombian grasped it briefly with gratitude, then admonished, "Go! You must hurry!"

The time was 0034.

Fifty-four

Detective Cummins put down the telephone receiver and turned to the others who had gathered in the small conference room. In his eyes were both pain and sadness.

"What'd they say?" a fellow detective demanded. "Where is he?"

Slowly exhaling, Cummins surveyed the ten Seattle police officers gathered in a semicircle about the oval meeting table. Some were standing, two against the far wall; all were white-knuckled and grim-faced. Finally he spoke, but in measured tones. "They think he's headed this way—with Harris. They're in her car."

Several of the narcotics detectives began speaking at once.

"Are they on to us?"

"What do they think they know?"

"Shit! We're all fucked!"

"Wait a second," Cummins cautioned. "Be

cool. The chief should be here any minute. We can deal with this. Christ, we haven't done anything wrong. We've been doing our jobs, haven't we?"

"Hell, Cummins." It was one of the detectives against the wall. His arms were folded tightly, his jaw taut. "You stopped taking money early on. Your only crime is you looked the other way. But the rest of us—shit, I've got two kids and another one due next month. I don't care how legal everything was, it's always the line guys like me who end up taking the fall. And you know what, Miller will come out smelling like a fresh diaper while the rest of us . . . Hell, you get the fuckin' picture."

"Listen, all of you," Cummins implored. "I know Frank Milkovich. He's as honest as they get. You screwed up, yeah, you'll pay, but he's not a headhunter; he'll see what's been going on, and—"

"And what?" another said angrily. "Fred is right. Miller will fold on us in a heartbeat, and where will that leave us? In the goddamn unemployment line, that's where!"

"Or jail," another piped in. "You think the DEA is going to back us up? What a joke. We've been screwed with the royal big one!"

"Hold it." One of the women spoke up; she'd been silent heretofore. "You guys are panicking. Darby was the bad apple, not us. We can't be blamed for what he was doing. It's not our fault, and now he's dead. Let's calmly deal with this from that angle. We just have to figure a way to keep this quiet. It'll blow over. You'll see."

"Dreamer!" someone chided. "Once the press get wind of this—"

"They don't have to know," she retorted.

"Right, and how are you gonna keep the lid on?"

She cast her eyes downward in despair and the room went silent. No one talked, no eyes met; hopeless breaths were drawn through clenched teeth. Then Fred's agitated voice spoke up from the back. "Well, I'm going to say it. I know you're all thinking it. I can tell by just looking at your faces. Which one of us did it? That's the million-dollar question. Who did Darby, and who killed that Herrera chick? I think everyone's money is on Darby for doing the girl, but who did him? Was it one of us?"

Neighbors exchanged uneasy glances, then looked back to Fred. "Am I right? Talk about means, motive, and opportunity. Everyone in this room is glad Darby bought it. Come on, admit it—you know I'm telling it like it is. So which one of you did us the favor?"

"That's crap!" Cummins yelled. "You guys, look, no cop is going to kill another cop. It hasn't happened, and it just ain't going to happen."

"Bullshit," Fred retorted. "Everyone knows Darby wasn't one of us. He was really DEA, sent here to keep tabs on all of us. Hell, do you know what his real name was? Huh?"

There was no reply.

"Well, I do. I had an old army pal who went to work for the DEA. I got him drunk one night when he was in town and he let slip Darby's real name. It was Gary Fossick. He's been ten years in deep undercover for the Feds. But you know, he's not our problem right now. It's the weasel from IA that's got to be dealt with."

"What are you driving at?" the female detective asked warily.

"What do you think, Linda. Christ, don't be so naive!"

"Shit, Fred!" Cummins shouted. "Do you know what you're saying? Are you out of your mind? How the hell are we going to keep the lid on any of this when you're suggesting what I think you're suggesting?"

"I got an idea."

"It'll never work. Besides, we're talking fellow cops here. You—"

"Damn it, Jer," Fred cut him off. "Don't be the pure little virgin in all of this. We're a group. We sink or swim together. Listen, anybody could see what's been happening for the past five years. We're big boys. We've been used, but we also got ours. I say we put it to a vote."

"Not everyone is here!"

"Too bad. That's their tough luck. We've got to do something, and do it now. We've got to have our ducks in a row before Miller gets here."

Cummins looked at each of the individuals before him. Their expressions confirmed what he feared. He shook his head in disgust. "I don't believe this. You can't be serious."

The phone beside Cummins rang. He snatched it up. "Go ahead." The others strained to learn what was being said.

"I see . . . Right . . . Yeah . . . All right . . . You'd better get up here right away." Cummins set the receiver back down and looked up. "They're pulling into the parking garage now." His voice was trembling.

"Then it's time," Fred said.

"Wait—this is insane!"

"I want a vote," Fred boomed. "I want it now!"

Another member spoke up. "But what if they don't know what's going on? What if—"

"Hey, Richie is right," a second officer agreed. "I say we hold off a bit. Besides, if one of us did do Darby . . . shit, I don't want any part of that."

"A vote!" Fred cried, pounding his fist on the wall. "We vote now, or I go take care of it myself."

"I think Fred is right," the officer at the end of the table said.

"Yeah," another officer seconded.

Cummins grimaced. A majority of heads were now nodding in agreement. He sighed. "I think you're all dead wrong, but I was always taught that cops stick together. No matter what, we hold the blue line. If we vote, I'll go along. But the boss is going to have my badge in the morning."

"That settles it." Fred bolted forward to the table. "Here's what I propose we do . . ."

The time was 0104.

Fifty-five

The Ford Taurus pulled into a parking slot beneath downtown headquarters. Harris had many to choose from; the lot was nearly empty. The administrative offices were like that on a holiday; except for the emergency 911 communications center located two floors below, no one would be on duty in the building, save maintenance and sparse security. Harris turned off the engine, pulled her keys out of the ignition, and sat looking out. "So what do we do now?"

"Take a look at the files on the disk and see exactly what we got."

"No, I mean after we get the information. Where do we go, what do we do?"

Milkovich reached over and took Harris's hand. "You know, I've been thinking about that all the way down here. There's the justice department, the press, maybe we get a lawyer. Nah, forget the lawyer. Look, we get the password and confirm what we got up in my office.

Then I think it best we just sack out here till daylight. There's some blankets and a pillow we can snag in the break room. Thanksgiving or not, I got a contact in the attorney general's office. We can roust him in the morning and dump the whole lot of it into his hands. What d'ya think?"

Harris squeezed Milkovich's hand, then said with a halfhearted smile, "You know what, Frank, I don't give a damn about the DEA, Herrera, drugs, or any of this cloak-and-dagger crap. I just want the killers. Pretty basic, huh?"

Milkovich nodded and he leaned over to give her a kiss, but sensing hesitation, pulled back. "Something wrong?"

"I've just got a bad feeling. Do you think we were followed?"

"Of course we were. You gotta believe that Mustang was side-streeting us all the way down here. And God knows who else. But Christ, no one is stupid enough to try anything here."

Harris sighed. She reached into her coat pocket and pulled out her pistol. "This hunk of iron has been getting heavier by the minute." She reached under Milkovich's legs and felt for her holster. She pulled it out, placed her gun into it, then shoved the weapon under her seat. "Come on; let's go see just what we've got."

They exited and began to walk across the cold concrete, past several unmarked police cars. In seconds they reached the elevator that would whisk them upward into the structure. Harris entered first; out of habit Milkovich shot a backward glance, then followed her inside. He inserted his coded identification card, authorizing his entry, then punched the floor button he wanted. Moments later they were ascending to their destination.

As expected, they found the floor dim and deserted; only the hallway was lit, and with only every third overhead light. "Which way?" Harris asked. Milkovich took her arm and they both stepped out onto the freshly polished linoleum. The odor of cleaning fluids still lingered in the air. Harris nudged Milkovich and whispered, "Is it normal for the janitor to be working this late?" An unattended garbage cart filled with trash rested nearby.

"Yeah," Milkovich replied, unconcerned. "Come on, this way." And he led Harris down the long hallway to his office.

Upon arriving, he withdrew his key, unlocked the door, and they quietly eased in without turning on any lights. Quickly Milkovich proceeded to his computer and punched the power button. As they waited, they heard a door shut from a distant corridor.

"It's got to be George, the cleaning man," Milkovich said, responding to Harris's questioning glance.

"I think he's coming!" she whispered.

Milkovich quickly stepped around his desk and poked his head out into the hallway just far enough to confirm the source of the sounds. To his relief, the elderly Hispanic janitor was about fifty feet away propping open the men's-room door in order to pull his cleaning cart through. Milkovich moved into the light. "Good evening, George."

The short, gray-haired man jumped, but quickly relaxed when he identified the speaker. "*Buenas noches, Señor Milkovich.* Working late?"

Milkovich smiled, gave him a nod, and popped back into his office. This time, though, he flipped on the light switch. They did not need to conceal their presence now. He returned to his desk while Harris nervously scanned the various pictures and memorabilia hanging on the walls.

"Damn computer," Milkovich uttered.

Harris glanced over.

"The thing's so old, it takes forever to boot up. Say, you want a candy bar or soda, or something?"

"No, thanks."

Milkovich shrugged his shoulders. "I think I'll grab one. Be back in a jiff." He scooted around his desk and headed out down the hallway, past where the janitor was now working.

Rather than wait alone, Harris decided to join him, but lagged behind, slowing briefly at the men's-room entrance. There she cast a suspicious eye into the lavatory, but could hear only the reassuring swish of a damp mop on the tiled floor. Satisfied, she caught up to Milkovich as he was inserting a dollar into one of the vending machines in the break room. "So you really would like something. What's your pleasure?"

"Snickers," Harris admitted.

"Good choice." He made the selection and the bar plunked out as well as a couple of dimes in the coin return. Milkovich grabbed both. He pocketed the change and handed the candy bar to Harris. "Here, take half. It's all the cash I've got on me right now."

She was reaching out gratefully when a slight odd sound caught her ear. Harris froze and mouthed, "Someone else is out there!" She pointed in the direction of the elevator.

Milkovich cocked his head and waited for several silent moments. Then he whispered, "It's probably just George again."

"I don't like this, Frank. I'm sure there's someone else out there."

Milkovich conceded with a shrug. "Better get back to my office."

Cautiously, Harris and Milkovich edged out into the hallway and retraced their path. As they passed the lavatory, all was quiet; the janitor was gone. *Maybe*, Harris thought, *I heard him leaving after all. But where is he now?*

Upon reentering the room, Milkovich shut and locked the door behind them. Harris felt some relief as the door was secured, but her uneasiness still remained. She took a seat on the windowsill, then thought better of it and moved to the opposite side of the room. Meanwhile,

Milkovich was busily inserting Herrera's CD and simultaneously opening his e-mail program.

"So?"

"It's coming, it's coming. Be patient."

Harris let go a frustrated sigh just as the computer *bing*ed, indicating incoming mail. She moved close to Milkovich to view the screen as he rapidly scrolled through the day's accumulated messages.

"It's not here." There was distress in his voice.

Near panic, Harris leaned closer. "Are you sure?"

Milkovich began from the top again. "See?" He groaned. "Nothing newer than five o'clock last night. Damn!"

"Well, try the disk anyway."

With his mouse still in hand, Milkovich clicked the run command and the small green light on the drive lit up momentarily. A window opened on the screen requesting a password. The program proceeded no further.

"Shit!"

"Can we crack it?"

"Maybe in a thousand—"

Suddenly there was a tap at the door. Milkovich shot a glance at Harris and pointed for her to take a defensive position on the hinged side of the entry. The tap came again, followed by a strained voice. "Open up; we need to talk."

Milkovich thought for a moment, then carefully tiptoed, revolver drawn, to within arm's reach of the door bolt.

"Come on, Frank. We're not playing games here. Unlock the door."

Harris stared at her partner. *Who?* formed on her lips.

Milkovich raised one finger. He knew the voice, and wanted time to think.

"Frank, I know you're in there. Listen, man, people are gonna get hurt unless we talk, and now! Open this damn door."

"You alone, Jerry?"

"Yeah, but not for long. Open up, and hurry!"

To Harris's surprise, Milkovich reholstered his gun and flipped the bolt. As the door opened, Milkovich grabbed Cummins by the arm and yanked him in, shutting it behind him.

Cummins quickly surveyed the small room, then focused on his friend. "Frank, this goddamned place is disintegrating right as we talk. Christ, you've opened a can of worms." He paused, glanced nervously at his watch, and continued. "I haven't got much time. They're all crazy. We took a vote."

"A vote?" Harris was confused.

Cummins turned to her. His face was deadly serious. "They're planning on killing both of you."

"You've got to be kidding!" Harris cried. "We're in the middle of the police department. How the hell do they plan on getting away with it?"

"They've figured that in order to keep their involvement private, they've got to make something public, and it's you, Frank. You're going to be the fall guy."

Milkovich thought for a moment as a perverse smile creased his face. "Barricaded hostage . . . That's the plan, right?"

Cummins nodded. "They're going to trap you in this office and make it look like you went postal and took Harris hostage. Christ, you were an alcoholic and borderline Section Eight for years. People will buy it. Hell, even I might, given your history."

"How much time?"

"Just a few more minutes, Frank. I'm supposed to keep you busy while they're getting in position. You've got to get the hell out of here now, while there's still a chance!"

Bing.

"What's that?" Cummins whipped his head toward the sound.

Milkovich glanced excitedly at Harris. "It's the e-mail!"

Cummins looked toward the machine. "What's that?"

Milkovich jumped back around to the other side of the desk and grabbed his mouse. He clicked on the new message while Harris kept a cautious eye on Cummins.

"Bingo!" Milkovich tapped in the cryptic key and pressed enter. Immediately the disk drive lit up and the screen slowly displayed a long directory of files, all with incriminating labels.

"Do we have anything?" Harris was still keeping an uneasy watch over their visitor, unconvinced that Cummins was not acting out yet another ploy.

"Interesting stuff," Milkovich replied. He clicked the mouse several more times and scrolled through the subfiles and directories. "Very interesting."

Both Cummins and Harris eased closer.

Bam! . . . Bam!

The plate-glass window behind the three officers shattered as two full-metal-jacketed rounds ripped into the room. The first missed them all, but the second slammed into Cummins's right shoulder, tearing flesh and shattering his collarbone. It exited out his back and smashed into the light switch, short-circuiting the wires. The room plunged into instant darkness, save for the eerie blue-white glow of Milkovich's computer screen.

Cummins screamed as his body tumbled backward onto the floor. Instinctively, both Milkovich and Harris dropped for cover, and moved to either side of the windowsill as the cold night air rushed through the gaping, jagged hole. Cautiously, Milkovich raised himself just enough to try to identify the source of the shots.

Bam!

Simultaneous with the muzzle flash of the sniper's rifle, another bullet ripped into the side of the building, only inches from his head.

"Shit!" he screamed as splinters of shattered

concrete flew into his face. He dropped back down and grabbed his cheek.

Harris looked over, horrified. "Frank?"

He slumped and exhaled, "Jesus, that was too close."

"Frank. Talk to me. Are you okay?"

He turned and calmly gave her a thumbs-up signal, and then motioned for her to stay exactly where she was.

She strained forward.

"Goddamn it, Leah. Stay where you're at!"

Harris bit her lip, then gave a hesitant okay sign.

Measuring the room, Milkovich judged it safe, if he kept low, to slide himself over to where Cummins lay writhing on the floor. Again he signaled Harris his intentions, then slowly, inched his way over to the dark corner.

Even in the dim light, Milkovich could see the damage done by the high-powered projectile. The upper portion of Cummins's left shoulder had been nearly blown off; blood flowed freely. He grabbed hold of his friend's belt and dragged him to the cover afforded by his desk. As long as he kept his head below the tabletop, he could not be seen from the outside.

"Oh, Christ." Cummins moaned loudly as he fought to suppress the avalanche of pain. "Man, I don't believe this shit!"

Milkovich slipped off his suit coat, folded it twice, and placed it as a compress over Cummins's wound. "Can you hold this?"

"I . . . I think so."

"Press as hard as you can. It'll slow the bleeding."

Cummins nodded, but already Milkovich could detect the onset of shock. His eyes were glazing.

Cummins licked his dry lips, drew a breath, then said shakily, "It's no good, Frank. They ain't gonna let us out of here alive. Not till they get what you have there in your computer. They'll do anything. . . . We took a vote. . . . Oh, God, this hurts like a son of a bitch."

"Hang in there." Milkovich reached down and gently patted Cummins's good shoulder as his friend weakly continued.

"A vote. Jesus! I never thought they'd be so crazy as to try anything here. Where's the shooter?"

"Across the street, on the roof."

"It's probably Fred." Cummins gasped. "He must have grabbed one of our sniper setups. We got a shitload of equipment down in Narcotics now. The best that seized drug money can buy."

"The rifle, what's it got?

"Probably a three-oh-eight with a nightscope, sound suppression, and laser sights. He can see right in here, no fucking problem!" Cummins struggled for another breath as his hand, holding the makeshift bandage, started to go limp.

Milkovich looked over to his office door. The shooter's angle meant he could hit anyone who tried to get through the entryway. But even if they were to keep low and make it out the door, he reasoned, a reception party would probably be waiting on the other side.

Bam!

Another bullet blasted into the office, striking the edge of the computer monitor and disintegrating most of its plastic case. A shower of sparks saturated the room for a brief second as bits of plastic flew into the air.

Milkovich's mind raced. If they waited and weren't hit, then sooner or later the sniper would have to cease. But would the others charge the door? Of course they would.

Milkovich's eyes met Cummins's. They were glazing over in preparation for death. Jerry needed help. Minutes were what counted now. He grabbed Cummins's hand and gave it a gentle squeeze. "I'll get us out," he whispered. "But you've got to hang in there, okay?"

Cummins managed a feeble wink. His breathing had quickly shortened to shallow pants, while the rest of his body grew still; his makeshift bandage was now held just by its own weight. "What are you . . . going to do?"

Suddenly a slight smile broke out on Milkovich's face. He squeezed Cummins's hand one more time and said, "Just you wait, Jer. It's time to air the dirty laundry." With that, Milkovich let go of Cummins and slid himself over the shattered debris back around his desk to where Harris still remained crouched.

"How is he?"

"He'll die if we don't get him to a hospital in the next few minutes." He eyed the top of his desk. Surprisingly, the image on his monitor, though faded and flickering, was still readable. Further, his computer's keyboard was within reach, though to grab it would momentarily expose him to the crosshairs of the shooter's scope. With a catlike lunge, he leaped forward and upward, snatched his target, and fell back with it cradled like a baby in his arms.

Bam!

The shot came too late. The bullet whizzed by Milkovich's falling body, missing him and smashing into the center of his desk with a spray of splinters.

"Frank!" Harris screamed in horror.

Milkovich's head landed in Harris's lap. He looked up and beamed. "I got the bastards now." And he scooted himself around so he sat shoulder to shoulder with her, against the solid exterior wall.

Suddenly someone tapped at the door. "Milkovich!" a loud voice boomed. "We can make a deal. No one needs to get hurt. We can talk this one out. Are you listening?"

Milkovich squinted at the distant computer screen. Using just key controls, he managed to activate his Internet access and scroll his bookmarks until he reached the newest one, the FBI Web site he had archived the prior morning. He opened it.

"Goddamn it, Milkovich. Give it up. No one needs to get hurt."

Milkovich grabbed at his reholstered revolver. "Here," he said softly to Harris. He handed over the weapon. "They don't have much time. They've got to kill us, and do it real quick before there're any witnesses."

Harris nodded her understanding.

"Get ready; they'll probably try flash-bangs and gas. That's standard operating procedure for a situation like this. I just need another minute. Buy me that time."

Harris clenched her teeth and moved to the edge of the desk so that she kept a view of the door while remaining under cover from the sniper. She called out the first words that came to mind. "This is Sergeant Harris. I'm ordering you to lay down your weapons, now!"

Milkovich keyed more commands.

"Do you hear me?" Harris continued. "You can't get away with any of this. Give it up. I've got a man dying in here. He's a cop—don't you know what that means?"

"There!" Milkovich punched enter one last time.

Harris turned back to Milkovich. "They're moving around out there. I think they're getting ready to take the door." She looked scornfully at the snub-nosed .38-caliber revolver. "Shit! This little popgun of yours isn't going to do much if they're in full body armor."

Milkovich's eyes remained on the monitor. The light on the CD-ROM drive was lit, and he could hear the whir of Herrera's disk, spewing out its contents into cyberspace.

"Frank! They're lining up!"

"Just a couple more seconds."

He too could hear the heavy footsteps coming down the hallway. There, an entry team gathered for the charge, armed with fully automatic 9mm submachine guns and clothed head to toe in protective, bullet-resistant suits.

"Just one more second, Leah."

She closed her eyes for just a moment, and trained Milkovich's gun on the center of the door. Just then the little green indicator light went off. "Got it!" Milkovich exhaled with relief. "It's done."

"Sergeant Milkovich, make it easy on yourself," a calm voice reasoned from beyond. "Come out and no one else will be hurt. I guarantee that."

"Richie, is that you? You're in this thing, too?"

"Frank, open up. Why get anyone else hurt?"

"Richie, you know that's bullshit. You've got to kill us. There's no other way out for any of you."

"We can make a deal, Frank. Just open up."

Both Milkovich and Harris heard the clear metallic sound of several 9mm submachine gun bolts being pulled back and released, loading the first round into their firing chambers.

"Richie," Milkovich called out in a resolute tone. "Listen to me, pal. Listen very carefully to what I'm going to say."

He was met with silence.

"Richie," Milkovich called again. "Decock those guns, and all of you guys listen. The jig's up, you got that? The game is over, and I just took your king. Checkmate!".

Still, no sound came from the other side of the door. Finally someone asked, "What do you mean, Frank?"

"Get on your tactical frequency and call up someone down in your ops room. Have 'em take a look at the Web site the FBI put on-line for us to post criminal intelligence information. Take a long look before you do anything else. Do that for me, and while you're at it, get the medics up here for Jerry."

There was an exchange of heated whispers. Harris slid close to the door and cupped her ear to it. A bead of sweat rolled off her brow.

"What are they saying?" Milkovich mouthed.

Harris signaled silence, then shook her head. "They're not all buying it, Frank. They think you're bluffing."

Milkovich gritted his teeth and bellowed, "Goddamn it, Richie, get on the radio and check it out!"

Voices muttered.

"It's all there," Milkovich continued. "Herrera kept records on everything. Names, dates, pictures, your offshore bank transactions . . . Hell,

every time you blew your nose, he made a nota-
tion. It's all there, recorded for the whole world
to see. Even pictures and videos of you palming
lots of dough. Christ, by now every law enforcement agency in the country has a copy."

A radio crackled.

"Look, most of you can beat this—maybe
even walk scot-free—but you come through this
door, and . . . Christ, you don't want a cop-
killing murder rap!"

"Keep talking Frank; they're hesitating," Harris reported.

The radio crackled again.

Milkovich slid from behind his desk and
scooted to Cummins's side. The wounded man
was still now, although his pleading eyes still
contained a flicker of life. Milkovich gently
grasped the dying man's hand and gave it a
reassuring squeeze. "Come on, Jer, hang in
there, buddy."

Milkovich frantically called out, "For God's
sake, get the medics up here now! It's over. Everything. Cut your losses."

Harris braced, but instead of the ear-
shattering blast of the door being blown inward,
a long, eerie silence followed.

Suddenly a voice yelled, "Oh, man, he's
right!"

Moments later the air filled with the sound of
frantically departing steps, accented by a shrill
alert tone wailing from an abandoned handheld
radio. The desperate sound signaled to one and

all: *Shots fired, officer down—needs immediate medical assistance.*

For a moment both Harris and Milkovich remained motionless, unsure what might happen next. But the fading sounds confirmed their hopes.

"They're going, Frank," Harris stammered, elated but confused. "What'd you do to them?"

Milkovich struggled to his feet, then bent over and helped Leah to hers. With her still in his arms, he gave her a gentle hug and whispered, "I posted all of Herrera's information on the Internet. I used an FBI site that in turn posted a copy on every federal, state, and local police bulletin board in North America. In a few hours, the whole world is going to know about the DEA and the big pile of crap that this department stepped into." He hugged her again as a new sound mingled with the rest. The urgent wail of an approaching ambulance siren pierced the night air.

It was 0132.

Fifty-six

They rode down the elevator to the parking garage in silence, each immersed in private thoughts. A feeling of numbness, overwhelming fatigue, and melancholy had descended on them both. The medics had arrived in time; Cummins would survive, although Milkovich's coat wouldn't. He was now in a borrowed one, two sizes too small. But what of the others? What of the department? They knew that in a few short hours, it would be torn apart by scandal. The press would start a feeding frenzy. Politicians would sniff the stench and get upwind. Arrests, resignations, careers in ruin, and for what? All would be tainted, both the good and the bad. Maybe it was their exhaustion, maybe just their finely honed skepticism, but in the end it seemed to Milkovich and Harris that all that had happened in the last twenty-four hours had very little meaning. Just another day in the gutter of humanity, keeping the sewers free of clogging debris.

The elevator slowed, then bumped to a stop. As the door slid open, Milkovich, with a gentlemanly sweep of his hand, motioned for Harris to exit first. She gazed out at the numerous empty cars now filling nearby slots, then turned and looked at the scratches on his face, the dark lines under his eyes, and the day's growth of stubble on his face, "Jesus, Frank," she said tenderly, "you look like shit!"

Milkovich grinned, but held his tongue. Harris looked the same, but he knew better than to respond in kind. Instead, as they stepped out onto the concrete, he said, "Leah, I've really liked working with you. Whatever happens, I want you to know that."

As the elevator door slid shut, Harris stopped. She grabbed Milkovich and kissed him long and hard on the lips. Slowly, they pulled apart and faced each other. "Maybe," Harris said, measuring her words, "maybe, in the end, all we're going to get from all this is you and me." Harris paused, her eyes wandering across the garage floor. "God," she said. "Listen to me. I'm sounding like a dime-novel heroine."

"There's nothing wrong with that. I kind of like it."

"Ah, hell!" Harris looked fierce. The glaze over her eyes had momentarily faded, and a fire seemed to be rekindled. "Frank, you know, I really don't give a shit about Herrera, the DEA or any of the rest of that crap. Christ, over the next month or two all of our waking hours will be spent talking to FBI agents, attorneys, and the brass. That's a different world than mine and it does nothing for me. My focus is much simpler. Someone gets killed. I find the killer. No politics, no grand schemes of world dominance, no nothing. Just good, honest police work. Damn it, Frank, that's all I want; and right now I don't have it. All that we've been through, all of it, adds up to nothing. I've got no case, only a lot of suspects. Christ, what does any of this have to do with the killings? What's the goddamned connection? Is there one, Frank? And if there is, where the hell is it?"

They took more steps, then Milkovich stopped and said abruptly, "I know who killed them—all of them."

"What?" She whirled to face Milkovich, surprise and confusion furrowing her brow. As she did, she saw movement out of the corner of her eye. A shadowy figure had emerged from the darkened stairwell adjacent to the elevator—a specter rushing toward them, large-bore gun in hand.

"Stop right there," Sergeant Anderson ordered.

Milkovich turned slowly to face her. She stood twenty feet away, her semiautomatic pistol cocked and aimed at his forehead. He gave her a slight scowl. "I was just going to suggest to Leah that we go look you up in the morning."

Harris glanced from Milkovich to Anderson. Their eyes were locked on each other like boxers at the bell for round one. The gun was unwavering; the finger taut on the trigger.

"Sergeant Anderson," Harris said. "Didn't you get the word? The game's over—you lost. The DEA money deal . . . the whole world is going to know about it in a few hours. Put the gun down and we'll see that you get treated fairly."

Anderson's lips curled. "I don't give a rip about the DEA, this department, or any of those others. I've got my own problems to take care of." She paused and brushed her hair back with her free hand. As she did, Harris could see that her eyes were red, as though she had been crying. Anderson continued, "The gun in your holster, Milkovich—pull it out with your left hand and let it drop to the ground."

Milkovich looked at Harris, then back to Anderson. Although she appeared emotionally distraught, he had little doubt that she'd shoot—her jugular was pulsing.

Reluctantly, he complied. But he knew he had a hole card.

"And you, Sergeant Harris. Let your purse drop."

"I'm unarmed."

"I didn't ask that!"

Harris shrugged the purse from her shoulder.

"Now, kick 'em to me."

They did, but only halfway.

"So where are they?" Anderson demanded.

"Where's what?" Milkovich replied.

"Oh, don't give me that shit. You know what I'm talking about. Christ, you're the only idiot in this place who's got a brain bigger than a peanut. So don't screw with me and I'll make it quick. Just tell me where they are!"

Milkovich raised his hand slightly.

"Keep it frozen or I'll—"

"Or you'll kill us like all the others."

Anderson's demeanor sagged, although her eyes continued to dance wildly as she momentarily reflected.

"Her?" Harris blurted.

"Yeah, Christina Herrera, Darby, and—" Milkovich began the roll call.

"And Griggs," Anderson sadly offered. She stiffened. "Damn them all. Every one of 'em, especially that whore Griggs. Look at me. Look what she's done to me. I loved her. Can you believe that? I fell for her like I was some dumb-ass teenager at the high school prom. Christ almighty, she ripped the guts out of me with what she did. Don't you see, I had no choice. None at all, and all because that two-timing bitch and her pals couldn't keep their pants on for more than a fucking minute!"

Harris's face showed confusion.

"Ha!" Anderson's flashed a demented grin. "You got used too, just like me!"

"Darby?"

Anderson gritted her teeth. "What a prick.

You know, it was his and that bitch Christina's plan all along."

"To fleece her uncle?" Milkovich offered.

"Right on, Frankie boy. I knew you were the smart one. I like your style. You're a good cop, just like me. Now tell me where the gloves and the diary are, and like I said, I'll make it quick."

Milkovich's mind raced. From where she stood, Anderson could easily put bullets into his and Harris's heads without much trouble. She was known to be a crack shot. But maybe if they could spread out and get a little closer, she might get only one of them. He twisted his eyes toward Harris. He could tell she was thinking the same thing. He shifted his weight and gained half a step sideways.

"The gloves?" Milkovich said, distracting Anderson from his movement. "What gloves?"

"Oh, give me a break," Anderson erupted. "I know you picked them up. You're the only bastard with enough sense to have known their value."

"Because of the gunpowder residue inside them," Milkovich said, easing left again.

"You're damned right. One lousy detail and I intend to take care of it."

"But how'd you get Griggs to eat her own gun? There was no sign of a struggle."

Anderson cringed. Each mention of Griggs's name left her more unsettled. "That little spot behind Safeway," she said softly, "was where we always used to meet. It was our spot. She was waiting for me there. I told her we had to talk, that I just wanted to get a few things off my chest. That I needed to tell her exactly how I felt about her."

"You were in the patrol car that Gilroy saw coming in. That wasn't Griggs."

"Yeah, that piece of luck worked out pretty good. Of course, I had to bust my ass getting out of there before that dumbshit detective figured out what was going on. But the real trick was getting into the armory records just before I went out there, switching serial numbers on our guns. Then all I had to do was slip into the car with her and while she was staring ahead and not noticing, I pulled out my gun and—"

"But why kill her? And why the others?"

"They're all whores!" Anderson roared. "All three of them. Christina knew what her uncle was all about. That story about her wanting to be on her own and live like a student was all bullshit. Darby and she planned it all along so they could skim a bigger chunk of the cash flowing through the house."

"And the heroin?"

"Oh, you found that, too! It was hers. Wouldn't Uncle Herrera have had a shit if he found out that his little darling liked to smoke a bit of black tar? The little bitch! And Darby encouraged it. You know why? 'Cause when Christina got high, she liked a threesome."

"Which included Griggs?"

Anderson's mood darkened again. "That

young bitch had no sense. She meets Christina at school and the next thing you know, she's in the sack with 'em. And guess what, one of her little play pals was HIV-positive. And now I probably am, too!"

Harris's eyes widened with realization. Seeing this, Anderson cried with glee, "Yeah, Darby, or whatever his name was, would screw anyone— even you! But then, you're not going to have to live with this, either. Now where the hell are those gloves? I'm getting real impatient."

"You're can't get away with this," Harris said. "In a few hours there'll be Feds everywhere around here. You'll spend the rest of your life in prison."

"I'll take my chances," Anderson replied. She rocked back on her heels and tightened her hold on her weapon. "Besides, I've got a plan."

"Leah's right," Milkovich broke in. "You need help and we can get it. Maybe an insanity plea can get you out of all of this."

"Insanity," Anderson scowled. "You'd have gone crazy, too, if you'd been through what I've had to put up with. Naw, I'll take my chances the other way. Like I said, I've got a plan and it's real simple."

"Whatever it is," Harris said, "it'll never work."

"You don't think so, huh? Well, I'll tell ya, when Cummins and the rest of 'em decided to do you with that stupid hostage scheme, they put it out to the area units just like it was happening for real. So, like a good little supervisor that I am, I hustled down here to help out." She paused. With her free hand, Anderson withdrew her portable radio from its holder and waved it at Milkovich and Harris. She then let it slip headfirst to the concrete. The impact snapped off the short antenna. "Funny thing," she said speaking to herself. "My radio stopped working. Must've gotten dropped or something. See, no one has ever let me know that the hostage situation is over and it was all a ruse. So here I am face-to-face with the guy who is supposed to have taken you hostage. I ordered him to freeze. God, at least three times, I'm sure. But instead, he kept coming. I had no choice, don't you see? Pity, you were in the line of fire when he drew his weapon on me. It's the shits, but that's life."

"Shoot her," Milkovich spoke up, "and you'll never get to the gloves and diary in time to keep you off of death row. I'll see to it."

"Yeah, right. Ten to one, the stuff's in your car right here."

"Is it?"

"Oh, we're playing games now, huh?"

Milkovich's eyes bore down on his opponent. "Someone else is holding the items and knows their significance. Killing us is not going to do anything but get you a choice between a hangman's knot or a lethal injection."

"You're bluffing." There was now hesitation in Anderson's voice.

Milkovich caught it. "Am I?"

Harris used the moment to her advantage. She eased imperceptibly to her right.

A taunting smile crept across Milkovich's lips. "So who is going to blink first?"

Anderson's jugular quickened its beat. "You fuckin' asshole, where's the goddamn stuff?"

"Seems we have reached an interesting impasse."

"Fuck you."

Suddenly the whir of an electric motor broke the deadly air. Distracted, Anderson whipped her head sideways. "Now!" Milkovich shouted, and he dove for his revolver while Harris leaped the other way, rolling over the hood of a car and dropping hard onto the pavement.

Bam! Bam! The shots echoed like thunder.

Harris could see nothing. Although she was in a position to make a run for the emergency exit she chose to stay, creeping to the edge of her shield, steeling herself for a desperate lunge.

With a whoosh, the elevator doors slid open, framing Detective Gilroy. He had his gun drawn.

"Phil!" Harris screamed.

Bam! Bam!

The first bullet from Anderson's gun struck him dead center in the chest, the second an inch lower. Their combined force sent Gilroy backward, his weapon flying from his hand. It landed with a dull thud inside the elevator compartment, a few feet away from Gilroy's motionless body.

"Phil!" Harris cried in horror. Then she caught sight of Anderson. She was turning back to where Milkovich must now lie.

"Okay, Milkovich. It's time to finish you off." She pointed her gun downward.

"No!" Harris screamed. She leaped up and charged.

Bam!

A solitary shot reverberated. Incredibly, the gun in Anderson's hand slipped from her grasp. "Well, I'll be a son of a bitch!" She staggered forward a step before dropping to the ground, felled like a puppet with cut strings. Harris froze in her tracks. From where she stood, she could see a deep red stain spreading between Anderson's shoulder blades, just below her neck. Stunned, she looked back up to the source of the mortal wound. There stood Jane Fenton trembling just inside the elevator doorway, Gilroy's gun in hand.

Epilogue

Milkovich had been lucky. He had missed the grab for his gun, but Anderson had also been off the mark. Her two shots had gone wide, but not by much.

Both detectives now sat across from each other, wearily awaiting their order of hot turkey sandwiches in an empty section of the all-night restaurant. The first rays of dawn were now cresting the horizon. They were shell-shocked, exhausted, their bodies aching for rest. But Milkovich had convinced Harris they needed to talk, although their words by now were few and far between.

The waitress returned briefly with two mugs of draft beer. Milkovich gulped half the contents of his in one swallow. Harris looked on with a rueful smile. She was preoccupied with the sobering thought that she might be HIV-positive. She sighed. "You know, Jane is probably going to have to be in therapy for the rest of her life. Almost twenty years with the department, and that was the first time she ever fired a gun!"

Milkovich grinned. "I'll be happy to pay that tab."

Harris agreed.

"And Gilroy," Milkovich went on. "He's going to be one sore puppy."

"Well, it's a hell of a good thing that he put his vest on under his sport coat when he heard about the hostage situation."

"That's the truth! I thought he was a goner. Two hits dead center on the shock plate. I bet his whole chest is black-and-blue right now. Did you see his face when we got to him?"

Harris chuckled, and for a moment her eyes twinkled. "Those hits knocked the breath right out of him. For a minute there, I think he thought he *had* bought it."

"Well," Milkovich said slowly, "it's over now. "You got your killer and I . . . well—"

"Frank," Harris cut in. "You got the killer. I didn't do diddly-squat."

Milkovich reached out and took Harris's hand. There was a slight hesitation on her part, but as she felt the comfort of his skin against her own, a sense of relief enveloped her. "Frank, when did you know? I mean, when did you figure out Anderson was the killer, and not the others? I never saw it. The pieces might have been there, but I just never had a clue how everything added up."

He was silent a moment, savoring their close-ness, sorting his answer. Finally he replied, "The heroin in the dishwasher door yesterday morning . . . it shouldn't have been there. Not and be consistent with everything else. Then there was Darby. He wasn't family. So how could he be hooked into a Colombian drug cell? I just kept returning to those anomalies; it told me something, and it was quite simple. All the facts would never add up to a whole, because we were dealing with at least two different puzzles. No matter how hard we tried, they could never go together as one. Some pieces went here, and others there. Trying to come up with some grand conspiracy to cover everything was never going to work."

Harris nodded with understanding.

"You see, Leah, there were several universes at work: Herrera's, Darby's, and Anderson's." Milkovich paused and took another long drink, finishing the glass. "They were unrelated and probably would never have come into contact, except for a twist of fate. Left on their own, nothing would have happened; but like galaxies colliding, their contact destroyed everything. You know though . . ." He stopped and chuck-led. "It's kind of ironic that a couple of greedy, horny people were the impetus for what will probably obliterate the DEA and maybe the drug problem as we know it. Ah, hell, I don't know, and quite honestly at this point, I don't care." Milkovich squeezed Harris's hand.

She bit her lower lip and mumbled, "God, I'm so stupid at times." She added, "You know, there's a slight chance I'll test positive. There were a couple of times when we weren't exactly safe about things."

Milkovich gazed tenderly at the woman before him. "So what? We can deal with it." He gently cupped her chin and said slowly, "I think I love you, Leah Harris."

Suddenly Harris jumped as her pager sounded. She let go of Milkovich, grabbed the device off her belt loop, and drew it close. He looked on intently, dread souring his stomach. But a curious smile spread across Harris's lips and she leaned back and chuckled. "What a doll!"

"What?" Milkovich asked intently.

Harris was giddy. "It's Jane. She evidently managed to drag Dr. Reid out of bed and down to the ME's office an hour ago. She tested Darby for HIV . . . and he's negative! That means . . ."

"Thank God." Milkovich sighed with great relief. As he did, Harris turned off her pager and set it aside. She leaned close.

"Let's see, where were we?" Her green eyes were sparkling. "You said something. I'd like to hear it again."

Milkovich blushed. "I said . . ." He hesitated. "Aw, hell, I said, I think I love you, Leah Harris."

She waited for a moment, then replied, "And I think I love you, Frank Milkovich."

It was 0559, Thanksgiving Day.

Leah Harris and Frank Milkovich
return in Michael A. Hawley's new
pulse-pounding thriller!

An unsolved murder.
A prime suspect.
And a secret that makes this case
anything but open-and-shut.

Turn the page for a special early preview.

Silent Proof

An Onyx paperback coming in August 2003

"Your honor," the young defense attorney protested, leaning forward in her chair. She glanced briefly at the stooped middle aged man handcuffed and seated beside her, then glared at the prosecutor at the adjacent table. "I've just been assigned this case. I haven't had ten minutes with my client. I—"

"Ms. Quinn," opposing counsel cut in, "this is only a preliminary hearing. I don't see—"

"But you want my client held without bail."

"Under the circumstances—"

"What circumstances, Mr. Collins? I've seen no offer of proof. In fact, I've seen nothing. Further, this whole situation is outrageous. My God, Mr. Bakerman was about to walk out of the prison gate. He was literally a week away from being a free man. Instead he was slapped back into shackles and delivered here. He's done his time, over a decade's worth."

"This is a new allegation."

"New? Clifford Bakerman has been in prison for ten years. How could he have committed new crimes requiring detainment without bail?"

Ignoring her pleas, Richard Collins rose and motioned for the bailiff to take custody of a legal document he held in his hand. He then glanced back into the near-empty courtroom at several reporters scribbling notes. Seeing their heads bob up, he returned his attention to the judge and announced in a melodramatic tone, "There is no statue of limitations for murder."

The uniformed officer reached his side.

"Let me see that," Tessla Quinn demanded.

"I'll be the first, Ms. Quinn," the judge enjoined. It was early, the middle of another weary week of routine hearings. Apathy was weighing heavily upon the graying magistrate—at least until now. The sixty-eight-year-old woman had straightened, a sharpness returning to her eyes.

"There are copies for everyone," Collins said with satisfaction. He surrendered one set to the bailiff, and stepped toward the defense table to meet Quinn's outstretched hand.

She snatched the proffered folder with a jerk and immediately began speed reading the papers. Meanwhile, her client remained still and emotionless, seemingly detached from the whole proceeding. His hands were folded neatly in front of him as though he was about to say grace.

"Give me a moment to examine this," the judge said. Collins settled back into his chair, folded his arms and waited, his smug smile growing wider.

In addition to the media scribes, the court clerk, and the two bored jail guards stationed at arm's length from Bakerman, one more individual was present. Detective Sergeant Leah Harris sat alone in

the public area. Dressed neatly in a wool skirt, a
sweater, and comfortable pumps, the thirty-
something, muddy blonde looked on with intense
professional interest—her attention shifting like a
watchtower guard's between the two attorneys, the
judge, and the lone prisoner. At Harris's side were a
small leather briefcase, a raincoat, and folded um-
brella: all standard equipment for a damp October
day in Seattle.

Detective Sergeant Leah Harris knew both Judge
Helen Stromberg and King County prosecutor Richard Collins from numerous prior cases. However, the
young wisp of a defense attorney was a stranger.
Harris eyed her suspiciously, cringing at the ankle
tattoo showing through her nylons and the multiplic-
ity of rings protruding from both pierced earlobes.
The ink was no doubt still drying on her newly
awarded law degree. Yet the young woman was
standing her ground without sign of intimidation or
fear, challenging one of the leading legal minds in
the area. And while to this point Harris had remained stone faced, suddenly she too felt a slight
smile crease her lips. And not for the same reason as
Collins. This testimony was not going to be the cake-
walk she had been promised.

Judge Stromberg looked up. "I see that Sergeant
Harris is in the courtroom. Under the circumstances,
perhaps it would be best if we swear her in and
allow opposing counsel the opportunity to question
her. Any objection to that, Mr. Collins?"

He shrugged his shoulders.

"Good." The judge's eyes shifted to the Seattle detective. "Please come forward, Sergeant Harris, and
be sworn in."

Leah nodded, withdrew a file from her portfolio, and made her way to the witness stand, taking a seat as the bailiff came about.

"Would you raise your right hand, please."

Harris complied.

"Do you solemnly swear to tell the truth, the whole truth, and nothing but the truth, so help you, God?"

"I do."

Stromberg leaned in her direction. "For the record, would you state your full name and the city you reside in."

"Leah . . . Rae . . . Harris. I am a resident of Seattle, Washington."

"Thank you—Mr. Collins, you may proceed."

The prosecutor straightened and cleared his throat. "Sergeant Harris, for the record, would you mind stating the name of your employer, the nature of your position, and your background qualifications."

Harris nodded. "I have been employed by the Seattle Police Department for more than seventeen years and am currently a supervisor in the robbery-homicide unit. I have been in this position for three years, and in homicide as a detective for a total of nine years."

"How many murders have you investigated?"

"We prefer to call them death investigations. A suspicious death can sometimes turn out to be accidental, or even a suicide—or vice versa. We wouldn't want to prejudge."

"Certainly—but how many?"

Harris paused and reflected. "In the last nine years, I've probably investigated, or have been part of a team that investigated, at least four hundred deaths."

"That's a lot."

Harris nodded with pride.

"And what special training and education do you have for this job?" Collins asked.

Harris shifted in her seat. "I believe I've completed every investigator course the state police academy has offered over the years as well as those through the FBI. I have a bachelor of science degree from the University of Washington in abnormal psychology. I am also a graduate of the basic and advanced FBI academy and their profilers school."

"I also believe you are certified in numerous disciplines as an instructor and have also been an adjunct member of the FBI's serial killer unit."

"Your honor," Quinn broke in, "the defense is well aware of Sergeant Harris's qualifications as a homicide investigator and I have the highest regard for her talents—"

"Something we agree on," Collins sniped.

She ignored him. "For the sake of time, the defense will stipulate to Sergeant Harris being an acknowledged expert in her field, so let's stop with the fluff and get on with it."

"I am laying foundation."

"You're laying a smoke screen."

"That's enough," Stromberg admonished.

Quinn bristled. "Your honor, this whole proceeding reeks of self-promotion. As you well know, Mr. Collins is up for reelection, and he is using my client for his own ends. I'll bet right now, there are camera crews setting up outside in the hallway. Why else would he be personally handling this preliminary appearance instead of some junior deputy?"

Collins's jaw cracked. Tessla Quinn had struck a nerve. Even Harris winced.

"Your honor!" he boomed.

"Save the objection," Judge Stromberg sighed. Her face, too, had gone scarlet. She glared down at Quinn. "We'll have no more of that in my courtroom, young lady. Do you understand me?"

For a moment, Quinn remained unmoved, but then she nodded silently and retreated. She had made her point. The seeds of doubt had been planted and for a moment, the only sounds that could be heard in the room were the frantic scribbling of the two print reporters trying to capture every word she had just uttered.

Collins recovered. He turned back to Harris. "Defense counsel has been gracious enough to acknowledge your expertise in the field of homicide investigations. Therefore, let's proceed to one particular death, the rape and murder of a young teenage girl named Cindy Jo Sellinzski, occurring some thirty years ago."

Harris opened the file that rested on her lap. Just as she did, her pager, set on vibrate, went off.

Harris jumped, then caught herself. She looked to Collins for direction.

"Your honor, a moment please?" the prosecutor requested.

The jurist gave a pope-like wave, granting permission, and Harris reached to her belt loop and scanned the digital readout.

"Is there a problem?" Collins asked.

Harris scrolled though the short communication, sighed, and shook her head no. It wasn't the message she and Collins were waiting for.

The prosecutor drew a deep breath and proceeded unfazed.

"Okay, Sergeant Harris, we're back on the record. Let me first ask you, are you familiar with a murder investigation that occurred in 1975—Seattle Police case number 75–28956?"

"I am."

"And how is that?"

"It's an open homicide case."

"Even after nearly three decades?"

"Murder cases are never closed. Not until there has been an arrest and a conviction. Even on old cases like this, a routine review is conducted at least once a year."

"Could you therefore give us a brief overview of the circumstances?"

Harris shifted in her seat and began. "On August 23, 1975, at 0610 hours, officers from the Seattle Police Department responded with paramedics to a wooded area just inside the Woodland Park Zoo, near North Fiftieth and Phinney Avenue. An early morning walker had observed a bloodied, unclothed leg protruding from thick undergrowth, just before the footbridge over Aurora Avenue. He immediately went to a nearby pay phone and reported it."

"What happened next?"

"Law enforcement arrived first. A pair of officers checked the victim's vital signs and to their surprise found the victim, a eighteen-year-old female, to be still alive. But just barely."

"What were her obvious signs of injury?"

"Multiple knife wounds about the neck, breasts, and vaginal area. There were also contusions about the face, and her left ring finger had been severed."

"Severed?" Collins's tone was rhetorical.

"At the joint."

"I see, and what about the knife wounds? They were unusual, were they not?"

"Yes."

"As an acknowledged expert in the field, how would you characterize the injuries?"

"Several ways. The incisions on her neck were nonfatal, only shallow cuts. They were meant to simulate a throat cutting—apparently part of the perpetrator's fantasy."

"Objection!" Quinn fumed. "The witness is offering pure conjecture. There's no foundation for this."

"You laid the foundation," Collins snapped back. "You stipulated that Sergeant Harris is an acknowledged expert in her field."

"But—"

Judge Stromberg intervened. "Objection overruled. Mr. Collins is correct, Ms. Quinn—you opened the door. Sergeant Harris is allowed to offer her opinions. Go on, Mr. Collins; please continue."

The prosecutor grinned briefly. "Now, where were we? Ah, yes, the wounds. What about the other ones?"

"Most were shallow."

"By design?"

"I would have to believe so."

"And why is that?"

"Any one of them could have been fatal if they had been more than a hair deeper. Besides, if you plot their locations and connect the cuts, they formed a cross."

"A cross, or perhaps more accurately, a crucifix?"

"Yes, the latter would be a better characterization."

"I see." Collins cast his gaze towards the defendant and continued his examination. "We'll get into the significance of that later. Sergeant Harris, what about the missing finger—was it found?"

"No."

"In your opinion, why not?"

"It was a trophy. The perpetrator probably severed it as his last act before departing. A memento, so to speak."

"Quite a grisly one."

"But typical. It's been my experience in cases like these that the killer tends to collect something from the victim, be it an earring, a button, a lock of hair, or—"

"A finger."

"Correct."

"Had Cindy Jo Sellinzski been raped?"

"Yes. There was deep vaginal bruising."

"Then there was semen present and other trace evidence?"

"Yes."

Collins paused, hoping to detect some sort of reaction from Bakerman. But the man had not batted an eye. The accused was near catatonic in his stiffness, apparently withdrawn from the entire proceeding.

Harris noted this also. From where she now sat, she had a good view of the man. To her, he was extraordinary in his ordinariness. He had a bookish look, like that of a low-level accountant or government bureaucrat who had been tucked away for an entire career in an anonymous cubicle. Perhaps it was his thick glasses, Harris thought, or the weak chin and balding hair, but she was having a hard time imagining a killer lurking beneath this bland facade—even when a young man.

"Sergeant Harris—"

The detective's focus returned.

"You stated that the victim was still alive when she was found, isn't that right?"

"Yes, just barely."

"Was she conscious?"

"No."

"Did she ever regain consciousness?"

"No. She remained in a coma for a number of months."

"And then what?"

"According to the autopsy report, she died of a brain hemorrhage."

"As a result of her attack."

"That's what the autopsy report concluded."

"Very good. Now let's move on to Mr. Bakerman and how he came to be our guest here."

Harris nodded, and Quinn grimaced.

"At about noon yesterday, Sergeant Harris, did my office contact you?"

"Yes."

"In regards to what?"

"Information that had been received in an anonymous letter."

"Would you relate the essence of our conversation and what you did thereafter."

Harris cleared her throat and continued in a clinical, cool tone. "You asked if I or one of my detectives would come to your office, take custody of the letter, and locate and interview a Carl Alvin Eeckler, the individual referenced in the correspondence."

"And did you find Mr. Eeckler?"

"Yes, in our county jail. He was being held on a drug charge. You arranged to have him brought to your office, and his attorney, Mr. Stuart Malconni, accompanied him. After setting some ground rules, he agreed to speak with us on the matter."

"In exchange for what?" Quinn sneered.

"That is enough, Ms. Quinn," Judge Stromberg ordered. "I don't want to hear another word out of your until cross."

Quinn rolled her eyes—but only after the judge had glanced away.

"Proceed, Sergeant."

"What did Mr. Eeckler have to say?" Collins prompted.

"He told me he had been convicted a number of times in the past for various felonies and had recently completed a three-year sentence in the Monroe State Reformatory for burglary. Further, he had become an acquaintance of Mr. Bakerman's while there, owing to the proximity of their cells. They were neighbors for six months, and during a recent overcrowding situation, they had bunked together for several weeks."

"In the same cell?"

"Yes."

"So he had access to all of Mr. Bakerman's possessions?"

"Correct. There's not much that can be kept secret in close quarters like that."

"Understood. Now let's move to the point of all of this. The letter my office received suggested Mr. Eeckler discovered something while he was housed with his new cellmate?"

Harris nodded. "According to Eeckler, Bakerman was a voracious reader and also fancied himself a writer. Over time, he had accumulated quite a collection of books and papers, which the guards left untouched. One day last summer, Bakerman was in the prison hospital undergoing tests. Left alone, Eeckler glanced though some of the handwritten documents and came across one legal pad that contained a sort of journal or diary."

"Bakerman's?"

"Yes."

"And what was in this journal or diary?"

"Lengthy and detailed descriptions of sadistic sex acts involving young boys and women."

"Fantasies?"

"At first Eeckler thought so. They read like something out of a bad porn magazine. But the account of one of them sparked a memory—a thirty-year-old memory."

"How so?"

"In 1975, Eeckler was a high school student and working part-time at Woodland Park Zoo as a groundskeeper. He was on duty the morning of the Sellinzski murder and was questioned by police as a potential witness. The elements contained in Bakerman's narrative were so chillingly accurate, from what Eeckler remembered, that he came to believe that Bakerman had, in fact, commited the act."

"I see." Collins thought for a moment, then asked, "Besides this rather old recollection, was there anything else that made Mr. Eeckler believe his cell mate was responsible for Cindy Jo's brutal murder?"

"In the narrative, Bakerman describes not only severing the finger as a trophy, but also keeping one more item he found in victim's purse, which was still on the floorboards of his van."

"And it was?"

"A small religious card in a plastic holder. It was the Virgin Mary at Fatima."

"A religious article, eh?"

"Correct."

"Is that significant?"

"Your honor!" Tessla Quinn vaulted upward. "Enough is enough. Where is this stroll through ancient history going to end? We're not at trial. There is no jury here. This is a preliminary hearing. Where are their facts? Where is this so-called diary? Let's see it, and save all this fluff for later. If there isn't any more physical evidence, then let's all go home, including Mr. Bakerman. He's paid his debt; it's time to let him resume his life."

The judge raised an eyebrow and was about to speak when Collins whirled around and faced his opponent. "Ms. Quinn, would you mind not interrupting me while I am examing *my* witness? Or don't they teach proper courtroom decorum in *night* law schools these days?"

A reporter giggled.

"Enough of this petty bickering," Stromberg ordered. "Proceed, Mr. Collins. I would like to hear more about this diary. Is it in your possession? I do trust you have more than the word of a convicted felon for your probable cause."

Collins smirked. "The State does, your honor. I can assure you of that."

Harris's pager suddenly went off a second time. She grabbed and twisted the device so she could read the text of the newly arrived message, just one word and a first name: *Confirmed — Phil.*

Harris looked up and winked at Collins. He understood.